PRAISE FOR
THE FIRST TIME LAUREN PA

'Stylish, alluring, utterly gripping. An intricate, elegantly written time-slip tale that keeps you guessing until the last page' LISA O'KELLY, *OBSERVER*

'A stylish time-slip story *à la* Sliding Doors' *GUARDIAN*

'This stunning novel gives you many stories for the price of one. In dealing with grief, love, and luck – and the unfair way they are distributed – it is both very moving and very clever' MARK LAWSON

'Beautiful, extremely moving and expertly done, with a lightness of touch that belies the complexity behind the plotting. I loved it (and I cried several times!)' HARRIET TYCE

'So many wonderful and unexpected moments … such a unique voice. A very special book' SARRA MANNING, *Red*

Alyson Rudd was born in Liverpool, raised in West Lancashire and educated at the London School of Economics. She is a sports journalist at *The Times* and lives in south-west London. She has written two works of non-fiction. This is her first novel.

The First Time Lauren Pailing Died

Alyson Rudd

ONE PLACE. MANY STORIES

HQ
An imprint of HarperCollins*Publishers* Ltd
1 London Bridge Street
London SE1 9GF

This edition 2019

1

First published in Great Britain by
HQ, an imprint of HarperCollins*Publishers* Ltd 2019

ISBN
HB: 978-0-00-827827-4
TPB: 978-0-00-827828-1

Permission to use an extract from 'But Not Forgotten'
by Dorothy Parker granted by Prelude Books.

MIX
Paper from
responsible sources
FSC™ C007454

This book is produced from independently certified FSC™ paper
to ensure responsible forest management.

For more information visit: www.harpercollins.co.uk/green

Printed and bound in Great Britain by
CPI Group (UK) Ltd, Croydon, CR0 4YY

For Sam and Conor

PART ONE

LAUREN

Lauren Pailing lived in The Willows, a Cheshire cul-de-sac that was shaped like a dessert spoon and as warm and cosseting as any pudding. Every Wednesday morning, sometime between eleven and twenty-past eleven, a big cream van would park at the corner of The Willows and Ashcroft Road. Seconds later, Lennie, who drove the van, would spring out of the driver's seat, open the double doors at the rear and lower the wooden steps so that the residents of The Willows and Ashcroft Road could climb in and choose their groceries.

The contents of Lennie's van were unpredictable, so the housewives of The Willows relied on the local mini-market for the bread or biscuits or tinned ham they needed. But when the van arrived, they all made sure to purchase at least one item as a means of ensuring that it was profitable for Lennie to keep them on his route. So it was that Lauren and the other children of the two streets came home from school on Wednesdays to *Watch with Mother* and a whole array of unnecessary treats: bottles of cream soda, slightly soggy Battenberg cakes and gooey peppermint creams.

To the children of The Willows' dismay, Lennie took a break over the long summer school holiday – so generally speaking Lauren had to be off school unwell, but not too unwell, in order to jump into his van herself. And this she loved to do. Everything about Lennie enchanted Lauren: the twinkle in his eyes, his creased forehead, his Welsh lilt, the way he added up the bills on a small pad of paper with a too-small pencil. She liked that the van was stocked with as many extravagances as essentials, that the whole operation involved adults behaving like children. It was make-believe shopping; grown-ups pointing at a bag of sherbet dip as if it were a serious transaction.

The very best part, though, was the smell. To enter the van was to be instantly transported to a new world, one that was permeated with the scent of stale custard creams and old and broken jam tarts. Lauren supposed the van had never been cleaned, for there was not one whiff of disinfectant. It smelled only and seductively of years of cakes. It was so old-fashioned that there were no lamps in the back – so the labels of the packets and the bottles were illuminated only by daylight from the open doors or the light that filtered in through the thin curtain that separated the shelves of food from Lennie's cabin. This was why Lauren's favourite time to visit the van was on sunny days: when the tiny food hall would be filled with dust sparkling from its contact with icing and sponge fingers.

It was, for Lauren, safe light. Delightful light. She had been inside the van only four times but always felt completely protected. No Santa's Grotto would ever compare, no Santa's Grotto ever smelled as lovely. Above all, thought Lauren, no Santa's Grotto could resist the temptation to overdo the lighting. In the van, Lauren would stick out her tongue, and Lennie would smile because so many children tried to taste the floating sugar splinters, but Lauren seemed to be tasting the light itself.

The Willows was not unreasonably named, as three of the houses had willow trees near their front doors. The street comprised two rows of small semi-detached houses which fanned out to make room for five detached homes, the grandest of which sat at the apex, as if keeping a patrician eye on them all. The grandest house of all had a tall narrow pane of green and red stained glass depicting tiny sheaves of golden wheat above the front door – just in case anybody was in doubt as to its status – and its front and back gardens were twice the size of the rest. Lauren, along with her parents, Bob and Vera, lived at No. 13, the first of the detached houses on the right.

It ought to have been a place simmering with social tension and envy, but The Willows was nestled in aspirational Cheshire and, as the years rolled by, the residents socialised with ease. Every Christmas morning, the Harpers in the grandest house welcomed them all, even the family at No. 2 with their boisterous twin boys who fought each other from the moment they woke to the moment they fell, exhausted, asleep, for sherry and mince pies. Meanwhile, on sunny days, the children would pile into the centre of the spoon and whizz around on tricycles or roller skates. The summer of 1975, when it rolled around, was dominated not only about speculation on the whereabouts of the murderer Lord Lucan and the rise of unemployment, but also by the Squeezy Bottle War. Empty washing-up liquid bottles were turned into water pistols and many a child would scream as the contents, still soapy, were squirted into their eyes. With the exception of water fights, however, The Willows was a place of utter safety.

One Thursday after school the following summer, Lauren was sat in her bedroom on her sheepskin rug, making a birthday card for her mother and sipping occasionally from a plastic tumbler full of cream soda, each sip evoking the seductively sweet smell of Lennie's van. She was immensely proud that her rug was white; white like a sheep and not dyed pink like the one in the bedroom of her friend Debbie.

Lauren's current obsession was to create pictures with complicated skies. She was using the stencil of a crescent moon when, to her right, a thin beam appeared, which to most observers, had they been able to see it at all, would have looked like a sharp shaft of sunlight. Lauren knew better.

She sighed, and tried to ignore it by pressing her nose against her artwork and wondering how paper was manufactured and how so much of it was stored in her father's big steel desk which sat incongruously in the spare bedroom. She had once covered the desk with stickers of stars and rainbows and was still not sure if her father had been cross, or had pretended to be cross but quietly found it as loving a gesture as she had hoped. Grown-ups, she thought, were always secretive. They were so secretive that it was possible they all saw special sunbeams which, if peered through, granted tiny windows into other worlds, too. Lauren doubted it. But she, on the other hand, had been visited by these peculiar, dangerous sunbeams for as long as she could recall.

Two years ago, when Lauren was six, a steel sunbeam had

appeared in the kitchen, and Lauren's mother had walked straight through it. Lauren had caught her breath, waiting for her mummy to clutch her head and sit down trembling, perhaps even to fall through to another place, but nothing had happened – and so, over time, Lauren came to understand that the curious metal, rod-straight beams belonged to her and only to her. Experience also taught her that it had been a mistake for her to turn to her best friend, Debbie, one day and say, 'Look at that.' Debbie had looked and, seeing nothing, had called Lauren Ghostie Girl for an hour or so before forgetting, as six-year-olds tend to do, why she was saying Ghostie Girl at all.

The Christmas after the Ghostie Girl incident, during the school nativity – dressed as an angel and feeling so happy about it that she suspected she might just be capable of flight – Lauren had seen a plethora of beams slice across the heads of the audience. It was as though Baby Jesus were sending the school his approval for their efforts to make his stable cosy with a fanfare of light, and Lauren had turned her head to her fellow angels, expecting to see her own awe mirrored in their eyes – but she saw only glassy tired eyes or vain eyes or look-at-me eyes. No one saw what she saw.

But the unease never lasted long, and the next day, the whole of the next day, was spent choosing, then buying, then decorating the Christmas tree with felt Santas, silk angels, frosted glass icicles – no tacky tinsel – realistic feathery robins and white twinkling lights. Vera, Lauren's mother, had looked on, feeling inordinately proud that she did not have a child who wanted to throw a dozen plastic snowmen at the tree but could see Yuletide in an aesthetic way.

By seven, Lauren had noted the way adults responded to her

sunbeam stories and had learned to avoid mentioning them. She had also noted how her school friends were ignorant of these gleaming gateways, and that to insist they were real was to be met with teasing, laughter or annoyance. Still, it was hard for her to remain silent when sometimes such lovely things happened through the miniature windows.

'You look nice in a silvery silky dress, Mummy,' Lauren had said one night when her bedtime story was finished. She'd started to care about clothes, started to notice that her mother dressed a little more elegantly than the mothers of her friends. Fashion was such a grown-up thing and she wanted to show she could make sense of it – that she might only be seven, but she had style – and a light beam on the stairs that morning had revealed her mother smoothing down a magical-looking skirt. Vera did not own a silvery silky dress and she frowned as she closed the book.

'You mean, darling, that I *would* look like nice in a silvery silky dress.'

Lauren had been sleepy and off-guard.

'No, you *do* look nice, and the dress is more gorgeousy than anything the Bionic Woman wears.'

Vera considered herself to be a devoted, sensible mother but allowed herself to feel occasionally undermined by her daughter's murmurings. She wondered if Lauren wanted a different sort of mother, a prettier one perhaps or one that constructed more elaborate cakes. Vera wondered if being at home meant her daughter took her for granted. Then, she would wonder if, on the contrarty, Lauren resented her having a Saturday job, or if her daughter was simply lonely.

Vera was occasionally disconcerted by her only child. When

Lauren had been much younger, she had watched her tilt her head and squeeze her eyes as if peering through a crack in the wall, a crack that was not there. Quietly, stood to one side, Vera would watch her daughter peer, watch her smile or grimace, watch her sigh, watch her turn away. While Lauren was mesmerised, Vera would vow to take her to the doctor, to speak to Bob, her husband, to investigate what might be happening, but as soon as Lauren turned away and carried on with being a child, Vera scolded herself for worrying and did and said nothing.

Lauren, sitting proudly on her white sheepskin rug, studiously ignoring her sunbeam, was now the wise old age of eight, and had long absorbed the peculiarities of her life in the way that most children can be hugely accommodating of anything; be it abuse, poverty, neglect or boredom. She knew that up close the sunbeam currently piercing her carpeted bedroom floor appeared to be a streak of mirrored glass but that, when viewed closer still, so close she almost touched it, there would be no reflection whatsoever. She also knew, she had known for a long time, not under any circumstances to touch the mysterious ray of light.

For while it looked heavy and solid and glistening, her hand could glide straight through it as if it were indeed a sunbeam. She could even walk through it unimpeded, but to do so was to feel instantly cold with a sharp, nasty headache that lasted for hours and made it impossible for her to do anything but lie down and moan. As this had once prompted her parents to take her to hospital she knew better than to let it happen again.

It was not her headache that had so worried her parents as

the fact Lauren had mumbled through her pain about her other mummy. Her parents had stared at each other, perplexed and a little scared. If they, too, saw the beams, then they would surely not have been so frightened.

'I don't like my other mummy,' Lauren had whispered indignantly, her eyes squeezed tight, her hands cold to the touch.

It was true, on that occasion she had not liked her other mummy, but subsequently she had liked her just as much as the regular one. Gradually, Lauren had come to know many mothers, all spied with caution through the prism of the magic glass, just as she had learned to accept the views through her beams, which were usually pretty dull and often almost exactly the same as the scene would be without her magic glass. Only now and again would the view cause her to gasp – such as when she caught sight of her mother, supposedly in the boutique she helped to run on Saturday mornings, sat on Lauren's own bed throwing Lauren's own dolls at the wall and spitting with rage.

Noisily, Lauren devoured the last few drops of cream soda, put down her stencil and crawled from her sheepskin rug to the base of the beam, which had appeared at a forty-degree angle and refused to be ignored any longer. She aligned her eyes and slowly inched forward so that the shimmering stopped and the view began. Peering through, she saw the same bedroom in the same home she was sitting in. Taped to the wall was a child's painting of the sun shining down on rows and rows of pink and purple flowers. Lauren made a small scoffing sound and looked away to the wall in her own room, upon which was taped a much cleverer child's painting of a full moon hanging over a wild sea out of which darted flying fish with smiling faces.

It seemed that, like so many of the sunbeam views, this one was boring and fairly pointless so, carefully, and with a sigh, Lauren set to work again on her card, making today's crescent moon yellow but the stars silver, humming, 'Happy birthday, dear Mummy, happy birthday to you,' and not wondering at all who had painted the simple sun and the garish pink and purple flowers.

Nothing made Lauren happier than creating pictures for her parents. She was a perfectionist. Many a crayoned red-roofed house, colourful garden and smiling cat had been binned before she deemed it worthy of handing over. It mattered to her that, when her parents gushed their delight, the picture was deserving of such rapture. It was not about competition – after all she had Bob and Vera's undivided attention – but being an only child conferred a deep sense of responsibility. If she was all they had, then she had better be good. She had better concentrate on the job at hand, and not become distracted by strange other worlds.

Vera was delighted with her daughter's card, and she hugged her tightly. Lauren hugged her back.

'You're the best of all my mummies,' she said, forgetting her own rules in her haste to say the most loving thing she could on her mother's special day.

Vera stiffened but carried on hugging.

'Well, cherub,' she said, 'I'm afraid I'm the only mummy you've got.'

Lauren sighed contentedly and Vera relaxed. She reminded herself that she had had an imaginary friend called Tuppence when she was four. Lauren was, at eight, a bit old for such things, but Vera could tell her daughter was creative and with creativity came, perhaps, an overexcitable imagination.

It was such a lovely, long hug. Bob walked in and chuckled and said he had booked a surprise Sunday lunch for the three of them. This turned out to be not a silver-service affair, but cold chicken, tongue, ham salad and homemade coleslaw at No. 17 where Lauren's friend Debbie lived with her parents, Julian and Karen Millington, her bright pink sheepskin rug, and her brother, Simon. But Vera was amused by the conspiracy and the fact that Bob both shaved beforehand and cleaned the sink properly after having done so. She knew she would have to wear the long white silk scarf Bob had bought for her and that meant she could not wear the wraparound dress she had bought from her boutique with her fifteen per cent discount the previous day. She stood in front of the mirror before they left for lunch, Lauren by her side.

'Long scarves go only with long trousers,' she told her daughter, and Lauren gazed admiringly at her mother's self-assuredness, her smooth, blemish-free skin, her elegant neck, her tiny wrists. When she dressed her Sindy Doll she would think how much more elegant her own mother was compared to the doll, or the other mothers of The Willows and especially when compared to the other mothers inside the sunbeams.

It always thrilled Lauren to notice the differences between her and Debbie's homes. From the outside, they were almost identical, bar the fact that No. 13 had a green garage door and No. 17 had a white one. Inside, though, they felt unrelated. Vera was very partial to glass partitions and bold wallpaper such as the orange-and-brown paperchain pattern in the living room. Debbie's parents preferred solid walls and had placed textured magnolia on them.

As a giant trifle was hauled onto Debbie's dining table, a metal sunbeam appeared in front of the sideboard. No one but Lauren noticed it. She was used to this by now, used to being different. She sometimes felt pestered by the magic silver string, as though a smelly boy were pulling at her ponytail. She also was beginning to recognise that the nagging cracks of light lingered longer if not given attention. But it would not be so easy, she thought, to give this particular beam attention while in a packed dining room in someone else's home.

She ate her trifle with one eye on the beam, which was noticed by Karen.

'Have you spotted our wedding photo, Lauren?' she asked.

Lauren stopped eating mid-mouthful, wondering if it was rude to look at another family's photographs, then realised this would give her a reason to peer closer at the sideboard.

'Can I look?' she said, and sprang out of her chair. Fortunately, no one paid too much attention to the way Lauren cocked her head to one side and stooped oddly.

'I was so slim back then,' Karen twittered self-consciously. Karen liked Bob and Vera but Vera had arrived in platform clogs worn under maroon flared trousers, looking, to Karen, like some sort of film star, and she had had to tug at her own hair in order to clear her head and remind herself that it was Vera's birthday and she had every right to look a million dollars.

Lauren stared into the metallic gap. Through it, she could see Karen sitting in a chair, her eyes closed, her cheeks hollow, her lips pursed. She was bony and brittle like a twig. It made

Lauren feel sad. There was never a soundtrack to the visions, but Lauren could sense a weighty silence, a room enveloped with pain.

'Pass the photo here, love,' Karen said, keen to make sure Vera had a good look at how petite she had been on her wedding day.

Lauren had to loop her arm under the beam and lean back a little to ensure she did not touch it. Watching her, the quiet bored Simon decided his sister's friend was, like all girls, uncoordinated and a bit stupid.

Eventually the long hot summer of 1976 ended, school restarted and Lauren was placed in charge of the art and stationery cupboard in the corner of her classroom. This was dressed up as an honour but it really meant that the teacher could avoid having to tidy up. Nevertheless, Lauren took her role very seriously. She loved the trays of string, of glue, of poster paint, of crayons, the stacks of thick coloured paper, the pencils and pencil sharpeners, the hole punches. It was her domain and she even sort of liked how for a few seconds, as the strip light flickered into life, it could be pitch-black in there. It was a small windowless space that smelled of plasticine and turps and, oddly, of forgotten fruit gums, and not once had a rod of light appeared. And yet.

Deep into her cupboard duty one afternoon Lauren heard a scuffling outside her door. It sounded to her like mice so she turned sharply and noticed a luminescence clinging to the cupboard's keyhole. She bent down and peered through the gap and saw her classmates rushing to sit down as the teacher, beaming, lowered the stylus of the portable record player. This could mean only one thing. The record player was used to play just one record and one record only, 'A Windmill in Old Amsterdam'. This was how birthdays were marked in her school and the children would sing with gusto as the birthday boy or girl was more or less ignored. 'I saw a mouse!' they would shriek along with the scratchy old vinyl record.

Lauren felt left out. How could they? she thought. The Windmill song was taken very seriously. The teacher would wait for the children's full attention and only when there was an expectant silence would she ease the stylus onto the record. For the first time in her stationery cupboard Lauren felt lonely and left out. She would have to act in haste not to miss the opening refrain so she firmly and a little indignantly pushed the handle and stepped into the room singing, *'A mouse lived in a windmill—'* and then she stopped short. No child was at their desk, the portable record player was still on the shelf.

'Anything the matter, Lauren?' asked the teacher as a few children giggled.

'Was there…? Were you all going to sing?' she said in a whisper.

The teacher shook her head distractedly. Gavin was handing out sweets again, an eight-year-old version of a spiv on market day. Lauren stepped back into the cupboard and the door clicked shut.

'Well, I declare,' she hummed to herself defiantly. She had, after all, always known strangeness and was an adaptable soul. *'Going clip-clippety-clop on the stair,'* she mouthed as she found a spare drawer for the plastic beads that had spilled on the floor every time the class had an arts and crafts afternoon.

As she sat down for the glass of orange squash the teacher

handed out to the children at two o'clock every day a lattice of metallic beams dangled from the ceiling and Lauren took a deep breath to mask a gasp at its majesty. This, she felt, was an apology for the Windmill debacle, and it might have been the first spiritual moment of her life except for the fact that Tracy Campbell saw her gazing at the ceiling and began screaming that there was spider in their midst about to drop into her beaker.

Lauren saw no spider, and wondered briefly if Tracy saw spiders the way she saw metal sunbeams. But she soon worked out that where her classmates had imagination, she had something more tangible. Something that could not be shared, that was more dangerous than the wildest of daydreams and so much more compelling.

A week after her eleventh birthday Lauren was sat in a chair at the optician's.

Her parents had seen her squinting as she stood before the newly installed bookshelf in the living room. They had also seen her, head cocked in the kitchen, seemingly struggling to make sense of a cereal packet on the table.

'I don't squint,' she said sullenly.

The optician knew an easy sale could be made. The parents were very suggestible to something corrective being necessary, desirable even. But, after a thorough examination, he had to accept that there really was absolutely nothing wrong with this girl's vision. What's more, something about the child unnerved him. It was as if she could see through him, see him for what he really was – which was lonely, and obsessed with his receding hairline.

'She's fine,' he said brightly, and Vera shook her head.

'Well, that's good news, I suppose,' she said as Lauren rolled her eyes. She felt spied upon. She had tried to be surreptitious when peering through the shimmering rods, but clearly her parents had sneaked up on her. She would have to be even more careful. She did not live in a world where it was acceptable to see things that other people did not see although she was sure there was a world somewhere where it would have been just fine. In fact, the more beams she looked through, the more it seemed to Lauren that there were endless variations of life; that her glimpses were not big revelations but tiny clues. She was only ever peeking, not properly looking, at what might have been. Or what could be. Or what also is.

By now, she had stopped telling her mother about her other mothers. Gradually she had noticed the stiffening, the frowning, the flushing it induced in Vera and the last thing she wanted was for her mother to be unhappy. Vera, Bob and Lauren enjoyed a contained and contented life. There was no need to spoil it. But Lauren was maturing and starting to wonder what the point was of her visions. Was this to be her life, always ducking under the beams, always needing to see into them?

By the time she was twelve, the beams had begun to gang up on her. Now and again she would walk into a room and be faced with a wall of metallic slices. There could be fifty or sixty of them blocking her path. It was impossible for her to duck or jump or squirm past them. These were the only occasions when she felt intimidated by the visions. It was like finding her bedroom window fitted with iron bars or being trapped in a public toilet cubicle. Fortunately, it did not happen very often and so far it had not caused a stir but she did worry that one day it would. That the headmaster of her new secondary school would ask her into his office and she would be unable to step through his door. Or that the beams would multiply to the extent that they formed a wall of steel, trapping her so that she could not even see what was ahead, only what else might be around her.

Otherwise, school was just fine. Lauren had forged a reputation for being artistic and creative. Little did she realise that the vast majority of secondary schools would have had no time at all for her clever cartoons and bold montages, that most teachers would have told her to spend less time with tissue paper and more time on her spelling tests. It was a school that almost treasured its pupils and that made it, almost, a wondrous place to be. There were sports days, plays, concerts, film clubs and art exhibitions on a seemingly endless reel. No one wanted to leave. Its sixth form was full to bursting. It was a very happy place. Or at least it was happy in Lauren's day-to-day version.

She knew by now that she was seeing alternatives, through her glittering rods, to what was really there, and once in the corridor between lessons she had peered, making sure not to squint too heavily, and seen a bleak school corridor with no artwork and a runt of a boy being spat upon by larger, older children. There was not time for her to dwell on his features, but she tried to burn the image in her mind so she could recognise him if he was somewhere in her real school. But if he was there then he was not in her class and she never passed him in the playground.

It made her thankful that she lived in a kinder place. It

made her smile at the staff, make eye contact with the dinner ladies and share her crisps with her friends. This in turn made her liked and popular, which helped to fill the void left by the fact that she could not share her visions with anyone. Nonetheless, it could be lonely, and she thought of her Aunt Suki, who lived by herself, and wondered if, when she grew up, she would have to live by herself too, watching television alone and never joining in the laughter or tears of anyone else. When a beam appeared that night as she brushed her teeth, Lauren muttered a prayer to no one in particular that, when she peeped through, she might see in it her Aunt Suki laughing with friends at a sophisticated party brimming with handsome men, but all she saw was the bathroom she was already in – albeit a version that had a sink with a large brown stain.

By the summer of 1981, Lauren was approaching thirteen and beginning to feel the first stirrings of teenage claustrophobia. Her home was so quiet, so full of routine. Not even the Royal Wedding was enough to spice it up although it was nice that she, Vera, Karen and Debbie were able to watch it – all the girls cooing together while Bob and Julian went crown green bowling with Debbie's grandfather. A whole week could pass without a visit from Aunt Suki, without even the visit of a neighbour; so the visit of sunbeams, no matter how many, was a welcome diversion, even the ones where there was a young boy being cuddled by her mother which made her feel a spurt of jealousy. There were days when just bringing her father a mug of tea as he pottered about in his messy garage was a highlight of the weekend. Usually she disliked it when her parents chatted about politics but it was different when it was just her and her dad in the garage. Bob was mesmerised by Margaret Thatcher and Lauren deduced that he admired her, feared her and was baffled by her.

'How do you reckon she and the Queen get on?' he would ask his daughter, and they would engage in a role play that invariable ended with Bob mimicking the Prime Minister and saying something silly such as, 'Where there are biscuits, may we bring tea?' and the two of them would giggle helplessly.

'One day I'll sift the rubbish from the necessary,' he would say as he rummaged in yet another cheap plastic box for a spanner or a rusty pair of secateurs, and Lauren would look at the oil stains and the cobwebs and say, 'Of course you will, Dad,' and they would laugh conspiratorially, then walk together into the kitchen where Vera might be mashing eggs with butter, mayonnaise and cress for sandwiches – the clearest indicator of all that the three of them were 'going for a drive'.

It amused Lauren greatly that, during these drives, her parents derived so much joy from pretending that they did not know where they would end up even though she knew that they discussed in detail their next outing to make sure that they saw every stately home or went on every country walk at the time when it would be at its most beautiful. Lauren could appreciate the beauty of Lyme Park's architecture and the rhododendrons that lined the still waters of the local quarry but, all the same, she was bored of tagging along, no matter how tasty the sandwiches or how good a mood her parents were in.

It was not normal, she grunted inwardly, that an invitation to a treasure-hunt lunch at Easter at the home of Peter Stanning, her father's boss, should have been such a highlight in her life. But there had been plenty of other teenagers around her age there, and also a decadent sort of freedom to it all, with the youngsters permitted to roam as they pleased. Lauren had liked Dominique, a girl home from boarding school, who carried a camera around her neck and took photographs of tree stumps and discarded bikes. Dominique was the daughter of who Mrs Stanning referred to as 'dear old friends' and it struck Lauren that this was evidence of a class divide. The Pailing family did not have any 'dear old friends' whatsoever. They just had people who they 'used to know quite well', like the family who had lived near Lauren's primary school before moving to Leighton Buzzard.

'They have eleven bicycles in this shed but thirteen bike wheels,' Dominique had said to Lauren as they stood before one of the many Stanning outhouses, and Lauren had fervently wished she was capable of noticing such details. Later that evening, she told Dominique that she too was an artist, that she did not have a camera but liked to draw and to paint, and Dominique had replied that she, Lauren, possessed the greater gift. Yes, Lauren, thought, I really like Dominique. But then she disappeared off to boarding school and Peter Stanning did not hint that his wife would be hosting any more such gatherings. Lauren recalled how Mrs Stanning had been a distant sort of hostess, as if she had something much more important to be seeing to, while her husband had been friendly and attentive and had spent ten minutes looking for some Savlon cream to rub into Dominique's elbow when she scratched it while making space for her camera lens through a lattice of wild and thorny roses. Peter Stanning had looked Dominique in the eye and said, as if speaking grown-up to grown-up, that she should pursue her dream in photography.

In the absence of parties, Lauren increasingly gravitated towards the house across the cul-de-sac spoon where there was noise and the odd raised voice, the squabbling of siblings and the laughter of parents who liked a midweek nip of booze.

She always knocked, but no one ever physically answered the door. Instead Debbie or one of her parents would call out for her to come in, and sure enough the back door was always unlocked. Debbie had begun to sequester herself in the dining room on the basis that her brother had the largest bedroom and it was an *insult* to expect Lauren to perch next to her on her small bed. They would sit, instead, on uncomfortable dining chairs, trying to feel sophisticated as they leafed through magazines bursting with shoulder-padded women, and swapped gossip or pretended to complete homework as they sipped at too-hot Pot Noodles. Above them could be heard the heavy beat of Simon's music and muffled lyrics which made Debbie groan and pout.

'The Cure. Again,' She would sneer.

As the months passed, Lauren spent more and more time at Debbie's. She quietly considered The Cure to be intriguing. She inwardly relished the chaos and the fact that sometimes the music would be so loud that the furniture would actually bounce. Furniture never bounced in her house. At Debbie's, if you wanted to open a tin of hot dogs and heat one up you could do so without anyone telling you it would spoil your appetite. If the terrible twins from No. 2 rang the front door bell, they would not be ignored, as they were in Lauren's house, but chased down the road and even sometimes called back and asked if they wanted to watch the football on the telly, whereupon they would turn into identical pink-cheeked curly-haired cherubs, dunking their Jacob's Club biscuits into beakers of milk, glued to the progress of Liverpool in the European Cup.

And should Simon make an appearance in the dining room, Debbie would throw a coaster at him while Lauren would wonder what the music was that had now replaced The Cure in his affections and whether when he smiled at her it was in sarcasm or friendliness.

'You're tagging along with us to Cornwall this year, then?' Simon said one evening as he threw a coaster back towards his sister.

Lauren opened her mouth but could think of nothing to say.

'Hey, Cornwall's not that amazing,' Simon said and walked out.

Lauren and Debbie faced each other, their eyes gleaming.

'Did my mum speak to your mum?' Debbie said.

'I'll find out,' Lauren said, feeling as if she were the last to know about the most exciting invitation she had ever received, and she skipped home across the cul-de-sac after giving Debbie a hug, the first hug they had shared feeling like sisters.

'Were you ever going to tell me?' Lauren said as she burst through into the kitchen.

'Of course I was, sweetheart, I was just thinking it through, that's all. I think perhaps you're a bit young to be away for a fortnight.'

This was an understatement. In fact, Vera's instinctive response, when sat at the kitchen table nursing a cup of tea opposite Karen, who was busily dunking her biscuit and burbling about the beauty of the Cornish coastline, had been to laugh it off as a wild and ridiculous suggestion. Vera was as much fun as any thirteen-year-old could ask their mum to be but deep down she was panicked that Lauren was all she had. And, since she was thirty-six, Lauren was likely to remain all she had.

'It's not America, Mum,' Lauren said pleadingly. 'Can I phone Granny? You do know she thinks I should be busier in the holidays and this will make me much busier.'

Vera had no retort that made any sense. Beryl, her mother, was right. Lauren should be out and about with friends who had siblings. Vera wanted to tag along on the holiday, but Bob was bogged down at the office and would have been wounded had she left him to his own devices every evening for a fortnight. All the same, two whole weeks without Lauren would be torture.

'She'll be fine, she'll have fun,' Bob said, coming into the room and giving his wife a tight hug.

Allowing her only child to leave for a fortnight made Vera want to burst into tears, but eventually she had taken a deep breath and given her consent. She threw herself into packing a large suitcase with the attentiveness a trip to the Niger Delta would have deserved. Lauren stared at the plethora of ointments and plasters and double quantities of sanitary towels and instead of griping as a teenager might have been expected to, she shouldered the ridiculousness. It was her burden as an only child to indulge such behaviour. Only when on the road with her friend did Lauren make a joke about the fussiness of her mother. Only when she had waved Lauren off did Vera succumb to a couple of heaving sobs of love and self-pity.

Debbie's family had rented a huge house not far from St Ives. They were joined by Karen's sister and Karen's sister's best friend and her son Brian, who was a gangly twelve-year-old who stuck tightly to Simon as if girls carried infectious diseases. Slowly, they all relaxed and Lauren marvelled at the noise and laughter and the cheating at cards and the arguments over draughts. Other families popped by. Karen's sister even went on a date. It was all silly and riotous enough for it not to matter when it rained. The adults wandered around in a perpetual state of tipsiness, clutching glasses of wine or beer as Phil Collins played on a perpetual loop in the background. It was hypnotically loud and busy. They all ate when they felt like it and the nightly barbecue lasted for three hours, so that Lauren regularly lost count of how many sausages she had eaten.

On the second evening, Simon was placed in charge of flaming some fatty steaks. As Lauren settled into a canvas chair with a plastic glass of lemonade a thin glistening steel rod appeared in front of her nose. She sharply pulled back her head, fearful of touching it, of the holiday being cut short by the nasty headache such a collision would provoke, and then gingerly leaned forward to spy upon another world. She expected to see simply more sausages and perhaps a new face or two, so unremarkable had been most of her recent peeks through the glass. Instead she saw Simon, wearing a faded red T-shirt that suited him better than the black one he was really wearing, squirting lighter fluid onto the hot charcoal that caused a flame to angrily reach up and slap his face, and setting fire to his clothes.

Lauren closed her eyes as her heartbeat quickened. She breathed in deeply and opened her eyes. The beam was gone and so was Simon but then he emerged, really re-emerged, walking from the shed to the patio, a small can with a spout in his hands. He had changed out of his black T-shirt and was wearing a faded red one.

Lauren was both transfixed and horrified. She wanted to shout to him to stop but lacked the courage to do so. Simon paused and held the can close to his face as he read the label.

'Dangerous stuff,' he said to his father, who grabbed the can from his hands.

'Too right,' he said.

Lauren exhaled and spent the rest of the evening in such high spirits that Lucy, Karen's sister, kept asking what she was really drinking.

Breakfast was Frosties or slabs of white bread from the freezer toasted to never the acceptable colour. Lauren noted that Simon would tip back his head and let the dry cereal fall from the packet into his mouth and then take a gulp of milk while winking at her. At least she thought he was winking at her. It might have simply been that it was impossible to eat breakfast in such a fashion while keeping both eyes open.

This was life, she thought. She was growing up. She had experienced a short burst of homesickness on the first night that had been interrupted by a glistening beam piercing the end of her camp bed. Through it she had seen a toddler sucking at a bottle of milk, its eyes wide, its toes curling around the ears of a small white teddy bear, and the vision had instantly cured her of her loneliness. I'm not their baby, she thought indignantly, and they had better get used to it.

Eleven days into the holiday an old Jeep appeared in the driveway driven by a man Lauren had not seen before, but

Debbie and Simon and gangly Brian piled in and so she did too. There were no seats for the youngsters; they just sat on the back and clung on facing the way they had come. The lanes, banked by thick hedgerows, became increasingly narrow. Lauren could hear her mother wailing about how dangerous it all was and made a mental note not to mention this particular outing when she got home. Debbie started singing Kim Wilde's 'Kids in America' and they all joined in, even Brian, because they were in a Jeep and felt they could be in California, and because it was easy to sing a song by Kim Wilde because Kim Wilde couldn't sing all that well herself.

Then the driver veered sharply round a bend and braked as a tractor approached and Lauren was thrown out of the back of the Jeep and onto the road. And the singing stopped.

Lauren felt like a small hard rubber ball bouncing down some stairs. She felt her neck snap, painlessly, like the wishbone of the Christmas turkey. She felt warm blood trickling across her chin. She felt the world spin, the colours of the beautiful early evening dim into sludge brown, then grey, then black.

She opened her eyes slowly, not out of pain or the fear of pain, but out of a curious sort of trepidation.

She knew without thinking, without calculating, the way that she knew her name and she knew that ice was cold, that she had died.

PART TWO

LAUREN

Whereas other little girls in The Willows might have clasped their hands together and prayed to God or to Jesus or grandparents in Heaven or a pet in the afterlife, Lauren had formulated her own religion. It had never been taught to her at Brownies or Sunday School or in assembly. She had not heard it mentioned on television or in the conversations grown-ups had over cups of tea or gin and tonics.

Lauren had always had her sunbeams and they had always shown her windows to other places. She was sure that everyone had these other worlds but that, for some reason, no one else could see them. What was the point of it all, she couldn't be sure, but her beams suggested to her that instead of dying, she could shift.

Shifting was, she thought, more sensible than Heaven. More convenient than Heaven. More realistic than Heaven. Nicer than Heaven. Her Grandad Alfie had confirmed it.

'We carry on,' Grandad Alfie had whispered to her when she was eight or nine and had asked him if he would still be able to see her when he died.

'Where?' she had whispered back.

'Somewhere nicer, or at least somewhere where we aren't dead,' he had laughed throatily but Lauren had not laughed along. She had simply nodded seriously and he had stopped laughing and nodded too.

When Grandad Alfie had died, she had known he had not been ready to actually die. He was sprightly and funny and liked to beat younger men at cards. He had carried on regardless, she was sure of it. He had carried on oblivious to the silent tears of Granny Beryl, the misery of Vera and the sad hymns in the church.

That had not been her grandad's time and this was most certainly not Lauren's time. She was thirteen. She could not die. She opened her eyes. She was in a hospital bed and she was sore. She could not move her head, it was being held in place by a plastic contraption and it made her feel claustrophobic.

Her mother's face loomed into view. Vera was both relieved and panic-stricken. Vera looked different somehow beyond the frown of desperation, the fear of what her daughter's injuries might mean. Lauren forgot about the pain and mounting unease and stared and stared at her mother's face. Though it was not what she was expecting, she recognised the face. She had seen it pouting sadly through the magic glass.

'Hello, Other Mummy,' she whispered through cracked lips before sinking back into unconsciousness.

The next waking was an emotional affair. Vera stroked her daughter's cheek trying to disguise how hurt she felt that Lauren seemed, ever so slightly, to flinch. Lauren sneaked a glance at her mother's forehead. It was dirty. How ridiculous. Had she tried to apply her eyebrow pencil while driving?

'You've got… stuff… on your face, Mum,' Lauren said.

'Oh,' Vera said, disappointed, adding with false brightness, 'I'll go to the bathroom mirror.'

Vera returned having rubbed off the faint traces of rouge she had applied simply to disguise her anxious pallor so as not to worry her daughter but Lauren had slipped back to sleep. Vera waited until her daughter stirred once more.

It hurt to move but her right arm was unharmed, not even bruised, so Lauren gingerly lifted her hand to her mouth and licked her forefinger.

'Lean closer, Mum,' she said and gently rubbed at her mother's forehead. This time it was Vera's turn to flinch. She had never liked her mole to be touched.

Lauren frowned. The small but annoying mark on her mother's face was not flat but raised and rubbery and solid and not at all like a smudge of eyebrow pencil or an errant piece of melted chocolate. She squinted at Vera suspiciously and then at her own right hand. There was silence, while Vera realised that the spot her daughter was trying to rub away had always been there.

'What a funny thing to forget about, darling,' Vera said, again with forced brightness.

'I didn't forget,' Lauren said angrily but she was bereft more than angry and she wondered why she felt as if her mother were dead when there she sat, on the bed, breathing and talking and being so obviously loving.

Through her recuperation her parents, and her mother in particular, had been attentive and doting but Lauren had become frustrated by Bob and Vera's lack of a sense of fun. Before her holiday to Cornwall, Lauren had hated Benny Hill, but loved how her father had giggled like a schoolboy in front of the television. Mr Hill had now vanished from their lives, and so had the giggles.

'Have they stopped making...' Lauren started to ask, but discovered she suddenly could not remember the comedian's name. She closed her eyes and tried to picture his face but she could not even do that. The harder she tried the more distant he became and within the hour she had forgotten that such a man had ever existed.

Lauren had fractured her skull, broken ribs, snapped her arm and splintered her right kneecap. It had been sore, then boring, then sore again. It was Bonfire Night before Lauren felt able to walk outside. The Harpers in the grand house were holding what the invitation they had pushed through the letterbox called their 'annual firework party'. They had never held one before, but Lauren allowed this detail to pass without letting it annoy her. The Harpers had spent a lot of money on the display and the cul-de-sac residents cooed accordingly. Lauren, though, was more intrigued and impressed by the Harpers' stained-glass window which seemed both familiar and not. It was decadently large, and depicted a white dove against an expensive azure-blue sky.

Her father worked slightly longer hours than she recalled him working before the accident, and her mother did not go to work in the boutique on Saturdays. Lauren wondered why she thought she would work there, so little interest did Vera seem to have in clothes. Her mother was altogether just a little bit less outgoing since the accident in Cornwall. It must have knocked her confidence, Lauren thought. Her skirts were slightly longer, her jumpers less jazzy, but she was just as tender and loving and smelled the same. Yes, she smelled exactly the same.

Gradually, Lauren forgot that she must have shifted to somewhere else. So many things felt off-kilter but they were small things and the doctors all said she might have lapses in memory. She did not push the point, she did not tell them that there were no gaps in her past; that her past felt skewed. She did not want these tiny electric shocks of surprise; she wanted to feel she belonged, and so she willed it that her other mummy was simply her only mummy, Dad was Dad, and Debbie was Debbie.

Lauren clung to sameness. It brought her disproportionate joy when she found a small black lacquer box at the back of her wardrobe and knew what she would find inside. She had had a six-month spell of collecting buttons in primary school, and she smiled at how tacky they looked compared to how magical she had thought them four years earlier.

If only the same were true of the garage, which was lined with long splinter-free wooden shelves, upon which were stacked neat wooden boxes bearing brightly coloured labels indicating items such as 'torches and matches' or 'anti-freeze'. She stood, watching Bob proudly fishing out a nail from a box of nails that were all the same size, and wondered why she pitied him. She brought him a mug of tea one cold Saturday morning and he was grateful and he smiled and told her how lucky he was not to have a stroppy and thoughtless daughter, but then there was a silence and she walked away feeling less warm inside than she had expected to.

Debbie's mother Karen was changed in other ways – ways that everyone, not just Lauren, could see. It was the guilt she felt over the accident in the Jeep. For weeks she was unable to be in the same room as Lauren without bursting into tears, and Vera, who had originally been tempted to freeze her out of their lives, was melted by her neighbour's remorse and they became closer friends than they had been before.

The next summer, the curtains were tightly drawn against the sun so that Bob and Vera and Lauren could watch the tennis from Wimbledon, cheering on John McEnroe and rooting for the bespectacled but pretty Jocelyn Evert, and through a tiny gap popped a concentrated shaft of sunlight fizzing with dust. Lauren felt a bolt of indigestion. It was like the unannounced visit of a long-forgotten friend.

It took the crack in the curtain to make Lauren remember that she used to see a different sort of sunbeam, magical thick ropes of metal that were both fascinating and cruel. She sighed at the shock of the sunbeam and let it go. She could not even remember if the beams had exhausted her, entranced her or worried her. In the weeks that followed, she had dreams about the few occasions on which multiple beams had appeared, blocking her path as if angry with her, but the dreams ebbed into different dreams about vapour trails and knitting and a sports day tug-of-war. She stopped noticing the mole on her mother's forehead and started noticing the boy playing the lead in the sixth-form production of *West Side Story*.

Before long, Lauren was able to walk, limping still, past No. 2 without giving any thought to who lived there. The fact that it was a house bereft of any twin boys stopped registering with her. She had accepted, and then forgotten, that the twins had not moved away. They had never lived there. The twins, in this world, had not been born and, perhaps because they had never existed, Lauren was able to absorb their absence as easily as anyone can accept that they left their keys to the left or the right of the table lamp. There was no significance. They were not even a memory, they were the wisp of smoke from the corner of a distant dream.

Mr and Mrs Cork, who did live at No. 2, were on the quiet side, but after an initial moment of uncertainty Lauren accepted that she had known them all her life. They smiled at their neighbours and wrote thank-you notelets to everyone who gave them a gift to mark the arrival of Jonathan, their first child, whose birth had been either 'difficult' or 'botched' depending on who you spoke to. Jonny would grow to become the mascot of The Willows, the child welcomed into every home because everyone felt a little bit sorry for him but also a little bit amused by his sunny stupidity. And not a day passed that Mr Cork did not wonder what sort of son would have been his first-born child had a different midwife been on duty that night.

Lauren liked to listen to her parents chatting to each other. She yearned to be older, to be free to do anything at any time of her choosing, to be able to talk about politics and money and know what it meant. She noticed that although her father left the house at twenty-past eight every day and arrived back home just after six thirty in the evening, it was the details of her mother's day which filled the conversations. She wondered if her father was involved in very secretive work or perhaps had a role that was too complicated for casual conversation. Or perhaps his work was so very dull that Vera's trip to the hairdresser's was a more enriching topic of conversation.

Lauren watched him closely. Was he bored? Vera always asked him how he was when he returned home and he would give an economical reply, exhale and then, brightly, ask what had been happening at home. It was one of the puzzles of adult interaction but just as Lauren thought she was close to solving it, everything changed.

Bob arrived home later than normal one December evening, his shirt rumpled, his hair ruffled. Peter Stanning, his boss, had gone missing. Lauren had, for no reason she could fathom, looked at her advent calendar while she digested this exciting but troubling news. Just two windows were open. She felt she had, right there and then, started a countdown; that Peter Stanning had to be found by Christmas Day.

The police had interviewed all the staff at Bob's office, the rumours had grown more intense and more upsetting by the hour, and suddenly all they spoke about at home was Bob's work, Bob's day, Bob's world. As they decorated the Christmas tree, her mother winding cheap tinsel around the branches in what was, to Lauren's mind, an annoyingly gaudy manner, she thought about the tree in the Stannings' house. If your father was missing did you even want a Christmas tree?

Bob became the celebrity of The Willows simply because he was the only person in the cul-de-sac who knew Peter Stanning. Bob was an accountant. Peter was an accountant. Such dramas did not usually unfold in the world of spreadsheets and tax breaks but there was no disputing the fact. Peter had gone missing. Peter had two sons, Peter had a wife who liked horses and growing strawberries, Peter had a sharp brain and a weakness for slapstick comedy. Bob was slightly worried that he could not be sure if he liked Peter all that much or even knew him properly but it felt right to speak of what a great boss he was. Great chap, very smart, very reliable.

There was so much chit-chat about the missing Peter Stanning that Bob felt reality begin to slip. Christmas Day came and went and still he was not found. The anecdote about the sandwiches Peter forgot and left in a drawer to rot and to stink; was that his story or one he was regurgitating? Bob thought he could smell the rotting chicken as he related the tale but this was Miranda the receptionist's reminiscence, not his, wasn't it?

Lauren turned it all into her school project. She produced a cartoon strip that began with Bob and Peter staring at a large graph on a wall, then incorporated the first visit of the police and then the imagined home life of the distraught Stannings. She painted a parcel wrapped in gold-and-red Christmas paper with a gift tag that read, 'for Dad, Merry Christmas.' She had to blink away tears as she wrote the message in a delicate but not trembling hand. She hoped he would be found in time for the start of the new school year so that her storyboard could be completed with a happy ending but Peter Stanning remained missing.

For her fifteenth birthday Debbie took Lauren and her other, less important friends to the cinema to see *Merry Christmas, Mr Lawrence* because they thought it sounded mature. Lauren had bought Debbie a pair of cream leg warmers which the others fawned over as if they were all suddenly living in 1944 and Debbie had been given silk stockings. Julian paid for them all to have a Chinese banquet at the upmarket Mr Yee where Debbie declared her love for David Bowie complete. In the window of Mr Yee's there was a poster asking for information about Bob's boss.

The New Year's Eve of 1983 was a quiet affair. Peter Stanning was still missing in the spring of 1984. Debbie was still Lauren's closest friend and Lauren was impatient to be grown up, to be in love, to be free of the pain in her knee. Since the incident in Cornwall she had been keen to turn the pages on her life rather than dwell in the moment. Only when drawing or sketching or painting did she slow down, enjoy the task at hand, concentrate on the present.

Sixth Form was, really, Dance Form. Led by Debbie, the girls would attend any disco going to be Madonna or Chaka Khan. Lauren, longing to feel love or be loved, wondered if, had she been able to wear heels after her accident, she would have had better luck with boys. She was buoyed enormously to discover that the female students at the art schools she visited all wore pumps or flat boots or trainers and that they looked sexy and cool and desirable. She wondered if her art project, Peter Stanning is Missing, was cool too, or a sixth-form assignment to be binned.

Lauren leaving home was hard for Vera when it came. Bob, too, was emotional. He ran his finger along the tiny windowsill of Lauren's small halls of residence room and inspected it for dust. Vera sniffed the air not knowing if she was expecting to smell drugs or a blocked drain or Cup-a-Soup. Lauren was impatient to explore but paused to hug them both, to promise to phone the next day, to love them forever.

In the car on the way home Vera and Bob agreed they had raised the sweetest, most talented of daughters and inwardly they both wondered if they loved her too dearly and whether life in The Willows would be too quiet, too dependent on knowing the date of her next trip home. Right now, a sibling for Lauren would have helped enormously. None had come though, thought Vera, none had ever come, and she let the tears, large dramatic tears, plop onto her lap as Bob, blinking, concentrated on the road ahead. He switched on the radio for distraction and although there was emotional discussion about the Hungerford massacre that had taken place a few weeks earlier, an incident which had been of political and human interest and therefore one both he and Vera could discuss with equal insight, he could hear only a jumble of meaningless and boring words.

'I just, I just… love her too much,' Vera said out loud and Bob took one hand off the steering wheel to squeeze his wife's arm.

It could be worse, he thought to himself. Peter Stanning, for example, was still missing and the house-to-house enquiries had long dried up. And the Jeep, the bloody Cornwall Jeep, well, that could have been an unthinkable thing.

BOB

Back in Lauren's first life, it would be her birthday soon. Bob could not find the words to describe how much he was dreading it. His daughter had already had one dead birthday, six weeks after Cornwall, but it been just another grotesque day among many. Now that Vera had stopped drinking and started caring about the house and the garden and cooking and even the boutique, this birthday could be a setback. He was scared to mention it, scared not to mention it.

He was so grateful to Peter Stanning. He had been stoically kind to them, especially when they began to feel isolated. It had been agony in The Willows. What had felt cloistered was now confining but it was impossible to contemplate leaving Lauren's room behind for another child to inhabit. And they lived opposite Karen and Julian who had not lost either of their children. Debbie was damaged emotionally but neither Debbie nor her brother had suffered more than bumps and bruises when the Jeep had braked.

The resentment and grief from one side of the spoon mingled poisonously with the guilt and indignation from the other. Ten months passed and then a 'For Sale' sign was put up in front of No. 17. Eventually, the removal van arrived and Debbie with her pink sheepskin rug left for a new home, a new school and the hope of new friends who would not fall out of the back of a Jeep.

The rage that had been directed towards Karen and Julian altered its trajectory and Vera began to blame herself. She stopped eating properly and began to drink heavily. Peter Stanning limply handed over another pot of jam as Vera poured him a Scotch which he barely touched. Bob tried to talk about the office. He was back at work but leaving early to keep an eye on his wife.

'Tell me about your kids,' Vera had slurred at the petrified Peter.

'They, um, they're great kids, Vera, thanks.'

'And would *you* let them go off in the back of a crappy old truck?'

'No, Vera, I wouldn't but I *would* let them go on holiday without me and the wife. Anyone would have done that.'

Vera glowered. It left Peter speechless. Bob cleared his throat. Peter stood up to leave as Vera scratched at the table top with an old butter knife.

'I didn't want her to go but I let her go,' she said, the mother's guilt seeping from her lips, her eyes. 'What if I had put my foot down? She'd be here now. Sat here, right here.'

Vera stared at an empty chair and then put down the knife and slowly pushed her glass to one side.

'I've drunk enough. I'm sorry, Peter. You're a good man.'

'Don't be sorry,' Peter mumbled and there followed a strained, normal conversation about the weather and the deliciousness of Peter's wife's fruit preserves.

Vera stood and smiled politely and walked with him to the front door. Peter did not know her well but it seemed to him that Bob should be more worried about this suddenly calm, reserved Vera than the angry one who blamed herself.

'Any time you like tomorrow, Bob,' Peter said.

'You should go in early tomorrow,' Vera said a week later. 'I'll have a lie-in and potter in the garden and fix us some dinner and I'll be fine.'

Bob was relieved. He felt torn between doing the right thing at home and the right thing at work, and work was so much easier to bear than the quietness of their home. After Peter left, Vera cooked him one of her mild fruity curries, the first she had prepared since the accident and they watched the BBC news still reporting on the fall-out of how Labour, led by Michael Foot, were humiliated in the 1983 General Election, by a Tory party that had to Bob's surprise elected Margaret Thatcher as its leader. Vera did not say how little any of it mattered and even nodded at the political analysis on offer. It felt like the start of something, a life worth living perhaps and he was sure he had Peter's gentle interventions to thank for that.

But it was Lauren's birthday soon and so, as they sat on the sofa in front of the TV, he plucked up some courage.

'Love, I'll take the day off next Tuesday. Maybe we can go and see Suki or drive somewhere quiet and go for a long walk. Whatever you want, love.'

There was silence and then Vera turned and kissed him on the cheek.

'Thank you,' she said but she did not think ahead to the long walk, she thought back. Back to that moment when, alone in the house, with Bob at work and her daughter on her first holiday without her, Vera had pouted into the mirror. Her complexion was youthful, her skin smooth and unblemished. She had a mole close to the top of her left shoulder and she often wondered how she would feel if that mole had ended up on her chin or her cheek or her forehead. One of her teachers at school had a strange sort of wart on the tip of her nose and Vera had thought it ridiculous that it had never been removed.

She was young enough yet for another baby, she had thought. She was feeling upbeat about life, about miracles. Bob was planning to leave work as promptly as possible so they could walk to The Plough together and find a table outside. It had been a shimmering day of unbroken sunshine, the pub would be packed even on a Wednesday. Afterwards they could try for a baby, she thought as she applied Tweed perfume to her wrists and neck. She had walked past Lauren's bedroom and wondered if the weather was as lovely in St Ives for her. She resisted the temptation to sit on her daughter's bed and absorb the scent of her, of her clothes, of her craft box. She'll be home soon enough, she had thought to herself teasingly, and then the phone rang.

Karen began speaking in a slow, strangulated voice and then grew increasingly hysterical. Julian, who had been loitering guiltily outside the door, took over but by now Vera was deaf. It was panic deafness. She really could not hear a word after Karen mentioned a terrible accident.

Oh Vera, there's been a terrible accident.

Vera's throat became tight, she could feel it tighten now, and she had replaced the receiver without saying goodbye. She stood, paralysed, forgetting to breathe. There was a rap on the door and a voice through the letterbox.

'It's me, Monica Harper. Open the door and I'll take care of everything, my dear.'

Vera inched slowly, not sure how to make her legs move, towards the voice of the poshest of her neighbours, who it seemed had been contacted by Julian.

Vera did not know Monica that well at all, only really seeing her at her annual Christmas party, but it transpired that she was calm and efficient and gentle and somehow bundled Vera and Bob onto a train, with overnight bags, to be met by Julian, whose eyes were so cloudy, guilty, hurt and red that both Vera and Bob knew instantly that their daughter was dead.

Everything, in fact, was dead. The friendship with Karen and Julian died. The innocence of Debbie died. Poor Debbie had stretched out to catch hold of Lauren but managed only to scratch her best friend's arm. She would burst into tears in the middle of supper or the middle of class. She became the girl to be avoided.

Some people were kind, others avoided them. Bob's boss, Peter Stanning, not only gave Bob unlimited time off, but frequently drove round after work with fruit and his wife's homemade strawberry jam. Vera would stand at the upstairs windows glaring as the children of The Willows scampered and shrieked, threw balls and fell off scooters. Only Monica Harper would look up and smile at her and offer Vera a glimpse of life beyond bereavement.

Someone organised the funeral. It was not Bob and it was not Vera. Debbie cried the loudest and had to be ushered out of the church before the last hymn had been sung. Teachers said nice things about Lauren's art and Aunt Suki said nice things about Lauren's sweet nature.

Wreaths of flowers were knee-deep in places and the smell of them was pungent and cruel. The Harpers hosted the compulsory post-funeral gathering and even Vera could tell they did it faultlessly.

'Without you...' she said to Monica.

'I know,' Monica said, and kissed her on her forehead. Vera knew it was supposed to have been a healing kiss but the memory of it felt more like she was being given permission to leave behind the pain.

The day before Lauren's second dead birthday Vera waited for Bob to leave and then began rummaging in the cupboard under the sink in the big bathroom. She had squirrelled away a stash of sleeping pills and paracetamol tablets and needed to get going fast.

She had been saving them ever since that first terrible day and the ring of the phone. It had been more important than eating, the hoarding of the pills. Monica's kiss, the Stanning jam and the pills. They were all she had.

Vera had a jug of water to hand and a bottle of whisky. She had planned to swig them while stood at the sink but decided it might be easier to do it at her dressing table. She would be closer, then, to the bed. She counted in Laurens.

One Lauren and swallow. Two Lauren and swallow. Three Lauren and swallow.

When the room began to spin, she lay down with her pre-prepared ice-cold face towel to place on her forehead so she would not vomit and therefore survive. She carried on counting, carried on breathing and then, ever so slowly, stopped.

Bob was slightly later home than usual, wanting to leave everything squeakily efficient at work so he could concentrate on keeping Vera afloat the next day. It was breezy and orange and yellow leaves swirled in the bowels of The Willows as he placed his key in the door. It was quiet and he could not detect any signs of food being prepared. He shouted her name, climbed the stairs and as he reached the landing he smelled the whisky fumes. He paused, he couldn't blame her. He badly wanted a drink too. He tapped lightly on the bedroom door before opening it.

He did not panic upon surveying the scene. Part of him was instantly envious. His wife had escaped the torment. He was not sufficiently calm, though, to take her pulse. He was loath to leave her to go downstairs to the phone so he opened the bedroom window. The curly-haired twins were throwing conkers at each other.

'Hey!' he shouted. They looked up. He asked them to knock on the Harpers' door. They looked at each other quizzically before running off towards their own house. Exasperated, Bob ran down to the phone, made a call he later had no memory of making, left the front door open, then ran back to Vera.

Her face cloth had slipped onto the pillow leaving it wet as if soaked in her tears. He placed his head on her stomach, hoping she would reach down and run her fingers through his hair. When the ambulance crew arrived Vera's blouse was damp too, and Bob, for the first time since his daughter died, was unable to stop sobbing.

VERA

Vera awoke in a panic. She had dreamed she had taken pills and it had been so vivid. She clutched at her flabby stomach but she felt fine, just disorientated. Bob walked in holding their baby.

'I'm glad you were able to nap, love,' he said, 'but she needs a feed.'

Vera wriggled herself upright against the pillows. It was the most beautiful thing in the world to feed little Hope, and the most emotionally cruel. Hope had been conceived in a frenzy of desperate, angry, escapist lovemaking after the death of Lauren. She had promised herself she would kill herself if she could not have another child and she had doubted it would happen, but it had. The sibling had come along. She was too late to be a real sibling. But she was real.

She looked like Lauren but not too much for constant tears. Hope made everyone happy. Vera and Bob had asked Karen and Julian to be godparents and they had cried and cried and cried about it for days afterwards. Debbie ran endless, unnecessary errands for Vera. Aunt Suki had moved in for a fortnight to ease the load, which meant she made lots of tea and toast and answered the phone and the door and reluctantly pegged out washing.

'Oh, Bob, I'm so grateful and so angry all at the same time,' Vera said, 'and I'm worried Hope will know, she will be scarred or withdrawn or frightened of me or something.'

'Nah,' said Bob, smiling. 'She's the most loved child in Cheshire and we'll tell her about her big sister in the right way, of course we will.'

Hope needed to be loved. Her name had the ring of optimism but was drenched in tragedy. Her full name was Hope Lauren Pailing.

Hope's christening was in the same church as…

That was how they all spoke of it. 'It's in the same church as…' There was no need nor desire to finish the sentence. The service was intimate, and conducted at pace, as if those present were pushing against a great weight and they could only hold their arms aloft for so long to avoid being crushed.

There were more guests back at the house, where Vera was complimented on how slender she looked in her new dress. She even summoned a little twirl for Debbie, who was particularly entranced by the crêpe fabric that fell Hollywood style to reach the floor and the way ribbons of silvery silk were woven through it.

'You look so lovely in your silvery silky dress,' Debbie told Vera, in a low voice to avoid making her own mother jealous and she wondered why, when she said so, Vera had blinked rapidly.

Later, sat on the edge of her bed, Vera ran her fingers along the dress which now lay across the bedspread like a willing bride. The silver ribbons glistened in the light from the pair of chintz bedside lamps and she closed her eyes. She had bought the dress three weeks ago. Now she remembered that seven years ago, maybe eight, Lauren had mentioned a silvery silky dress.

Vera smiled sadly. She did not know it while in the shop but she had bought the dress to please Lauren. To fulfil her daughter's idealised image of her, perhaps. To keep their relationship a tangible thing, not just a painful memory.

Peter Stanning drove over with a hand-carved rocking horse and bundles of strawberry jam. He would have done more, but for the fact that he went missing when Hope was three months old.

Vera and Bob had no idea how helpful Peter Stanning had been until he disappeared from their lives.

'You know what, Bob,' Vera said when Peter's vanishing was less of an intriguing piece of gossip and more a fear for the man's life. 'Lauren would have cared about what happened to him. She was so mature, so caring, and she loved a puzzle. She would have been asking us every day, "Any news about Peter Stanning?", wouldn't she?'

Bob accepted all his wife's reminiscences regardless of whether they tallied with his own, but in this instance he really did agree. Lauren would have been fascinated, he was sure of that.

Hope grew up loving her big sister. It was a peculiar kind of love, the sort a teenager has for a distant pop star she has never met. Hope celebrated Lauren's birthday with enthusiasm, blowing out the candles her sister could never breathe over, eating the cake her sister could never taste, singing the songs her sister could never hear. Her favourite bedtime stories where the ones in which Lauren played a starring role. 'Little Red Riding Hood' became 'Little Lauren in a Red Cloak'. Rapunzel had a name change too. And every night Vera would hold out a photograph of Lauren for Hope to kiss before kissing it herself.

Aunt Suki thought it all sickly sweet and unhealthy, but said nothing. She had kissed a photograph of her niece just the once and it had made her maudlin, uneasy and embarrassed. The role of the dead was unclear, especially when it was a child that had died. There was something both touching and terrible in the way Hope would randomly grab at a framed picture in the lounge and plant wet kisses on the face of her sibling. But it made Vera and Bob smile, so Aunt Suki said nothing.

LAUREN

There was a long queue for brunch in the refectory. It was the queue of friendship. So many art students that first Saturday morning made lifelong pals while waiting for eggs and muffins. Lauren gazed about her. She noticed a tall slim man with wild dark hair wearing a crisp white shirt, its sleeves rolled up, and over it a tightly fitting woollen waistcoat. There were girls with dyed hair and spiked hair, girls with long skirts with wacky hems; one girl, Indian perhaps, who glided about as if in her own palace. Everyone had an identity. There was something distinctive about them all. She looked down at her ballet pumps and her simple dress. Maybe her ordinariness was her shtick.

Lauren's first queue friend was Ski, a serious boy of Russian descent who was adored by his mother. His father was less impressed by Ski's desire to study art. But it was Nina, a couple of weeks later, who rechristened Lauren 'Loz'. Nina was a livewire chatterbox and managed to spread the name Loz as quickly as the wind catches hold of wildfire in a dry forest. Lauren did not mind. She needed an interesting name to compensate for her nondescript image.

Lauren took an instant dislike to her tutor. He was five years too old for his tight green T-shirt and it took a good deal of willpower not to stare too hard at his thick rubbery lips. His name was Ossie Thomas-Blake and he held before him Lauren's portfolio.

'I like this,' he said confrontationally.

He was looking at *Peter Stanning is Missing* which Lauren had refined – but which was still, essentially, the work of a sixth-former.

'Too many students fail to find the narrative before they create,' OTB said. 'It is not enough to see a pretty sunset and want to capture it. *Why* do you want to capture it? That's what matters.'

Lauren nodded. She wanted to say that any cartoon strip would have a narrative but held her tongue.

'Is he still missing?'

'What? Oh, yes, he is. It's the biggest news to hit my village,' she said.

'Good,' OTB said. 'Relevant. You should try to find him.'

'I should?' Lauren was struggling now, wondering if OTB was winding her up, if this was a sort of initiation.

'Jeez, I don't expect you to actually find him but you should try to and then put the adventure into your work. Cartoon strips, abstracts, portraiture; anything that feels right.'

'Is that my first-year project?'

OTB smirked.

'That's your first-year project.'

Lauren left his studio bewildered. She had not come to London only to have to trek back home to Cheshire. She almost stamped her foot in frustration. London had been dizzying for the first week but now she felt addicted to the noise and the light, the fact you could buy a hot meal at any time of day or night. There was art everywhere, and theatre, and cinema and live music. Men would kiss while standing in front of posters that told them not to die of ignorance. In the student bar the chat would veer from AIDS to condoms to whether anyone would dare travel through a Channel Tunnel, or to snog Neil Kinnock, the Prime Minister so beloved of most of the students, or shake hands with Jeffrey Archer. Being in London was to be at the centre of the universe. Nothing was taboo. Her fellow students could believe in any god they chose to or believe in nothing at all. The only heated exchange she had witnessed was about the role of photography in a degree portfolio. The art the students produced ranged from overtly sleekly commercial to angry and minimalist and in between there was room for those who used oils and captured light as beautifully as Vermeer.

By contrast, Peter Stanning's absence had become boring, even the police seemed bored when they embarked on one of their shopping-centre blitzes, asking passers-by if they recalled anything unusual, had they seen this man behaving strangely? Had they seen this man? But perhaps that was the point: to be honest about an event that everyone was supposed to be worried or sad about. Or maybe she could jazz it all up, put Peter Stanning into all kinds of outcomes? Hiding in the Australian bush, living with another woman in Wales or dead in the boot of an abandoned car, the victim of mistaken identity.

Vera and Bob were as excitable as toddlers that Lauren came home for a long weekend before the end of her first term.

'I've come home for inspiration,' she said, 'and to see you, of course.'

Lauren made sure she pronounced the word 'inspiration' in a mock-Home Counties voice. She did not want her parents thinking art school had turned her head, given her ideas above her station, as Aunt Suki might say.

It was more difficult than she had imagined, explaining to her parents that OTB had made the disappearance of Peter Stanning her first-year project. It made her feel tacky and insensitive.

'I'm sorry,' she said.

Bob patted her arm. 'No, I think maybe your tutor chap might have a point. Anyway, you don't have to go around upsetting anyone, do you?'

'No, but you're probably tired of it all now, Dad; the last thing you want is me asking you questions about him.'

Bob beamed. 'But you can ask them over a meal at Mr Yee. It'll be a treat for us, really it will.'

Mr Yee had a fresh poster featuring Peter Stanning in his window, which seemed to Lauren to be a sign that her project was current affairs, not old news.

'Fire away, love,' Bob said as he stirred his wonton soup.

'Well, I'd like to know what you really truly think happened.'

'Ah,' he said. 'I keep changing my mind about that.'

'Right now then, what's your best theory?'

Lauren was aware that Mr Yee was listening, above them, at the raised counter where he prepared the bills. She could already envisage Mr Yee making a cameo appearance in her next cartoon strip.

Bob nodded and Vera, sitting across the table, tilted her head. Mr Yee held his breath.

'I think he had a secret, not necessarily a terrible secret, but something that took him away from where he could have been expected to be so the police have not looked anywhere relevant yet.'

Bob raised his hand. 'And. And, I think he was probably hit by a car and rolled down a bank to a place that can't be seen easily. He'll be found one day but it might take years. And. And, I don't want that to be what happened. I'd rather he ran away to a remote paradise and was happy but I don't think that was his style.'

Vera nodded, Lauren frowned and Mr Yee exhaled.

'Do you see his wife ever?' Lauren asked after the silence that followed. She knew Peter had been her dad's boss and not his friend but, still, it was strange that his wife was invisible to them all.

Bob swallowed a wonton. 'Never – and never did really. She was always busy with her horses as far as I could tell.'

Vera did not like horses, so it seemed to her perfectly likely that Peter had been having an affair with a woman who did not wear jodhpurs while smelling of manure. Otherwise, she agreed with Bob's scenario.

So did Mr Yee – with a slight variation. Mr Yee was convinced that Peter Stanning had been on his way to his establishment, keen for some Peking Duck pancakes and plum sauce, before being diverted to an ugly fate.

Lauren decided there and then that her theme would be about the 'not knowing' and the empty space Peter Stanning's absence represented in the lives of those left behind. OTB surely did not expect her to speak to the police or to Mrs Stanning. Before they left, however, she smiled at Mr Yee and asked him if Peter had been a regular customer.

'Best customer. Many Fridays,' he said. 'Such a nice man.'

'Did you speak to the police about him,' she asked.

'No, not police, not ever,' Mr Yee said which left Lauren feeling she had uncovered a clue; a tiny one, but enough to work with artistically.

When back in London she began to sketch Mrs Stanning, a woman she had never met and yet whose face she knew. A face which, for reasons Lauren couldn't understand, she pictured illuminated by April sunshine, smiling as she watched a horde of children aged from three to sixteen hunt for chocolates eggs and ribbon-wrapped five-pound notes. And Lauren framed the drawings with tiny bicycle wheels which she found time-consuming yet oddly soothing. The more wheels she drew the deeper she fell into a reminiscence of something that had never happened. Something to do with sunshine and bicycles that were not in use, and which were now just there as a giant art installation.

Ski did not live like other students. He knew people outside of college, he had money and he rented a basement flat that boasted a central living space big enough for parties. He preferred to lie on giant cushions with selected friends, smoking dope. Tentatively, Lauren joined in. She liked Ski and she did not want to be the one labelled as his prudish pal. She coughed, she spluttered, she laughed and finally she relaxed. Ski recited poetry and his accent became increasingly hysterical. Lauren recited a recipe for coq au vin and Ski giggled uncontrollably.

Nina recited a list of all the boys she could bear to sleep with and Lauren began to feel fretful. There was someone else in the flat, watching them.

'Who is it?' she whispered to Ski.

'It's me,' he said, spluttering with laughter as a thin metal rod pierced his neck.

He did not flinch. Lauren crawled closer, confused, and as she reached out to touch it something made her stop. Something made her tilt her head and peer into the strange piece of taught shiny string. Nina screeched.

'Loz has gone, she's off,' she laughed. 'Loz is going to bite you, Ski.'

Lauren did not hear her, she was looking at a basement flat without any cushions and with Ski having his jeans pulled down by an older muscular man. She gasped and fell back onto her bright orange bean bag.

'Déjà vu, vu, vu,' Lauren said, her head spinning. 'I feel all déjà vu.'

Nina screeched again.

'I'm nicking that, Loz. That's my theme. Fuckin' brilliant. Déjà vu means the same image repeated. Lazy art becomes clever art.'

Lauren sighed. 'I'm so jealous, I have to solve a bloody unsolvable crime and you get to paint one thing and make copies.'

'You'll just have to shag OTB, almost everyone else does,' Nina said and Lauren stumbled, disgusted, to the bathroom.

Lauren decided cannabis could not be her friend. Ski and Nina had just been extra jolly and relaxed while she had seen strangeness and felt strangeness. The beam bothered her a lot. It felt both peculiar and familiar and the vision she had glimpsed was as sharp as a cinema production. Most odd of all was that she felt possessive about it. It had been her beam, meant only for her, and she had not even wondered if Ski or Nina had noticed anything.

She tried to sketch it but it was impossible. The materials did not exist for her to convey the way the shimmering turned reflective and then transparent. The materials most certainly did not exist for her to convey how she was both fearful and transfixed, how she felt knowing as well as surprised.

She worried about Ski contracting AIDS like the men in the adverts even though she had no evidence, beyond what she had seen through the beam, that he might engage in sex with men. Even when he started dating the diminutive and blandly pretty Coral Culkin, an American student with seemingly wealthier parents than him, Lauren still was concerned for his health. She wondered if the seers and witches of old witnessed the sudden arrival of magic string and were similarly cursed with knowledge they did not want.

Try as she might, Lauren could not convince herself that the image was purely the product of smoking pot. It began to annoy as well as unsettle her. So she devoted herself to the missing Peter Stanning.

'Would be weird, Mum, wouldn't it, if he just turned up again?' she said to Vera over the phone on the wall of the kitchen she shared with those on her floor and which was so clogged by fat fumes and errant marmalade that the dial hiccupped its way back to zero which made making calls a long-winded process. She had been worried about the lack of privacy at first but there was always so much background bustling noise from chitter-chatter and music and the lift clanging and the kettle whistling that she could dial home unperturbed about eavesdroppers.

'Well, it would for his wife,' Vera said, 'as she is supposed to be dating a famous showjumper I've never heard of.'

Lauren decided to ignore this as she could not draw horses very well. Instead she produced a painting. Fuchsia reds and russet reds and one small white square representing Peter Stanning. OTB liked it but said it was a bit 'obvious'.

She returned to her desk and turned the white square into an opened window behind which was an image of a Santa hat. She smiled at the memory of Peter Stanning in costume, with a silky fake white beard, at the Christmas party in her father's office. She knew now what she would paint next; an advent calendar full of versions of Peter's fate, building to the climax of crucifixion. It was blasphemous, but she knew that OTB would adore it.

BOB

In a bleaker world in which Peter Stanning was not yet missing, and Lauren and Vera were not out shopping, not anywhere at all, Bob was alone in the house that had become the dark house on The Willows. Even the twins would edge away from its driveway. Nobody knew what to say. No one except Peter Stanning, who had seen it coming but had no way of warning Bob, none at all.

One day, Peter drove over with a small casserole prepared by his wife. He fiddled with the oven.

'Right, that will be warmed though in half an hour so, so in the meantime, let's look at our options.'

Bob blinked through bleary medicated eyes.

'I have one option, top of the list,' Bob said bitterly but not nastily.

'Yes, of course you have, Bob,' Peter said stoically and firmly but not unkindly. 'But allow me to talk through some others.'

He opened a notebook and cleared his throat.

'One. Sell up, buy a small flat closer to the office, work when you feel like it, come to supper at our place, let the staff be kind, find a new life. Slowly. With our help.

'Two. Family. You have a sister, anyone else? Maybe family abroad, maybe friends abroad? Sell up and travel to them, see the world, anyway. Find a reason to enjoy life.

'Three. New career. Leave us if it helps, work for yourself or a new company where they don't know you. Or retrain, take an Open University course, become a teacher or a librarian or an architect or a permanent student.

'Four. Do nothing, but know I'll take you back on at any time. When you are ready.'

He closed his notebook self-consciously.

Bob groaned and then swiftly sat up.

'I can't thank you enough, Peter. I, really – could you leave me the list? I'll think about things, I will.' Bob summoned a small smile. 'Maybe after the stew.'

'We're eating it together,' Peter said.

The two men sat in silence for a while, and then Peter emptied the bin and cleared some old food from the fridge before serving up the soupy beef.

'I think that was nice,' Bob said, 'but I can't seem to taste anything. Actually, Suki, my sister, asked to stay but I told her no. Perhaps...'

Peter seized on the idea.

'Yes, absolutely, even if just for a few days, Bob. I know it would be better than you being on your own so why not call her now? I can speak to her too if it helps.'

Oddly, Bob thought it would help. He handed the phone to his boss. Between them, Peter and Suki concocted a plan to keep Bob from festering.

'But she can't sleep in Lauren's room,' Bob said in a sudden panic.

'No, of course not, Bob,' Peter said. 'She'll do everything required to make the spare room what she needs.'

Bob had been sleeping alternately in his daughter's room, his and Vera's room, and the spare room. They were all a bit smelly and somehow Peter knew this. He went upstairs and opened the window to the spare room and stripped the bed. He had told Suki to bring her own bedding.

Suki was a limited cook, but it was hardly appropriate, she decided, for the pair of them to be dousing pancakes with Grand Marnier or flambéing steaks. Suki was a limited housekeeper too, but even she could tell the place needed a good hoover. After vacuuming the entire house, she decided she had been enough of a martyr and called on the neighbours and devised a rota. She would look after Sundays and Monday mornings, but everyone else would have to chip in with something the rest of the week. The mother at No. 2 yelled at her twin boys to offer to wash Bob's car, and when Suki realised that would be the most she would get from her she accepted the offer with a forced smile.

'We don't know him,' said the couple who had recently moved into No. 17 and found The Willows to be a morose sort of place.

'In that case, you can just drop off milk and bread on Thursday mornings,' Suki said. 'If he doesn't answer, leave it outside the door.' And with that she left them gawping, railroaded, and even more regretful that they had chosen this house over the smaller one near the church. Suki found The Willows stifling and dull and told Bob it would be a diversion, and good for him, to sell up. He mumbled something non-committal. Suki smiled, sadly. Bob was the quietest, least interesting person she knew but she was fond of him, always had been, and it angered her that he was being made to suffer.

'We should visit Vera's mum, don't you think, Bob?'

Bob was startled and for the first time in weeks felt something other than self- absorbed grief. Beryl would be having just as awful a time of it as he was. Maybe worse. But he could not bear to phone her so Suki took charge of their sombre trip past Stockport to Marple Bridge and Beryl's damp stone cottage.

At least, Suki thought it was damp. Everyone else thought it a sweet and cosy sort of place, but as soon as they walked in Suki began to feel uncomfortable. Every side table and shelf was stacked with photographs. Vera and Bob on their wedding day, Vera holding baby Lauren, Beryl and Alfie holding baby Lauren, Beryl holding baby Vera, Lauren on her first day of school, her uniform slightly too big, her briefcase slightly too formal. The telephone, instead of being on the hall table or in a corner, sat incongruously in the middle of the polished round dining table at the back of the living room. More than any photograph, it told a picture of loss. No more chats about nothing much at all with her daughter or her granddaughter.

To Suki's surprise, the visit was a success. Bob tried to cheer up Beryl and Beryl tried to cheer up Bob. Bob told her about his 'options' and Beryl told him she had none unless she considered leaving the country to stay with her sister and her family in Canada but as she had not been invited she could not, really, consider it much of an option at all.

'Funny place to want to live, don't you think?' she said to Suki.

'Utterly ludicrous,' Suki said and for the first time in a long time Bob gently chuckled.

It was a turning point. It was as if one chuckle had broken the spell of pain and inertia. Bob decided he could have a future and it only took him two years to decide which one. It was not on the list made by Peter Stanning but it was in the spirit of it. Bob rented out No. 13 The Willows because he could not bear to break the ties completely, and bought an apartment in a trendy conversion overlooking the River Mersey and not too far at all from Suki. He did not retrain, but set himself up as a consultant, working on projects for Peter's business and for smaller clients.

When Peter vanished, the December after presenting Bob with his life options, Bob helped out from a sense of duty, but gradually he expanded his private client base and cut his ties to his old firm. He liked to be busy but he also liked knowing he could cut away for brief periods and wallow and weep without letting anyone down. One Sunday each month he let Beryl cook him a roast chicken, and one Saturday each month Suki let herself take him out to a pub or the cinema.

Was it living? Suki wondered sometimes how her brother's mind worked, whether he could forget for a while about his wife and daughter or if it might be worse if he could forget only to have to remember and suffer all over again. There was something very contained about Bob, she thought. It was like being with an acrobat, a man treading the high wire and wanting to appear confident and calm but knowing one lapse in concentration could lead to a catastrophic fall. His laughter was measured, his smiles were tempered, his eyes could twinkle but only dimly. She remained, all the same, very fond of him.

'Do you fancy seeing *Prizzi's Honor*?' Suki asked Bob on the phone ahead of their regular Saturday outing. His wife had been dead for two years and his daughter had been dead for over three but, still, there was a remnant of it being somehow inappropriate to spend too much time wondering which film they should see.

'Seen it, Suki, very good, though.'

Suki paused. How had he seen it, the film had only been in cinemas for a week?

'I went with Rachel,' he said.

'Who the fuck is Rachel?' Suki said.

Bob laughed.

'I think I somehow ended up on a date,' he said.

'In that case no movie for us on Saturday, we're meeting for a drink,' Suki said.

Rachel was deep into divorce proceedings and had employed Bob to untangle the financial mess of her marriage. There was a large house on The Wirral, a large house near Lake Windermere and a flat in Menorca to be sold off and all manner of stocks and shares and registers which Rachel had not even known her name was attached to.

Rachel had a golden tan, long legs and expensive hair and when she met Bob she realised how much she wanted a solid man who did not travel, who was straightforward and honest and serious and highly unlikely to have been secretly shagging another woman for the past seven years. The fact that Bob did not notice her tan, her legs or her hair made him desperately attractive to her. The fact that Bob was sad and damaged made him irresistible.

Suki wondered how protective she should be. Rachel could

be a shallow vulture or exactly what her brother needed. She rattled off her questions.

'How old is she?'

'Er, forty.'

'Children?'

'Nope.'

'Does she have a brain?'

'She knows a lot about Menorca.'

Suki paused. Was Bob humouring her?

'OK, I'm sorry,' she said. 'It's just, well, you know.'

'I know,' he said.

Eventually, Rachel was introduced to Suki. Bob's sister had low expectations. Yes, she was attractive and very golden for someone living on Merseyside. She was dressed immaculately in beige and cream and her eyes glazed over when Suki made a quip about Thatcherism. Just as Suki gave up any notion she would be able to stomach Rachel for the length of any meal together, Bob's new friend let slip she had bought a dilapidated building and was refurbishing it to become a women's shelter.

'I was lucky,' she said. 'I could afford to disappear for a few days while I recovered from being let down by Gary and in any case Gary's not the violent type. But there are plenty of women who ought to leave their husbands and can't because they are too poor or too afraid.'

Suki was intrigued and by the end of the evening had agreed to join the executive committee of the nascent charity. By the end of the year they were firm friends. Bob would sometimes lean back in his chair as the pair animatedly discussed the charity's progress and feel he was living someone else's life. Vera and Lauren were sometimes so far away that he needed to reel their memory back in like a fisherman scared of losing a big catch. The remembering hurt but the notion of forgetting was terrifying.

And then, remarkably, he found himself discussing marriage. He half wanted his sister to dissuade him but if anything Suki seemed to be as fond of Rachel as he was. Bob was content with things as they were but also knew that was not allowed. No one was allowed to drift. Things had to be headed somewhere. In a muffled way he heard conversations about a new life together, starting afresh, commitment, cementing the relationship. It was true. He was in a new relationship. Sometimes he woke and wondered who he was. Sometimes he woke and he did not feel sad and he had Rachel to thank for that. If she needed them to be married, so be it.

LAUREN

Lauren's student days were almost done. Her friends were plotting, planning, leaving, stagnating, worrying. The answer to almost every question was to party. She found herself at the entrance to a nightclub that was grubby to the point of extreme elitism. She groaned. Her knee hated heels and hated dancing. Just this once people said – or maybe she was the one who said it. Let's end this thing in style.

Everyone had their arms in the air, there was jumping, swaying, gyrating to Inner city's 'Big Fun'. She liked it. No one but men had heels on and even the ugly were sexy. Everyone is ugly, she thought, everyone is sexy. Ski placed a tablet on her tongue. 'I know,' he said, 'but just once, Loz, just one, just for me.' He swallowed and smiled, Nina smiled, so she swallowed and smiled and soon the music was in her belly, warming her with love.

'*I love*,' she shouted to Ski, and then it appeared.

Across the middle of the dancefloor there hung a row of metal strings that had no end and no beginning. She gasped. There was beauty and danger and familiarity. And fear. And love. She swayed closer to the beams that were glittering mirrors and then suddenly magical glass. She peered into the rod that was closest to her eyeline saw the same dance floor, the same bar, but in place of students were lots of middle-aged men and women dressed in school uniform and dancing provocatively. The women had their hair in silly pigtails and wore short skirts and shirts that were too tight and the men were just drunk enough not to laugh at themselves.

She peeled away and turned her back on the beams, which she sensed were reproducing. She wanted love not peculiarity. But then she was twirled around again and the compulsion was too strong. She tilted her head and saw an empty supermarket with a solitary woman mopping the floor. The overhead lights flickered and the woman looked over her shoulder as if only just at that moment realising she was alone in a big building. Lauren wanted to hug her but then she mopped her way out of view and Lauren was left staring at an aisle of breakfast cereal and teabags.

She stepped to her left to peer into another kingdom but it was without illumination of any kind. She moved on to another beam and saw dancing much like the dancing she was part of right now. On tiptoes she peered into a big kitchen with sweating men wiping down tables and sealing bin bags, and then she lost her balance and was pushed forward into the shining lattice, pain searing through her temple, and it hurt so much she passed out.

It hurt so much that her parents travelled down from Cheshire. It hurt so much she mumbled about glass and light and visions and not caring who heard. It hurt so much she promised Bob and Vera she would never take drugs again in her life. It hurt so much she knew it was not the ecstasy. The tablet had unleashed something that was part of her, just as the cannabis had back in Ski's flat. She would have been terrified except for a nagging sense of continuity. It has always been there, she thought. It is always there. It is part of who I am. She stared at the mole on her mother's forehead as if it held all the answers before falling into a deep recuperative sleep and dreaming of angels carrying her to a Heaven that looked just like home.

Her parents had returned to The Willows worried but triumphant. They had known all along that London was dangerous. Vera had ached to bring Lauren home and install her in her small bedroom with its sheepskin rug and she could not understand why, even though her studies were at an end, her daughter felt the need to stay in the capital a week longer. Every time the phone rang, Vera hoped it was Lauren, hoped it was Lauren with the noise of a railway station in the background and her only child raising her voice to tell her she was about to step onto a train and could Bob meet her the other end because she had all her belongings with her.

The phone did ring but the line was crystal clear. Lauren was very permanently in London.

'Is Peter Stanning still missing?' she asked Vera, to lighten the mood. Her mother sounded close to tears.

'I'll visit soon, Mum,' Lauren said unable to think of anything else to add.

'I'll put your dad on,' Vera said.

'Tell me the news, then,' Bob said.

'Well, I can't quite believe it, Dad, but I've got the first job I applied for. I'm assistant to an art editor at an ad agency.

It's not a big one or a famous one, you won't have heard of it but that might be a good thing really, but I think Mum is… disappointed.'

Bob lowered his voice. 'Jan's daughter is back home from finishing university in Edinburgh, and you know the Weller boy, he's been back from college for two years and is still with his parents now. I think your mother thought you'd be coming home too, at least for a few months. But she knows this is great news. She'll be OK, and we're so proud of you, you know that.'

Lauren sighed. The burden of being not just an only child but one they had almost lost, not once now, with the Jeep, but twice, thanks to the ecstasy, never grew lighter but she had too much to do in London to spare time for a trek back home. She had to find a flat, buy work clothes, find *herself*, really. This was the grown-up world and she wanted to be calm and ready for it.

Before the night in the club she had been living with Ski, but he did not want a permanent flatmate and could be disconcertingly moody, and Nina had, to everyone's astonishment, secured a place on a post-grad course in New York, so Lauren scoured advertisements until she arrived at an address in Paddington where the door was opened by a twenty-something man in pyjama bottoms and a T-shirt.

He grunted then smiled and turned towards two women who had walked into the hall.

'Can we have this one, please?' said the man, whose name was Luke, as he ambled upstairs.

The women tutted and fussed, apologised for Luke's behaviour, made her a mug of tea and quizzed her about every inch of her life story without seeming nosy at all.

'We share the big double bedroom at the front,' one of the girls, Kat, said as the other girl, Amy, nodded. They went silent then, looking at Lauren for signs of disgust or discomfort.

Lauren took it as a cue to ask questions about the household. Were there other couples? What jobs did they have? How long had they lived there?

They drank more tea, laughed a good deal, and then Luke appeared, fully dressed, his hair damp from the shower.

'Have they done a character assassination on me?' he asked.

'You are Luke and you are twenty-five,' Lauren said, 'and you are a social worker and do more good for the world than all the people Kat and Amy know put together but you never, ever put food back in the fridge.'

Luke pouted and Lauren felt herself fall in love right there and then, but she had not asked Kat and Amy if Luke was single, or if they would hate her to be in love with him, or even if everyone fell in love with him. I'll find out soon enough, she thought.

Ski offered to help her move in but all he did was lean against a wall, smoking and nodding as Luke, Kat, Amy and a post-grad student only ever called Jeffers carried Lauren's suitcases and bedding and art to her second-floor room.

Lauren had shared a house in her second year with three girlfriends, all art students, and of course she had lived with Ski, but this felt different, much more grown-up – a rite-of-passage moment. She had two days to settle before starting her new job. Her career. Her proper life.

Luke, predictably, was the spaghetti-sauce man, while Kat and Amy provided Sunday roasts even if no one else was in and Jeffers was a dab hand at chicken breasts in a variety of sauces all of which contained copious amounts of cream. This left Lauren to summon a specialty. She phoned Vera in a panic, who, pleased to be needed, calmly talked her daughter through the baking of fish as well as the creation of a salad Niçoise.

The Paddington house had an old-fashioned pantry as well as a fridge and when she first opened its door she became transfixed by the smell of stale jam tarts and old butter biscuits. It was such a familiar and happy sort of smell. She held the doorframe and closed her eyes and felt herself hurtling down The Willows on a tricycle then being walked back up the cul-de-sac again, hand in hand with her mother towards a large van, and she smiled at herself for having such an odd daydream. She opened her eyes when she thought she heard a man's voice, a Welsh accent. But when she walked into the hallway there was nobody there.

Lauren's office on Charlotte Street was airy, her immediate boss a short compact serious man in his thirties whose shirts were beautifully ironed, and her workmates were bustling and busy but they smiled and were welcoming. On the streets outside people wore acid-washed denim and big jumpers but in the office the staff were either impeccably suited or wore stylistically independent T-shirts with clever slogans over expensive leather skirts. The only faux pas was to not know what your own style was. One night, a few days in, she joined them for after-work drinks before travelling home for Luke's Thursday-night pasta. Even my knee is happy, she thought, having spent an entire day without noticing even a twinge.

Jeffers opened a bottle of port to toast her first four days in gainful employment and the fact that Thursday was the new

Friday. As she drifted towards drunkenness a beam of silvery light cut across the big sagging sofa. Lauren lurched forward and then stopped, filled her glass with water and drank it quickly, refusing to be drawn towards the apparition. She drank another glass and another and then made coffee. As she sobered up the metallic light ebbed and she was filled with an indescribable sorrow. She had let someone or something down, and she went to bed confused and unhappy. In the morning, though, she remembered none of it, except that she was a maudlin drunk and needed to limit her alcohol intake.

VERA

Lauren had been such a talented artist, Vera couldn't help but think, upon being presented with Hope's latest creation. Hope was hopeless at drawing but besotted with trying. She would endlessly present her parents with pictures of stick men with fried red hair and trees with giant apples and tiny branches. And every time it hurt. Every time Vera would remember the grace of Lauren's earliest attempts to depict a house or a garden or a cat, the way she coloured in so neatly and always added her own little flourish to even a join-the-dots page.

She bought her a miniature keyboard to encourage a different passion, but Hope was uninterested. She encouraged her to help make cakes, but Hope's inquisitiveness faded quickly. One evening, though, as Bob sat with a large cumbersome calculator at the kitchen table, Hope sat on his lap and began to ask questions about numbers.

'I wish the tooth fairy could bring me a calculator,' she told Vera a few days later. Much to the annoyance of the parents of her peers, that was exactly what the tooth fairy brought

Hope on her next visit, and Vera and Bob's maths prodigy was unleashed.

Or, at least, they had a child that liked numbers – but Vera was prone to exaggeration and given her still-evident grief no one reined it in. One lazy Saturday morning Vera found Hope staring into the middle distance and slowly moving forward.

'Don't do that,' she said sharply and Hope burst into tears.

'I'm sorry, sweetheart, naughty Mummy, silly Mummy,' Vera said breathlessly, bundling Hope into a giant guilt-ridden cuddle.

Vera waited for Hope to say it, to start speaking about another mummy, but she said nothing other than she had spotted peppermint creams in the cupboard and could she have one pretty please.

It helped, though. It helped Vera accept Hope as Hope, a slightly dumpy child with a beaming smile, a desire to please and a fondness for the times tables. Aunt Suki breathed out properly for the first time in years. Hope could be Hope. The endless comparisons were coming to an end.

'I've asked George Stanning to come over for supper,' Bob said abruptly. They did not entertain much. Vera was not cross, just surprised.

'Why?' she said, but not acerbically. 'I mean, I didn't even realise you knew him.'

Bob frowned. He did not know either why he had invited Peter's eldest son over. George had been in the office and had been asking questions about the business that had turned into questions about his father and it had dawned on Bob that he, of all the people in the building, had known Peter the best or at least the longest. Peter had been such a rock after Lauren's death and in return he had offered nothing to George or the rest of the family when Peter had gone missing. He groaned a little as he recalled taking George for a pint and how the poor boy had to mature fast. 'Missing presumed dead' was not a phrase much used in Cheshire. Like everyone else, Bob had refused to contemplate what such a state of limbo would mean to Peter's family and they had certainly not really discussed it in the pub. It had been, now he thought about it, more a case of George cheering Bob than of Bob cheering George; and he remembered how typically male they'd been, reminiscing rather than addressing the future.

'And anyway why would a teenager want to spend an evening with us?' Vera added.

'He's not a teenager, he's twenty-one,' Peter said, 'and, well, he said he wanted a proper chat about the business, and from what I can gather he does not get on with his mother's new man and well, why not, eh?'

Hope appeared. She had started watching *Coronation Street* and treated it as a documentary, as a way to see into the lives of grown-ups.

'Was Lauren divorced?' she asked and Vera, instead of stifling a sob, laughed out loud and planted a kiss on her daughter's forehead.

'Oh, Bob, you explain what divorce is.'

Bob, smiling, told Hope about grown-ups and weddings and breaking friends and as his daughter became bored and wandered away, he took hold of Vera's hand and repeatedly kissed it as she laughed and laughed to make up for all the laughter their home had lacked for so long. It was fortuitous happiness because George brought his girlfriend, which rattled

Vera, but she hid it so well that Bob felt a surge of protective pride. Vera avoided any young women of a parallel age to Lauren yet somehow here was one in her living room drinking the gin Bob had somehow known to buy in for their guests. Worse still, it soon became clear that it was Vera's job to talk with Felicity while Bob and George discussed the future of the firm. It all threatened to become too much to bear when Hope crept down the stairs in her fluffy pale blue pyjamas, stood before Felicity and sleepily said, 'Are you my big sister?'

Vera gasped involuntarily and blinked rapidly at Bob for help, but none was needed. Felicity had been well briefed and she scooped Hope onto her lap and stroked her hair.

'Hello, pretty one,' she said. 'I'm not your sister but I'd like very much to be your friend. My name is Felicity. Would you like me to read you a story in bed, to help you get back to sleep?'

Hope beamed and nodded as did Vera and the pair of them ascended the stairs hand in hand.

'Fels loves kids,' George said. 'She's training to be a nurse. She's amazing.'

Later, as she cleared the table, Vera felt a small burst of liberation. She had room for warmth towards Felicity. After all, she looked nothing like her Lauren would have looked by now, and Lauren would not have gone into nursing. And George, who had his own troubles, adored her, needed her, perhaps.

'Have you spoken to George about his father?' Vera asked Bob as they lay in bed, the last people in The Willows to retire, it not being the sort of enclave that saw much in the way of midweek entertaining over supper.

'A little,' Bob said. 'But more about the practical side of

things. I think he must sometimes feel angry that Peter just vanished, I mean angry towards him, leaving them all like that.'

Vera chose never to think about Lauren's funeral, partly because it was a blur, but she knew it must have helped her come to terms with reality. Meanwhile poor George had had no father to bury, and must always be wondering if there could be a chance Peter might be found, alive if not necessarily well. In the darkness, as if he could tell she was trying to make sense of all their grief, Bob took Vera's hand.

BOB

After a small civil ceremony, Bob and Rachel set up home not far from the sea. The house was a detached Victorian villa of blackened brick which Rachel told him was classy. She was attentive and happy. She was always busy but would fall into his lap in the evenings and knead his shoulders as if he had been hunched too long over paperwork. Which he rarely had. Bob deliberately kept his workload modest. He liked to go for bracing walks and watch nature at work. The sight of a washed-up jellyfish would put him in a good mood for hours. The beige foam at the water's edge made him grin. And when he came home, Rachel and Suki would be chatting away and he wondered how he would feel if he had to walk into a cold house with no noise, no people, no family. He would joke to clients that Suki and Rachel were the married couple and he was a convenient alibi. Sometimes a client would smile, sometimes a client would look puzzled and sometimes a client would sneer with a salacious glint in his eyes.

There was a girl with a whippet most days in the sand dunes. She wore a bobble hat and a denim jacket through the autumn and early winter and, once Christmas was over and the winds started to bite, she wore a ludicrously huge baby-blue woollen scarf. Sometimes she smiled a tight wary smile if he was close by and sometimes he did not even notice she was there. Then the scarf came off and then the hat and one still, windless day in March 1988 notable only for being the last day of tin mining in Cornwall, she plopped herself down next to Bob as he sat on top of a dune gazing out towards Blackpool Tower on the horizon.

Without the hat he would not have recognised her, but the whippet jogged his memory.

'Do you know, we are often the only people on the beach,' she said.

'That won't last long,' he said, not turning to face her. 'There'll be kite flyers, paddlers and ice-cream munchers galore soon.'

She studied his profile and guessed he was around forty. She glanced at his left hand and saw that he did not wear a ring – which could mean anything, of course. Still, she liked his voice and his thick dark hair, so decided not to ask the question – and vowed to have a full-blown kiss with him before…

'April Fool's Day,' she said.

'Is it?' he said.

'No, you daft beggar, it's the sixth of March.'

'Thought so,' he said which was, to Andrea, the girl, both annoying and intriguing. Still, she had to stand up and leave before he did so she placed the lead on the whippet and walked for a few yards before turning round. Bob was still not looking at her. He had forgotten her. He had forgotten everything. He felt cleansed here, free of the past, free of the present. He could stare at the changing light, the rolling clouds, the twinkling movement of the water and think of nothing at all.

Three days later, the temperature dropped and the skies were a steel grey. Andrea, back in her bobble hat, ran close to the water's edge, her dog seemingly disappointed in how little competition she provided over their hundred-metre dash. She knew he was there, high up, not really looking at her and she weighed up the pros and cons of turning her back to the sea to stand and wave at him. She decided she could not resist so swivelled on her heels which made her sink into the wet sand and lose her balance just as an extra-large wave hit the shore.

Her backside was wet now and cold but she remained on the muddy sand, annoyed enough to punish herself. Suddenly he was there holding out his hand. She had no choice but to take it. This was not part of the fantasy she had concocted.

He was frowning.

'Everything all right?' he said.

'S'pose,' she said. 'It's your fault.'

'Of course it is,' he laughed.

'I was turning to wave to you, you know, to be friendly, and now I look an idiot.'

'You should get home, have a hot bath,' he said.

'Yeah, I guess,' she said. 'I'm Andrea, by the way.'

'Hello, Andrea, I'm Robert,' he said, and in that moment he knew there was a germ of flirtation or subterfuge. He had not called himself Robert since his wedding day.

Wedding days, he said to himself. Wedding days.

LAUREN

'I will never drink port again,' she said to Luke the next day as they stared at the toaster waiting for the ping.

'Jeffers is always doing that,' Luke said. 'He'll give us anything but wine. It's his thing.'

She watched him butter his toast and noticed how graceful he was, how beautiful, beautiful enough to be someone in fashion or film but he was probably off to save a life.

Jesus Christ, I am in love with him, she thought, and kept on thinking all day.

Luke was, she concluded, unattainable. She was not in his league in terms of looks or in terms of integrity but there was something else, a much larger obstacle. He was diffident, he floated as if totally blind to his appealing qualities while simultaneously possessing a composure that only comes with being self-aware. She imagined him as a spoilt, irresistibly cute child, winning trophies, captaining the school team, never suffering self-doubt. Perhaps he could come to love her gradually if she learned to bake cakes and took him to the cinema.

Their toaster moment became a precious and rare one. Days and evenings passed when she simply never saw him. When he did sit down to eat with them he did so distractedly and Kat and Amy excused him for failing to produce a single pasta dish for a month. They knew him much better than Lauren did and their adoration only served to deepen her attachment to him.

Lauren began to construct fantasies that would make him want her. As Christmas approached, she pictured him confessing he had nowhere to spend it and imagined that they would travel to Cheshire together as the snow began to fall, forcing them to stay in a quaint hotel with a real fire in the last available bedroom. He was the least needy person she had ever met, however, and would probably happily spend Christmas Day by himself in the London house.

Sure enough, when the time came, she was sat on the packed train alone, then soon holding a glass of sherry at the Harpers' house and being asked the same three questions over and over.

'No, no one special. Yes, it can be glamorous but mostly it's lots of hard work. I know they miss me, I miss them too.'

The Harpers had carols playing from speakers she could not see and there were plenty of people milling around she could happily never speak to again, and yet she was expected to make small talk with them once a year. Debbie had found herself a boyfriend and was in Truro with his family. It was the first Christmas Debbie had been absent from The Willows and Lauren missed her terribly, even though she had barely thought about meeting up with her again beforehand.

A balding man in a bright red jumper decorated with

snowmen told her about his time at university and how he rejected a job in London to be able to help his ailing mother. He acted as if he knew her well and yet she did not even remember his name or which house he lived in. She nodded, feigning interest, hoping the terrible twins would knock over a plate of mince pies and create a diversion.

'Are the twins coming?' she asked Mr Harper as he replenished her glass.

'Twins?' he said. 'Not aware of any. You'll have to ask my good lady wife.'

She was about to tell him that he must know the twins but then she realised she could not recall what they looked like or their names or even if they were part of The Willows. Perhaps they were in a book, she thought, and she might have been bewildered by her confusion but her father squeezed her hand tightly and asked if she wanted to stay or leave with them. She rolled her eyes and linked arms with him.

As she and her parents left, Mrs Harper called out to Lauren.

'Good luck, my dear,' she said almost wistfully.

Lauren waved her thanks and stopped to look at the Harpers' Christmas decorations. Having a small pine tree planted in their front garden certainly helped and it was bedecked with large red bulbs and heavy glass baubles. Lauren smiled at the earnestness and enthusiasm of it all. She cocked her head slightly as her gaze drifted towards their large stained-glass window.

'It wasn't always a dove,' she said to Vera who was stood alongside her. 'What happened to the wheat?'

Vera squinted.

'It's always been a dove,' she said. 'You had me worried there for a minute.'

Lauren was not convinced, but she let it go. Maybe I've just outgrown the cul-de-sac, she thought to herself. She used that theory as the explanation for everything that felt strange. Each time she walked into the kitchen she felt as if something were missing; each time she walked into her bedroom it felt as if she were trespassing. The fact her parents had done nothing to remove the brown stain in the bathroom sink annoyed her. She let her fingers run along the thick golden tinsel on the Christmas tree in the living room and told herself to be less snobby about her loving home.

Later, Vera produced a photograph of Lauren, aged seven, dressed as a shepherd for the school nativity play.

'Look what I found,' her mother exclaimed.

Lauren gazed at the picture and shook her head.

'You know, Mum, I don't remember it at all.'

'Well, you were only seven,' Vera said, 'and you didn't want to be an angel for some reason.'

Lauren smiled weakly and gazed at the tree that was weighed down by miniature Christmas crackers, its foil-wrapped chocolate reindeer and yards and yards of tinsel.

As a break from the endless turkey and stuffing sandwiches, they drove to Mr Yee's. The poster depicting Peter Stanning was still there and, when there was a quiet moment as the number of customers thinned out, Mr Yee tapped Lauren on the shoulder. She followed him to his desk and he pulled out a large grey scrapbook.

She thought for a moment that he might be a shy artist, keen for someone who had attended art school in London to deliver an encouraging verdict but Mr Yee had collected cuttings, all of them about the disappearance of Peter Stanning.

'Very nice man,' he said.

Lauren turned the pages carefully. She had read most of the reports since his disappearance and seen most of the available photographs but she paused before a double-page spread which showed scenes from the Stanning home that she had not come across before. There was a beautiful landscaped garden, stables and a large outhouse, its huge doors wide open revealing a discarded wheelbarrow and a row of bicycles of differing sizes. Without thinking, Lauren counted them with the tip of her fingernail.

'Why you do that?' Mr Yee said.

'I have no idea,' she said.

Luke was thinner when Lauren returned to London and Kat and Amy fussed all the more over him.

'Christmas is a terrible time of year for him,' they said in unison and for a minute or two Lauren saw past how tragically handsome he was and understood that his job was quite possibly indescribable. She joined in the platonic fussing and helped her housemates prepare a post-Christmas Christmassy supper while feeding him smoked salmon on triangles of sliced brown bread. Jeffers opened a bottle of Fino which he said would go well with the salmon and the five of them slowly sank into a warm and gentle alcoholic stupor as they swapped festive tales and Luke, at last, became serious and told them about an artificial tree under which was a box containing a dead puppy and a five-year-old boy made to sleep in a baby's cot. Amy burst into tears and Kat glared at her, then softened as she pulled her gently upstairs. Jeffers ambled off to find brandy and Lauren was left alone with Luke.

She so wanted to say the right thing but she hardly knew him really.

'Do you get… I mean, do they teach you how to handle the sad things?'

'Not really,' he said quietly. 'If you need that sort of help then you're in the wrong job. You can't get sentimental. I cope, I suppose, because I know that by being hard I help more people. You don't save kids by crying. Or hurting.'

It was the most grown-up thing she had ever heard. She touched his hand lightly and he did not flinch. She sighed and tried to sound upbeat.

'In that case, do you ever get a holiday?'

He smiled.

'Oh, you bet,' he said. 'Cheapest skiing I can find.'

To her dismay the first thing that occurred to Lauren was not how glad she was that this saint of a man would get a break but that her knee would not let her ski.

'I take it from that face that you hate skiing,' he said.

'I'll never find out,' she said, pointing to her leg.

'Well, you can go for walks and drink lots of glühwein,' he smiled as Jeffers walked back in peering at a label on an expensive-looking bottle.

The next morning she woke with the same thoughts she had fallen asleep repeating.

Was that an invitation or a casual, meaningless, throwaway remark? Should she say something? She decided she couldn't. He would find his bargain break and either mention it again or not. It did not stop her from buying a new dressing gown so that she could be presentable at weekend breakfasts. It did not stop her pretending she had made too much toast, would he like some? Too much bacon, would he like some?

Meanwhile, Luke trundled around in an old stained T-shirt and crumpled pyjama bottoms in a daze, and Lauren knew he ought to smell bad but he didn't, and she wanted to ask him to go for a walk to Kensington Gardens but she couldn't, so she went alone and gave herself a strict talking-to about how having a crush was a waste of energy, but it made not a jot of difference.

BOB

The hail had ceased and the sky had turned silvery so Bob placed a paperweight, a gift from Suki in which floated the seed head of a dandelion, one of his daughter's favourite flowers to draw, on his spreadsheets and left the house. He had recently bought himself a bike, so depressing did he find the need to drive to the beach. Short drives were an irritating if inevitable element to life in the countryside, but it felt somehow grubby to drive past the pines and their squirrels to the dunes. It was what old people did or those with toddlers. Or perverts, perhaps. The bike was much better.

Andrea was not there and he realised he had no idea what pattern she kept. He had no regular time slots for the beach. Sometimes she was there and sometimes she wasn't. Maybe she was there on the days even when he sat for hours on end which could imply she visited the coastline every day with her dog and that to see her all he had to do was hang around long enough.

But I'm not here for her, he told himself as he walked out towards the water's edge. The wind hurt his ears and made his eyes sting but he liked that. He imagined the salt in the air cleansing his skin, killing germs, scrubbing away at the dark thoughts he rarely had but knew were inside, ready to consume him, to punish him for his second chance at life. Vera had not wanted a second chance and he respected her for that but Lauren had not been given the choice. She was so young, he sighed, too young to really know what life could be. He turned around to ease his right ear and give the other one the opportunity to be attacked. The girl with the whippet was walking towards him.

'I know why you wear that hat so often,' Bob said, his hands cupped over his ears.

She was pink-cheeked and smiley.

'It's useful,' she said, 'for keeping my hair out of the way when kissing.'

Bob wanted to say something witty but was stumped and she filled the silence by lifting her heels and pressing her lips against his. It lasted about three salty seconds and then she called out 'Walter!' and she and the dog raced back inland, leaving Bob with whistling in his ears, a headache and a surge of elation.

He cycled home feeling a weight had been lifted and partially grasped that it ought to be the other way around.

'I'll run you a bath, birthday boy,' Rachel said, and she laughed at how startled he was.

'I bet you didn't even notice the gifts on the table, did you?' she said but she was not cross.

'Sorry,' he said.

'You will be if you're not dressed for a night out by seven,' she smiled.

He lay in the bath he needed if did not want and wondered at his wife's serene confidence that she knew how to celebrate a birthday he had no interest in celebrating. He let his mind drift back to the day Lauren, aged six, had burst into the bedroom with a card she had made that was huge and unsubtle but also incredible. It was covered in all manner of tiny pieces of material, a mini-collage that had, said Vera, taken her a week of painstaking effort to make.

'My angel, you are the cleverest little girl in the world,' he had said. And he remembered the proud look on Vera's face, the look that said, 'We made this angel, Bob, you and me.'

He had been drifting ever since their deaths, he knew that. He also grasped that he was fortunate to have found such a palatable way to drift, that he could have been broken and lonely. He was grateful to Rachel. She was so calming. He knew most women would have thrown a plate to the floor if told their new husband would not wear a wedding ring, but Rachel had understood. She still understood. Instead of giving him the silent treatment he had anticipated, she had smiled and told him her own father had never worn a wedding ring because it was 'not manly'. He was grateful, almost as much to Suki for her steadfast humour and loyalty; but this girl had made him feel real. Andrea had no knowledge of his past but had been nice to him anyway. There was a freedom in being anonymous, in being flirtatious, in being flirted with. In kissing. Kissing in a vacuum.

The bath was cold. As he climbed out he mulled over the way time would slip from his grasp, that he could look at his watch and find that he had lost an hour, maybe several, and that this was wasteful or at least it would be if there was not part of him that willed away the hours until he too could die. His admiration for the route Vera had taken would never diminish. Bob, he said to himself, you are a coward. Bob, you seem to be continually handsomely rewarded for being so.

He did not want to rush back to the dunes. He had a sense it could be no better than this, knowing she was there, prepared to kiss him again perhaps, the sea spray trapped in her eyelashes sparkling, teasing. But it was a day of clear skies and brisk sunshine and he longed for the gulps of air that would taste of driftwood and salt.

He reached her well before the sea came into view. Andrea was on her way home, the whippet on a lead. He braked sharply and then stood before her, which startled her but she seemed pleased.

'Walter the whippet?' he said.

She stroked Walter's head.

'Is it a weird coincidence? Is your middle name Walter?'

He laughed. 'I think I would have hated to be a Walter when a kid, but it's a fine name.'

They were framed by tall pines which kept them in shadow and Walter, Bob noticed, was shivering.

'I'll walk with you for a bit,' he said.

'OK,' she said.

It was not OK. All she could think to say was to ask him if he was married, which irritated her because she was not the least bothered when he said that he was. That was his business, not hers. Meanwhile all Bob could think about was the way Walter appeared to be some sort of chaperone, ruining the mood, making them walk.

'Let's time it better,' she said at last. 'I'll be on the sand by two tomorrow.'

And with that she walked more quickly and he hung back for a moment, then cycled towards the beach, glad to be alone, glad to slouch and laze and wonder at the straight simplicity of the horizon.

He shared a late supper with Rachel and Suki, who had spent the day with Beryl. They chattered about their visit as if it was the most natural thing in the world for his second wife to visit her own second husband's mother-in-law from his first marriage. Was it natural? They had not even told him they were going.

'You might have mentioned it,' he said.

'We did mention it,' Rachel said breezily but she must have noted the sulky tone because she changed the topic to nurses' pay, mainly because Beryl had been singing their praises. She knew Bob had backed their industrial action and she knew too that Suki would launch one of her pseudo-Communist attacks on the system which would shake the walls and make Bob forget all about the perceived treachery.

He did not quite forget and lay in bed grumpily considering how his life was being lived for him by his sister and his spouse. He felt as if the only decisions he had made completely independently in years were to visit the beach and buy a bike. I'll shag Andrea, he thought, although he did not mean it. It was the thought that was defiant. That will be my decision; to contemplate being with her. Christ, I didn't even have a say on this being our bedroom, and why the hell is there a toy snow leopard at the end of the bed? He dreamed of Andrea walking a leopard instead of a whippet, of thin bones washing up onto the shore, and of Andrea wailing that Walter had been eaten but not realising that the culprit was obvious.

The next day he was sat on the highest dune by one o'clock. Walter found him first, then Andrea sat down next to him.

'No hat,' he said.

She stared at him, a faint smile in her eyes. He still felt defiant. He was surprised.

'No hat, so I'll have to do this,' Bob said as he pushed back her hair for their second kiss.

In his head he did much more but he dared not spoil everything by being crass.

'One-all, as my dad would say,' she said.

He looked about them and an image from a music video featuring Stevie Nicks being sexy on the beach popped into his head. If they were to have sex on the sand he would need props. A huge blanket, some beers, warmer weather.

'Oh. You. Are. Transparent,' she said but she was laughing. 'Ask me out. I do own a dress and I might have some nail varnish somewhere.'

He sat up straight.

'Andrea, I'd like to take you dinner, if you'd let me.'

She looked at where his wedding ring should be. She had not meant to but it stalled the mood.

'Would lunch be easier?' she said.

'Yes,' he said softly, 'it probably would.'

He cycled home feeling as close to a cad as he had in his entire life. To think he had thought driving to the beach was a grubby, dirty-old-man thing to do. This was worse. Had he really said that? If Andrea had any sense at all she would back out of their crappy date, ignore him at the beach and train Walter to bite a chunk out of his backside.

But he did not yet know Andrea. She was not a dreamy romantic. She was bored, in need of a few dates and if those dates came with the backdrop of subterfuge then so be it. She counted herself fortunate that the only man to regularly frequent the beach on weekdays out of season was reasonably attractive and intriguing. Still, she was no sap and she made sure she and Walter changed their routine to baffle Robert and make sure he did not take her for granted. To have ducked the beach entirely even for a day would have been out of the question. Her father, to whom Walter truly belonged, thrived on her stories of the trek to the dunes. He would pat his dog and seek veracity.

'Did you really, boy?' he would say.

'An old tennis ball?'

'Did you stop for a drink from your bowl?'

Andrea bore it all with no ill will. Her dad was recovering from a stroke, unable to walk much at all, and she knew his greatest wish was to be with them on the sand, throwing sticks, poking at dead jellyfish. If she was not prepared to walk Walter for him he would have been desperately distressed.

She liked that her and Robert's only point of contact was the beach. It gave their budding romance an ethereal quality. It was not bound by normal rules. She wondered if having lunch would kill it dead or liberate it further. She made herself just one pledge. She would not have sex in his car.

The following week they stood at the water's edge, having what Andrea's young cousin would call a massive snogathon.

'Let's make a vow to kiss only in beautiful places,' she said.

'In that case, let's fly to Paris,' he said, and she laughed but he was almost serious.

'Or Blackpool Pier,' he added, nodding to the tower in the distance.

'I love funfairs,' she said. 'So shall we?'

They did. They whistled through the air on the roller-coaster, ate fish and chips, kissed on the pier and then checked into a large garish hotel where they were given a spacious, draughty room with peeling wallpaper and a creaking bed covered in a deep pink eiderdown – but it had a sea view from huge windows which allowed them to kiss in a knowing, ironic sort of way. This amused Bob because they hardly knew each other at all but there were tiny slivers of his persona he believed only Andrea had ever seen and hoped the same was true for her.

An hour later and Andrea was asleep. She had woken very early to ensure Walter could have his daily escapade before they set off. Bob was plunged into loneliness the minute she dozed off. The room became chilly and ludicrous. He wanted to snuggle close to her but did not think they knew each other well enough for that so he ran himself a bath he knew in advance would be either shallow or tepid but he had not brought a newspaper or a book and he had to do something.

It was almost dark when he dropped her home. They had not exchanged numbers and they both liked that the beach, or perhaps Walter, would decide their fate. As he drove away Bob wondered at how he could feel both elated and troubled at exactly the same time. The car radio suffered a static attack in the middle of a news item about British soldiers killed by the IRA so he drove in silence, the taste of candy floss on his lips, the sound of a half-full rollercoaster's screams reverberating in his head.

LAUREN

She watched him haul his bags into the taxi.

'You not coming, then?' he said. This seemed to Lauren to be a cruel thing to say. Had he invited her properly of course she would have joined him. Was she supposed to have nagged him for flight and hotel details?

'I think I'm booked on a different package,' she said. 'You are going to Andorra, aren't you?'

Luke laughed.

'Next time,' he said. This, too, was cruel unless he had no idea how she felt. Emboldened by her own stupidity, she tapped him on the arm and leaned up to kiss him. He did not offer his cheek. Instead they enjoyed a proper smackeroo, as her Aunt Suki would say.

'Now that is a nice farewell,' he said, and then he was gone.

She joined Kat and Amy a few hours later at the kitchen table. They warmed their hands on mugs of tea or instant coffee as if they were taking a break from the ski slopes themselves.

'He really is remarkable, isn't he?' Kat said. 'He was in an avalanche a few years ago and still he goes skiing.'

'It wasn't an avalanche, Kat,' Amy said. 'He went the wrong way and got buried in snow.'

'But he nearly died. I'd never go near the bloody stuff if that happened to me.'

'He's just being rational, I guess,' Lauren said. 'I was in a car crash but I don't avoid cars.'

Kat and Amy both turned to her, their eyes wide. They knew Lauren had been in 'an incident' and that was why she limped sometimes but she had never introduced the topic before.

'Were you very young?' Amy asked, trying to sound both nonchalant and sympathetic.

'I was thirteen. A funny age really. I think the age bit matters because in many ways it feels like a dream and in others it feels like a giant life-changing moment. My parents, for example, they were changed by it. I think they thought I had died or would die and they've been sort of uptight ever since. Sometimes I think of them as pre- and post-crash parents and I want the pre-crash ones back.'

Lauren smiled self-consciously and Amy tried not to look disappointed. She had been hoping for the violent detail not the psychological impact.

'But yes,' Lauren added, 'Luke is very brave. We already knew that.'

At work she was accused of looking dreamy and she confided in Patti, the friendliest of the girls in her team, that she was possibly in love.

'Yeah, I tried that last summer. Waste of time,' Patti said, but she smiled and added that Luke sounded interesting.

At the other end of the room, Gregory, her boss, watched

the two women nattering and he allowed himself an indulgent couple of minutes imagining the topic of their conversation. Perhaps, he thought, one of them has a crush on me – and then he noticed a piece of fluff on his jacket, hung on a hanger on the wall next to his desk, and stood up quickly to pluck it off.

A week later Luke was standing in their hallway, dishevelled and smiling. She wanted to reprise the kiss but Kat and Amy were fussing over him, offering to take his clothes to the launderette. It seemed plausible then, to Lauren, that if the house could handle one couple it should be able to handle another, and she wondered if Kat and Amy actually thought he deserved better than her.

As they sat round the table, like an old-fashioned family, eating the oh-so-lovingly prepared roast chicken, Amy handed Luke a letter which he inspected reluctantly.

'Your mother?' asked Kat.

'Hmm,' he said, and not for the first time Lauren felt left out but she wanted to be bolder. They had kissed after all.

'Does that mean bad news?' she asked and she held his gaze knowing that Kat and Amy were throwing her disapproving glances.

He sighed. 'Not really, it's just that she's so bloody formal, always acting as a go-between. Via letters. Like we live in 1902 or something.'

'Go-between?' asked Lauren, and she was sure she heard Kat hiss.

'Yeah, don't talk to my dad. He doesn't like my... life choices.'

With this Amy steered the conversation to skiing, which left Lauren musing that maybe Luke was titled and supposed to be in charge of a thousand-acre estate rather than saving drug-addled teenagers from abusive step-parents. Or maybe he had been expected to join the army. Or the Church.

Jeffers cleared his throat and wondered if they should not hold a house party before he went into Finals Preparation Hibernation. It was his way of announcing he would soon be bookish, reclusive and against all partying, which they understood in some way, and it made them fonder of him. When asked by friends why they were throwing a party they all said it was to launch Jeffers' FPH and nobody, strangely, asked what on earth that meant.

Amy and Kat took charge and decided upon the theme of Block Colour.

'Which means everyone will wear black,' Luke said.

'Which is fine,' said Kat, 'because one or two will wear white and one or two will be in green or yellow and it will all look crazy and superb.'

Lauren was nervous. Ski might not come, or else he might come with ten very odd friends. And what about her office; should she invite only Patti, or everyone from the team? Mostly she was nervous about those Luke would invite. The Block Colour Party appeared to be a form of exposure. They all led very different lives and she wondered how their worlds would interact. As she handed Gregory the invitation Kat and Amy had asked her to design, she shrugged apologetically.

'I have no idea if this will be fun or not, so please don't come if there is a chance it will affect my career,' she said in a jokey voice although she partly meant it.

Gregory was, though, delighted to be involved. Everyone assumed he was an uptight, serious sort of guy but he liked boozing. He liked a bit of a dance. And he really liked a sartorial challenge. He was one of the first to arrive, dressed head to toe in deep brown. His shirt was crisply ironed and he was particularly proud of his brown satin tie which had been more difficult to source than he expected.

Amy, cream, and Kat, black, were thrilled with the seriousness of his effort and pampered him for the rest of what was the most peculiar house party Lauren, turquoise, had, or ever would, experience.

Ski, black, brought just one friend, orange, announced he was gay and almost burst into tears when Lauren said she'd thought he was, though she didn't add that she'd suspected as much ever since she'd had a vision of him in his flat with a man. It was not clear if Ski was teary because he had hoped to surprise her or because he was touched by her intuition.

Jeffers, denim blue, spent the entire evening lining up shot glasses and filling them with different varieties of vodka, washing them up, drying them, then starting again. The food comprised hundreds of cocktail sausages baked in honey and sesame seeds and separate bowls of tomatoes and celery and mozzarella balls: Block Colour Food.

Someone connected to Luke, grey, turned up in black jeans and a red T-shirt and was heckled until he swapped his top for a black vest he found in Luke's cupboard.

Patti, black, brought her much older sister, black, who spent the evening glowering against a wall while Patti explained she was a writer who needed to observe. The writer took a long time to roll each cigarette she barely puffed upon and Lauren, newly enamoured of peach vodka, noticed a beam of silvery light appear in a rare halo of smoke above her head.

Lauren did not gasp. She had, very vaguely, expected something odd to happen. She walked over to the writer and whispered in her ear.

'I am going to look at something that is just above you. No need to move.'

The writer's eyes flickered then closed as Lauren used a small stack of books to reach over her. She peered at and then through the metallic string as naturally as a nosy neighbour peers through net curtains. She saw pointed trees bending across a starlit sky that was a warm, inky blue. There were no buildings, no people, just a plain and serene beauty. It was a place she could aspire to live in but she was not even sure it really existed. She climbed down off the books and thanked the writer, who grunted.

People were dancing now. Luke gyrated slowly and she inched closer, her hips mirroring his hips until he placed his hands on her shoulders and kissed her before shuffling out to the kitchen.

Patti took hold of her hands.

'I'm in love with him too,' she said. 'I mean, who wouldn't be?'

This, to Lauren, seemed to sum up her dilemma. Luke could be with anyone he chose so why would he bother choosing someone?

BOB

The beach could never be too crowded, not even on a warm still day in June. It was not that sort of beach, but it was certainly busy as they sat, their backs against a dune, him gazing at her toes.

'You have very lovely feet,' he said.

'Why thank you, Robert,' she said teasingly and then she stiffened. 'I need to discuss something with you,' she said, and she did not wait for his acquiescence.

'My mum is taking two weeks off work at the end of the month and she says she insists that I use one of them to get away. She'll walk Walter, see to Dad's lunch and stuff, and I do want to do something, find a cheap flight maybe. Anyway, before I start booking stuff, do you want to come with me? Can you come with me?'

Bob had no realistic excuse to offer Rachel for being away from home. On the other hand, she was so tied up in her various projects that she might not mind at all if he found an old friend who wanted to meet up. The real trouble was Suki. If he invented a pal from school she would know he was lying. On the other hand, his sister knew little about his old office. She had met Peter Stanning, and was very pleased to have done so given his subsequent notoriety, but no one else.

'Give me the dates and I will come with you,' he said, pleased to sound so certain and feel so free.

Rachel did not seem interested in the convoluted reasons he had rehearsed as to why he was joining some old work colleagues for a conference in Spain, although his chest tightened when she said had he given her more notice she would have accompanied him and amused herself by drinking sangria by the pool and flirting with the waiters while he wasted his time in an air-conditioned hall.

Twelve days later Bob and Andrea were in Barcelona where they sneered at the beach for being nothing like as impressive as their own but were otherwise overwhelmed by the bustling long nights and oil-drenched sausages. Their hotel room was hot and noisy but pretty and they loved it that way – and the only means to fall asleep was to have sex they were too drunk to really want.

Andrea was witty and lively. She dragged him down narrow alleyways in case there was a courtyard worth seeing at the end of it. She had a basic grasp of Spanish he had not expected her to have and had bothered to read up on the history of the region. On the plane she had finished reading Orwell's *Homage to Catalonia* and pressed it into his hands saying, 'Your turn, Robbie.'

Not once did she say 'I love you' and not once did she ask him if he loved her, yet they held hands and stopped to kiss whenever they got close to something either of them pronounced beautiful. He thought of her as free and young but she was simply making sure she squeezed as much as possible from this interlude in her humdrum life. She was not madly in love with Robert but this trip was the happiest she had ever been and as she brushed her teeth on their last evening she thought she could, perhaps, become a little besotted with him.

At the airport, as he held her bag and passport while she nipped to the bathroom, he realised he did not know for sure her age and birthday. What had she said? *Don't worry, Robert, I'm in my twenties.* Sometimes she looked thirty, he thought, and sometimes sixteen. He looked around and opened her passport then closed it again. It was a violation, like peeking at her diary. He would not be so sly.

'Did you look at my dreadful photo?' she asked breezily.

'Almost,' he said, 'but it felt like prying.'

'Go on,' she said, 'let's swap.'

They swapped. She guffawed but only because that is what people do when they see a lover's passport photo for the first time. He sniggered and then stopped sniggering to read the information.

She was indeed called Andrea and she was a British Citizen.

And then he froze. Her date of birth made no sense to him. It felt as if he was staring at hieroglyphics. He blinked. What was wrong here? September '68?

She snatched the passport from him, misunderstanding his grim expression.

'OK, so I'm almost twenty. There's nothing wrong with that.'

He did not answer. He was back at the hospital. Vera was cradling her newborn daughter.

'She'll be one of the oldest in her class,' Vera had said.

'And therefore one of the cleverest,' he had said.

It was 20 September, 1968.

He snatched the passport back again and scoured the page for Andrea's exact date of birth.

29 September, 1968.

He was having sex with a girl the same age as his daughter. Nine days younger than his daughter.

'I never lied,' Andrea said. 'Why are you so pissed off?'

He stared at her, his stomach churning.

'No, no, I'm not pissed off,' he said but her expression told him he would have to say something. 'It's something else entirely,' he said. 'I'll explain later, when we've landed.'

She was silent. It had been such fun and now it was spoilt. She could not think what it was in her passport that had spooked him. She told herself she did not even like him that much but as that had the unexpected effect of making her tearful she turned away from Bob and examined their fellow passengers, trying to eavesdrop and discover something diverting.

He closed his eyes on the plane and wondered if he was the sort of man who would have an affair with a girl the same age as his daughter if that daughter were alive. He could not solve the riddle. If Lauren was here, then Vera would be here and he had no idea if his and Vera's marriage would have lasted but he supposed it would have lasted just fine. They would have become grandparents one day. *It would have been just fine.* But he had never watched his daughter grow older, and neither Suki or Rachel had grown-up children. He thought of Rachel and her childlessness and he sighed; of course, that is why we have a cuddly toy on the bed. Just occasionally Rachel would flinch at a soap storyline revolving around a pregnancy; just occasionally she would hold the cuddly leopard too tightly.

He had never dwelled on her sadness. She had given his the priority. His loss was greater than her loss. He needed to be better at being her husband. As Andrea fiddled with her seatbelt, he understood he needed to be better at being a boyfriend, too, and that he was, effectively, trapped into being utterly dreadful at both.

He wanted his old life back, the one that would have been just fine.

LAUREN

Patti and Lauren stood side by side as Gregory carefully brushed the sleeves of his jacket, then put it on and left to meet the writer in reception. They turned to look out the window to watch them walk together hand in hand across the road and then down a side street towards lunch.

'Incredible,' said Patti. 'I didn't even know my sister liked men.'

'But nice,' said Lauren. 'I don't think I will ever meet Luke for lunch. Or brunch. Or dinner.'

'I really don't see why you can't just ask him out. Ooh, you could double date with Gregory and Lydia, how could he resist that?'

Lauren smiled. It sounded so easy but if he declined they still had to live in the same house. It felt risky, potentially awkward, and she pictured the kitchen falling quiet as she walked in, with Amy and Kat frowning disapproval, Jeffers shifting uncomfortably in his chair and Luke not really noticing her. Except. Except they had kissed. Who kisses someone in a meaningless way? It had to count for something.

'Actually,' Patti said, thoughtfully, 'the problem might be that you are a sort of family in that house. You could end up being his little sister or something. You should suggest meeting him from his work, or he could come here and do a Lydia.'

Yes, thought Lauren. Yes. Part of her inhibitions stemmed from Aunt Kat and Aunt Amy and their entrenched belief that no one could be good enough for the beautiful, saintly and it had to be said, complicated, Luke. The nearest pub to her office held a comedy night on the first Monday of the month. She could ask him to that. Yes, thought Lauren. Yes. I can ask him to that. I will ask him to that.

Their paths did not cross for a few days and then, one month on from the Block Colour Party, as her self-confidence had grown to almost the point where she might tell Luke something about her heart, Lauren found a ballet dancer on the landing. At least it looked like a ballet dancer. It was a slender, pixie-like thing with glossy auburn hair in leg warmers and a lace vest. And a wash bag. Why did it have a wash bag?

It put its hand to its mouth.

'Oops,' it said. 'Is it OK for me to use the bathroom now?'

Lauren's pulse began to rattle.

'Ah, er, yes. If you are quick, I mean, who are you?'

The dancer rose up on her tiptoes and announced herself as Tabatha.

'Tabatha?'

'Yes,' the dancer said, her hair swaying in slight indignation. 'Tabatha, as in Tabatha, girlfriend of Luke.'

Never had Lauren taken such an instant dislike to anyone.

'So nice to meet you,' Lauren said icily. 'How long do you think you'll be?' she added, nodding at the bathroom door.

Tabatha glided past her whispering she would be just five minutes, maybe less, the implication being that one as lovely as she did not need to dwell in front of bathroom mirrors.

Lauren felt the double whammy of betrayal and jealousy with none of the upside of having been in a relationship with Luke in the first place. As he stood beside her in the kitchen that evening offering to chop onions, she could not stop herself from feeling deeply wounded, betrayed even.

'I met Tabatha this morning,' she said, trying to keep her voice level and light.

'Oh yeah,' Luke said. 'Now she really was a big mistake.'

This was not what Lauren had been expecting.

'She won't be moving in, then?' she said.

Luke groaned. 'Let's just say I woke up today feeling... not good.'

'About Tabatha.'

'Yes, not good about Tabatha.'

The dancer was never seen in the house again but Lauren was wary now of Luke, fearful he might be incapable of even a minor level of commitment.

'I need a break from thinking about him,' she confided in Patti, and so the pair of them planned a blitz on big theatre productions and films in Leicester Square which left them broke but bedazzled and diverted. In the hours Luke did not occupy her thoughts, life was good. Gregory, her boss, was indulgent and happy. Her work itself was fulfilling and creative and outside the office she had time to laugh and feel lucky.

She tried not to drink too much and not to think about why she needed to avoid becoming drunk. She had an idea her accident, the fall from the Jeep, made her vulnerable to hallucinations and that alcohol exacerbated something in her brain but she felt no desire to discuss this with a doctor or a friend. She really wanted never to think about the accident but if it was not her knee then it would be a headache that reminded her. She had an idea that if Luke had fallen off the back of a Jeep and survived he would have taken up car rallying and counted each day a beautiful bonkers bonus but try as she might Lauren could not find a way to count her blessings.

The accident was a very private thing and that was about all she was certain of. The really strange part was that she had no memory of the mechanics of what happened that day, or what happened when she drank too much only that something peculiar sometimes occurred to her. I'd probably be burned as a witch four hundred years ago, she thought, not the first time.

It was Easter, 1991, and her parents wanted her home but she did not want to be in their house. The Christmas visit had unnerved her; her memory had felt marginally fractured. It simply did not feel like home any more. She suggested they all meet in a hotel, have a four-day holiday together. Somewhere halfway between Cheshire and London.

'Birmingham?' Vera said. 'I'm not staying in Birmingham.'

'No, Mum, how about, well, not halfway exactly, but somewhere like the Cotswolds or Bath or something? I mean, you used to love all those National Trust places. There must be so many you've never visited.'

'You are funny, Lauren,' Vera said. 'We only went to one stately home and you're still holding it against us.'

Lauren laughed. 'I must have been so bored it feels like we went to loads of them,' she said.

The notion did not fulfil Vera's desire to cook for and pamper her daughter but at least Lauren was making time for them and plotting a little trip might be fun. So it was that the Pailings stayed in an elegant hotel in the centre of Bath, where the weather was kind to them. Lauren wanted none of the unsettling disconnectedness of Christmas. She was sure she had simply outgrown The Willows and that it had nothing to do with her parents, but as they settled down to afternoon tea, with Bob clumsily spooning a generous helping of bright red strawberry jam onto a tiny scone and Vera examining a delicate cucumber finger sandwich, Lauren felt slightly uneasy in their company.

Vera liked to reminisce but as soon she tried, Lauren steered the conversation to the present. It felt like safer ground, and Bob was, in any case, keen for once to talk about his work and a Peter Stanning Memorial Fund that had been established to help disadvantaged kids through school and their accountancy exams. Lauren struggled to keep a straight face. How many kids were out there, she wondered, who, rather than dreaming of becoming an actor or a footballer, were hoping against hope for a big break in accountancy?

Instead she said, 'Poor Peter,' and Bob and Vera nodded.

'Lovely chap,' Bob said, although by now he really had forgotten what his boss had been like.

Vera, smoothing some crumbs from her lap, tapped her husband's knee.

'I've always thought he went missing because of love,' she said. 'I think he kept an affair so secret the police had no idea where to look for him and he kept his home life so secret from his mistress that she had no idea who he was or where he lived and so when he vanished she assumed he had, you know, emigrated, or decided not to cheat any more.'

'She would have seen his photo in the paper, wouldn't she?' Lauren said.

'Not every woman reads the paper,' Vera said solemnly. 'Or maybe she was...' here Vera lowered her voice because the waiter was swarthy-skinned, 'foreign.'

'But what happened to him?' Lauren said, trying not to smile.

'Oh, how am I expected to know that?' her mother said, cross that her theory was not in itself enough. 'Anything could have happened to him. The point is no one knew where to look.'

BOB

In the end they drove straight from the airport to the beach. He took her hand and pulled her away from the path and into the pine trees. They walked for a while across the carpet of shed needles and the nutshells discarded by the squirrels until they reached a sandy patch of sunlight and sat down. In the distance they could hear a woman calling for a dog and further away still they could hear the whoops of children playing hide and seek.

Andrea drew her knees up to her chin.

'I don't like being here without Walter,' she said.

He squeezed her hand.

'Me neither,' he said.

He decided to be honest. He hated to talk about Lauren and Vera but he had, he felt, no choice.

'I'm not sure why I kept going,' he said. 'But people were kind and then Rachel and my sister took charge of me, I guess.'

Andrea took a deep breath.

'So what's the bit that's freaking you out?' she asked.

He had assumed it was obvious and he flushed slightly.

'You are the same age as my daughter. Don't you think that's...?'

There was silence between them. Eventually she spoke.

'It's not creepy unless you let it be,' she said. 'I need to get home now.'

'Of course,' he said.

As they pulled up outside her home she kissed him on the cheek.

'I'm sorry you lost your family,' she said. She pulled her case from the back seat and walked towards the front door. He could see it opened before she reached it but he was already pulling away and he did not look back.

He fantasised as he drove home about coming clean with Rachel but what would be the point of that? He had read somewhere that people who confess to affairs do it to cleanse their soul and make themselves feel better rather than trying to be honest and fair with the people they have betrayed.

Rachel hugged him tightly.

'I missed you,' she said, laughing, as if it were a big surprise to her that she would have done so.

Even so, she had managed to move some furniture around and there was antique clock in the hall that had not been there before he left.

'It needed the clock,' she said sweetly but firmly before changing the subject to the charity ball she and Suki were planning.

'You can make your new conference buddies buy a table and bring their wives,' she said.

'Yes, I'll do that,' he said, feeling cornered and miserable and hoping she would forget about his rediscovered colleagues or that the ball plan would fall apart.

*

But the ball grew like an aggressive tumour. The local paper got in touch, Rachel was interviewed about her battered and fearful wives. The picture they published was not of Rachel and Bob but of Suki and Rachel looking strident and empowered.

She showed him the tickets. They were very grand, stating a cocktail reception would be followed by dinner and then dancing to live music and that all proceeds would go towards Rachel's Refuge. He badgered his clients in the hope that if he could sell one table Rachel would forget about the Spanish connection. After a few false starts, Eddie Hough, who ran a small chain of DIY stores, agreed to buy a table and provide a voucher for the auction. Bob could tell the DIY voucher was not quite the kind of item Rachel wanted for her glittering fundraiser but she was gracious in thanking both of them.

He dreaded her telling him she was a table short and that she would phone his old company herself if necessary. He dreaded Suki deciding theirs was a project that the rich Stanning family should support. Both women were too busy, though, to be so conniving, and he concocted a tale of a conflicting events which, in the end, he never needed to use.

He avoided the beach for a few weeks. Andrea's voice played in his head. It was only creepy if he let it be creepy... but there was more to it than that. He was resentful that Andrea could be so vibrant, so alive. He had made the connection to his daughter and there was no way of reversing it.

Bob missed the place and came to the conclusion that none of this was Andrea's fault, he could at least be civil with her, still walk with her and Walter perhaps, so he cycled seaward and came up against a throng of families. The beach was teeming with people, most of whom were licking at Mr Whippy ice creams. It was the school summer holidays and it was sunny. He felt far more exposed than when the beach was empty and concluded he would need a dog of his own if he were to walk with ease. In the meantime he clambered up the quietest dune and surveyed the landscape. The most fun was definitely being had by the under-tens and dogs. He half fancied an ice cream but was too self-conscious to queue up for one so he cycled home. He had a client meeting anyway.

Rachel was at the kitchen table sorting though some paperwork.

'How's the charity bash coming along?' Bob asked her, hoping not to be told there was a glitch.

'I'm so pleased with it all, Bob,' she said, and for a few seconds she looked sweet and innocent and pretty rather than composed and mature and sleekly attractive.

'How would you feel about us getting a puppy?' he asked.

VERA

Bob was the least Machiavellian man in all Cheshire and yet his small act of kindness in inviting George for dinner had led to big things. George Stanning, a young man with the void of a missing father to fill, had expanded the firm so grandly and adroitly that it had divisions, and Bob was now managing director of its accountancy branch. Elsewhere there were mergers and acquisitions and new business initiatives. George was rather adept at spying a failing company that was merely suffering a blip, taking it over and brusquely nurturing it to profitability.

Vera, meanwhile, was the least aspirational woman in all Cheshire but even she could see that she and Bob had outgrown The Willows. If they lived in the Harpers' house, maybe they could absorb the new car, the dinner invitations, more easily but they did not live there; they lived on one side of a dessert-spoon-shaped cul-de-sac which seemed to grow smaller by the hour.

Bob did not even hint at the differential in their lives, knowing that leaving The Willows meant leaving behind the adolescent perfume of Lauren, whose room remained her room, with a sheepskin rug that Vera took outside to shake every week, but Vera knew when he suggested hotels to guests, met them in restaurants, it was to avoid the tiny provinciality of their home. And so, one evening, she handed him two sheets of paper.

'What do you think?' she said quietly. 'Fancy viewing either of them?'

Bob deliberately remained equivocal.

'If you think they are promising then no harm in it,' he said but inwardly he rejoiced. It was time to move on. In a few days he would tell Vera they could afford much more than the price attached to the two houses she had shortlisted. Heck, he thought, we could afford to buy both of them.

Hope was now nine and found talk of moving house unsettling until Bob promised her a bedroom with an en suite bathroom. Hope had a friend with the same and had been impressed to the point of speechlessness.

Vera had just one request. She wanted a view. She was not too picky about what was in the view as long as it was bucolic and soothing, so as soon as details arrived of a Grade II listed house with woodland to its right, rolling hills to its left, a village pub to its rear and five bedrooms, three of which had en suite facilities, the deal was sealed. It took Vera a while all the same to comprehend that most of her new view also belonged to whoever bought the house.

'We've never owned more than one tree Bob,' she said, 'and now we own a… a wood.'

'A magical forest,' corrected Hope.

'Yes, a magical forest,' conceded Vera although she knew

real magic would be needed for her to cope well enough to pack up Lauren's clothes and art, strip her room bare.

But help arrived in the form of Suki, who appeared with several large boxes all covered with a deep lacquer. Stencilled upon them were the words 'Lauren Pailing'.

Vera was deeply moved. This was preferable to dumping Lauren's things into any old cardboard box. The two women embraced.

'Will you help me?' she asked Suki.

'I would be honoured to,' Suki said.

It took them five consecutive afternoons not just because of the tears and need for breaks for cups of tea but because of the lingering over what Lauren had drawn.

'I would never wear a skirt like that, it's so matronly,' Vera said of a sketch among many sketches of friends and family. 'And I don't understand why this puppy keeps cropping up. We never even discussed getting a dog. And look, here it's me – it's definitely me – but I have my arm in a sling. What a strange thing to imagine.'

The two women gazed at a series of small paintings of grand venetian blinds through which could be seen a blazing light. 'What an imagination,' Suki said, 'there's something religious in them, like an afterlife or something, and she was what, twelve, when she did these?'

'I think she would have studied art at college,' Vera said.

'Undoubtedly,' Suki said. Suki looked again at the drawing of Vera with a sling and realised it was a drawing of Vera holding, in the crook of her arm, a tiny baby wrapped in a cream blanket. She said nothing of it to Vera.

LAUREN

Gregory tapped Lauren on the shoulder.

'Let's go for a coffee,' he said. She felt mildly sick and wondered if she was being let go. Had she made a costly mistake on the camcorder advert?

He explained that he was setting up his own agency with three partners, including Tim, the voraciously ambitious account executive who never made small talk.

'You'd want Tim on your side, not the opposition, every time,' Gregory said.

He smiled. He could tell that she had not twigged what he was about to ask her.

'We'd like it very much if you would join us at Pilot, Lauren. We cannot improve your pay in the short-term, but we'd match it, and we'd like to think before too long you'd be much better off financially – but more importantly you'd be part of something exciting. Thrilling. Yes, I'd call it thrilling.'

Lauren flushed with gratitude. Thrilling was right. This was the most thrilling thing to have ever happened to her and she stammered her thanks.

'Have a chat to your friends, family first,' Gregory said, 'and also, come and meet the others. We're having a drink on Thursday evening.'

The house was full when she arrived home but there was no one she felt able to talk the offer through with and for the first time she acknowledged that she was not the right fit for Luke. Whatever she said about her possible new job would sound self-indulgent to someone who spent every day either with the disadvantaged or discussing them.

She phoned her parents. Vera made a weak joke wondering what the chances were of her new office being in Chester but Bob was more practical.

'I can tell you're flattered, love,' he said, 'but it is a risk. You should ask for share options. You need to be tied in to future success because if there is a future it will be partly thanks to you.'

Lauren sensed he was right but her throat dried as she asked Gregory about shares.

'Of course,' he said as if she had asked if she would be allowed to use the bathroom during work hours. And that was that. Another beginning, she thought, although she wondered quite why she viewed it that way. It is, objectively, a progression, she told herself, but she could not shake the idea that she had been offered a fresh start.

The work consumed her. Gregory set a fine example. He was meticulous, energetic, enthusiastic. Tim was demanding but so astute it did not seem to matter. The remaining two partners were, having more existing wealth, less visible, but no less impressive when inside the small, stylish new offices on Charlotte Street.

Gregory had engineered a generous private health scheme

which required Lauren to undergo a full medical and answer a plethora of questions. The scheme was so generous that elements of her pre-existing condition were covered and she found herself on a long course of physiotherapy for her knee, which made very little difference to the discomfort she suffered, but it was worth the try, she supposed.

The doctor asked her if she had any anxieties, irrational or otherwise. She held his gaze. It was so piercing and the examination had been so thorough that she half expected him to ask if, when she returned to her childhood home, she felt displaced.

'I don't think so,' she said. 'I don't want to die, but I expect most people feel that way.'

For a short while the doctor babbled about the responsibility felt by an only child and gradually Lauren came to see that he only appeared perceptive because he covered practically every inch of a person's body and mind. At some juncture he was bound, accidentally, to hit a nerve.

The day after she had helped map out a campaign for a pizza chain client, Tim pulled up a chair beside her.

'They absolutely loved you,' he said. 'You're very good at working out what clients want but do not have the capability of expressing for themselves.'

Before she could absorb the compliment and respond, he sprang up and dashed outside. She shook her head and smiled. He is a peculiar one, she thought, but admiringly, and then he reappeared.

'Also,' Tim said, 'I'd very much like to take you to dinner either this Friday or Saturday evening. Could you let me know which, if either, is preferable?'

Again she smiled. Six months ago she would have worried if that constituted a date or a meeting but she could tell. This was a very busy man asking her out on a date.

He booked a boisterous Italian near Covent Garden where she ordered Scampi Provençale, her go-to dish on dates or meetings in Italian restaurants, as she knew she could eat it without splashing her dress or slapping spaghetti or tagliatelli onto her cheek or chin. She wore black. She hardly ever wore black. Why am I wearing black? she wondered and decided it was to signify to Tim she knew this was a date. A date and not a meeting. It was a good thing, she was sure. Tim did not seem sure even though it was a Saturday night, but why else would a man and woman in their twenties be together, her wearing black, him wearing an open-neck expensive grey shirt, on a Saturday night?

The waiter brought them coffee and Amaretti biscuits. Tim carefully unwrapped one, smoothed out the paper, made a cylinder and stood it lengthways on the white tablecloth. He then picked up the candle and carefully set fire to the tip of it. The flame glowed pink and when all that was left was a charred carcass, the paper soared delicately into the air.

'Did you make a wish?' he asked her, and she wondered whether that might be the first of a range of subtly romantic gestures or the sum total of what he could offer.

'I take it you've been here before then,' she said, 'or do you set fire to most things in the hope they'll look pretty?'

He laughed.

'No, I'm not a pyromaniac very often, and yes, I have been here before. With a delightful blonde with big blue eyes and a tendency towards naughtiness. And her mother and my father.

Lottie is my half-sister and she is a spoilt but not unpleasant ten-year-old who loves the Amaretti biscuit trick.'

Lauren thought it sounded so exotic, to be part of a complicated family with some kind of controversial history. Her only intriguing relative was Aunt Suki, and Lauren was not even sure why she thought her intriguing in the first place.

'My mother has a mole on her forehead,' she said in a half-whisper and then stared at her wine glass. Before Tim could respond, assuming he would have been able to respond, she added, 'I do seem unable to handle too much alcohol. You should know that before even wondering if you want to eat out with me again.'

'You and Lottie have *so* much in common,' he said and Lauren felt a strange, flirtatious sort of comfort in being with him. As if he might even be her new family. She pinched the back of her own hand and warned herself against ever saying such a thing to her parents.

BOB

Suki insisted they find a rescue dog and as neither Rachel nor Bob could summon enough good reasons not to, the three of them, one week later, stood in front of a small caged enclosure which housed a medium-sized mongrel who was pale cream bar one grey smudge on his forehead. He had been rejected, they were told, for his colouring, which showed the dirt.

'He might have a bit of greyhound in him,' said the plump, breathless sanctuary owner. 'He's ever so sweet. Do you have children?'

Rachel smiled tightly. 'No,' she said. 'I think we just need to know if he'd enjoy the beach. That seems to be the main requirement according my husband.'

'I'm sure he'd love it,' she said. 'He's called Rascal but what people tend to do if they don't like the name is pick one that sounds similar but more to their taste.'

'Yes,' said Rachel. 'I'm not sure about Rascal as a name. It would seem to encourage him to be naughty, don't you think?'

Bob laughed and the dog wagged his tail. Bob liked him. He looked like a distant cousin of Walter. After the paperwork, which surprised him, was complete and their home had been assessed, which surprised him even more, Bob was at last able to go to the busy beach with a companion. Now, it was acceptable to drive there. The newly christened Pascal was not yet a year old and Bob was not sure how obedient he would be nor how tired he would become and, sure enough, on their first outing, Pascal was an utter wimp, reacting nervously to the screams of small children and the reversing of a nearby car. All he seemed to want was to sit next to Bob and for Bob to rub his bony chest.

Bob did not mind. He sat on a quiet dune and took in the view.

'Not to worry,' he said to Pascal, 'pretty soon we'll be on our own.'

The school holidays ended and the ice cream van vanished even though it was a still, glowing sort of September. Bob had brought some dog treats and decided to let Pascal off the leash. As he did so his heart lurched in a sudden panic that he would dash off into the distance, never to be seen again. But Pascal was not at all keen on being abandoned again and stayed close by. Bob felt almost tearful with relief.

'Well now, are you going to introduce us?' she said.

Andrea and Walter had crept up on them and, instinctively, Bob first gave Walter a treat and then kissed her on the cheek.

'Still creeping you out then,' she said, but sadly, not with bitterness.

'No, no,' Bob said. 'It's my problem, my stupidity, I'm so... so fond of you. I'm just really sorry.'

There was a long pause and then he introduced his dog. She did not even ask why he was called Pascal. Everyone else had. He was starting to think Rascal was a far superior name even for someone French.

'Can we go and sit over there?' she asked, pointing to the nearest dunes.

'Of course,' he said and they sat, flanked by their slender dogs, while three lads threw a frisbee at the water's edge.

'I'm afraid I have some bad news,' she said.

'Is it your father? Is he OK?'

'He's fine, improving slowly, I think, thanks. Robert, I'm pregnant.'

He felt nothing. The words held no meaning. It was as if he had been knocked out by a heavy boulder. The imminent pain was so great that he was numb, confused. Only as she rubbed her knees, waiting for a response, did he slowly begin to comprehend, to feel panicked.

'Look, I'm pretty sure I'll have an abortion but I don't want my mum and dad finding out and I don't want to do it alone and I guess I felt you should know because, well, I don't hate you.'

His mind drifted back to Vera telling him she was pregnant. They were engaged and they brought forward the wedding. No one was very shocked. Vera was happy, he was worried about still feeling like a child himself, but when Lauren was born he felt so grown-up, so responsible, so determined to provide a good home. Instead he let his only child go off on a holiday without him. He was too busy at work to even consider tagging along and if he had been there he would not have allowed her onto the bloody Jeep.

'You're crying,' Andrea said.

'So I am,' he said, and he placed his arm around her. 'Thank you for telling me and thank you for not hating me.'

They sat in silence until the silence became so solid neither knew of a decent way to break it. Eventually, Bob suggested they walk back to the car park. They made gentle, polite small talk.

'Can I meet you here tomorrow? You choose the time. I need to think, I mean, if I say something now I might regret it, say the wrong thing. I want to be what you need me to be.'

He looked so forlorn she forgot that she was the one with the far greater immediate burden.

'I'll drive you both home,' he said.

'No. Nice to meet you, Pascal,' she said.

Later that same day, while staring uncomprehendingly at a client's tax return, he began choking on his mug of tea. Abortion? But it was his child they would be destroying. And now his only chance of another child, a chance he had not known he wanted to take or even contemplate, was like a hand appearing at a cliff edge, hauling him back from the brink.

LAUREN

There was no subterfuge at the office, because Tim was far too busy for it, and anyway everyone seemed to know he and Lauren had been to dinner a few times. And because everyone knew, nobody gossiped about it. Gradually, they became a couple, often leaving the office together, to catch a quick supper before a late film or jump on the train to Tim's elegant flat.

'The children of divorced parents join the property ladder sooner than their peers,' he told her the first time she gazed upon his first-floor living room with its oak floor and stylish rug. He even had a cleaner but was nervous about telling her in case she thought him a spoilt brat.

At Christmas, before she left for Cheshire, he bought her a soft dove-grey dressing gown with a label attached that read: *'To be left at all times at No. 53C.'*

On New Year's Eve he asked her to move in with him. She was not crazy, madly deeply in love, but she was in love, and so she said that she would.

Kat and Amy were gracious when she told them and Lauren smiled to herself. If Luke was to move out, they would fall to the floor weeping, she thought. She hardly saw Luke these days but when she did she worried that he was too thin and pale. She suspected that he sometimes forgot to eat.

He hugged her tightly, though, when she told him, and whispered, 'I hope you are in love, don't settle for contentment.'

'Don't worry about me,' she said, and she assumed that was part of his problem, that he was waiting for someone or something perfect.

Jeffers was the only one who told her to keep in touch and she hoped for the others it was implicit. But maybe not. None of them grew tearful as she placed her key on the table and she thought not only had she outgrown The Willows, but she had also outgrown this kind of London. Tim's London was more grown up, more expensive, more thoughtful, more serene.

It was the 16th of February 1992, in a world that was very like so many others.

'Thank goodness you didn't move in on Valentine's Day,' Tim said. 'It would have cheapened it, made it tacky. This can be our own Valentine's Day from now on.'

Lauren shook her head playfully and was about to say, 'No wonder you're not one of our copywriters' but she thought better of it. Instead she told him that her parents would be visiting London the following weekend.

'Obviously to meet you,' she said. 'Ostensibly to see *Five Guys Named Moe*.' She paused. 'They even said not to worry if we were too busy to meet them. They've gone all polite on me since I nabbed a proper boyfriend.'

Tim booked the Italian and Lauren realised it was his default restaurant when he felt nervous. Vera and Bob loved that it was vibrant and that they could not find much to complain about in Tim.

'Is he handsome enough for her?' Bob asked his wife on their train home. 'I'm not in a position to know these things.'

Vera thought he probably was.

'Is he clever enough for her?' he asked. 'I mean, our Lauren is very talented, she couldn't be living with someone who was ordinary.'

'Lauren says he is very highly regarded,' Vera said, wondering if Bob wanted Tim to fail these benchmarks so he could advise their daughter against becoming too seriously involved.

'Does this mean they are going to get married? Is this how it works nowadays? You live together and then get wed?'

Vera sighed. 'I don't know, love,' she said. 'Let's not worry about it, though, let's be glad she is happy. She seemed really happy, don't you think?'

Bob was forced to concede that she did but deep down he was hurt that no one acknowledged that it was a tough thing for him to have to take, his only daughter living with a man who was a stranger to him.

'They're really nice,' Tim said, 'and they seemed pleased we waved them off at the station. Anyway, my turn next. And there's more of my lot.'

Lauren met his family in dribs and drabs and she was petted and made welcome by them all apart from Lottie, who scowled and squirmed and behaved like a jealous ex-girlfriend.

'How long are you going to live in Tim's flat for?' she asked Lauren.

'Oh, until he throws me out, I suppose,' she said. 'Which might be weeks and weeks so I'd like us to be friends.'

Lottie stormed off to her room.

'Oh, she's a jealous little flower,' said Tim's stepmother with a tinkling laugh. 'She won't like it either that I think you're marvellous.'

Lauren wondered whether she imagined it: Tim stiffening as if to indicate it did not matter if his stepmother approved of his girlfriend, that only his mother would know if she was right for him.

His mother Beatrice was hard to pin down. She was an actress, the sort that determinedly portrayed her job as hard work and discriminatory. Her favourite words were 'ageist', 'sexist' and 'fuck'.

'It's an exhausting life,' she said to Lauren when they finally met. At the Italian restaurant. 'Oh darling, do that lovely thing you do with the biscuit wrappers,' she said to her son.

Lauren thought she was fascinatingly self-absorbed but not at all unpleasant. Tim seemed to both adore and fear her. At the end of the evening she clasped all their hands together at the centre of the table.

'I'll give it all up,' she said, 'if you need me to be a hands-on grandmother.'

Lauren spluttered with laughter as Tim groaned.

'No, you won't, Mum,' he said.

'Just try me,' she said, a little too sexily.

BOB

'I'll come with you,' Rachel said.

'Oh,' he said.

'He's my dog too, Bob,' she said, smiling.

'Of course he is,' Bob said.

'I have heard of dogs that get sick in cars,' she said as they drove to the beach.

'It's not far enough for that,' he said.

They parked the car and walked across the slatted wooden path and then he turned right, towards Blackpool, instead of his usual left.

'It's much nicer this way,' Rachel said, turning left.

There was no sign of Andrea. Perhaps she was watching them from the dunes. Rachel held his hand.

'Everything OK, Bob?' she said. 'You've been really quiet lately.'

He wanted to tell her everything and nothing. He wanted to weep.

'When the ball is over, we can go away somewhere,' she said, 'somewhere peaceful, leave Pascal and Suki together in the house.'

'Sounds good,' he said. But he could not go anywhere. Not yet. And then he saw a familiar figure striding across the dunes.

Andrea could have walked over to them and said hi and Bob could have explained how he had started chatting to her about her dog and then told his wife about her poor dad and Rachel would have seen nothing to be suspicious about at all and then Andrea would have dashed off back to her poor dad and Bob would have said what a kind young woman she seemed to be and Rachel would have said how women always turned into carers and that would have been the end of it.

But that is not what happened. Andrea, keeping her distance, simply said,

'Hello, Robert.'

And instantly, Rachel knew.

Rachel saw how Andrea was quietly seething. She saw how Bob was squirming. Rachel also saw there was something bigger at stake than a flirtation or an affair. She was not sure what it was, but there was an urgency behind the girl's flickering eyelashes. And then as the wind attacked the loose sand and the sky darkened for the first time in weeks, Rachel stepped backwards.

'You're pregnant,' she said.

Amid the silence a tear trickled down Andrea's cheek.

'I haven't got a tissue,' she said.

Rachel pulled one out of her coat pocket and handed it to her neutrally.

Bob turned to face the horizon.

Andrea blew her nose.

'I'm sorry,' she said to no one in particular.

'I expect you have lots to talk about,' Rachel said and began to walk back to the car park.

'Does she have car keys?' Andrea asked.

'I think so,' Bob sighed. 'Bloody hell, bloody, bloody hell.'

'Go after her,' she said. 'I'll be here tomorrow.'

'Thank you,' he said. 'Please be here. Thank you.'

VERA

She would often wake and wonder what they had become. After neatly folding Hope's hockey kit and driving her to the bus stop that served the private coach to her new private school, Vera would turn her attention to running the house. That she lived in a house that needed running was still a source of amazement to her. They had insufficient furniture for a start and so much land that there seemed to permanently be a man in overalls somewhere doing something Bob was far too busy to be even trying to do.

Vera had so wanted a view but the price of it was lack of privacy. She needed to clear at least one day each week when no one at all but her would be on their land so she could meander in peace and solitude. Too often she felt like a wicked queen from a fairy tale about possessions bringing unhappiness. Their life was, in theory, so blessed with money and beauty, yet it brought her bouts of unhappiness. Especially when she pondered how Lauren would have lain on the grass with a sketch book and drawn the wood and the hills and the sky.

And it was not even a normal kind of longing or grief, for if she still had Lauren she might not have had Hope and would she really trade Hope to have Lauren back? She half dreaded it when Bob said they were having people to dinner and half grasped at it for the diversion. George and his new wife, the lovely Felicity, were coming this evening along with Harry, George's younger brother, and Stanley, who was another of George's trusted lieutenants, and his wife, Caroline.

Vera was aware that George had reached the realm of the mega-rich but trusted that Bob and Vera were not pleasant to him because of his wealth but because of genuine loyalty and fondness. What she liked most about George was that although he was driven in a manner that meant he would often appear with shadows under his young eyes and a restlessness that was unnerving, he was still a little shy, and honest in his ruthlessness towards business.

Harry was only twenty-one and was clearly dragged along by Felicity as a means of ensuring he ate properly and took a break from his studies. Only when he stood alongside Harry did George look robust and healthy and an average kind of guy. Harry was thinner, taller and possessed an intellectual intensity that made even the most thick-skinned individual think twice about raising the topic of a new film or the pop charts or what the new royal baby would be called.

Harry had completed his physics degree a year early and was working on a PhD in the field of quantum chromodynamics. It seemed perfectly obvious to Vera that Peter Stanning's disappearance had resulted in both his sons striving to fill a gap in their lives that could never be filled and perhaps, given she understood voids better than many, that was why she found herself throwing expensive brandy at pieces of chicken for them. The real glue for the evening was Hope, who adored Felicity, adored her virtue, her clothes, her posture, her calmness, her humour, her sunniness in the face of George's focused energy and Harry's distracted brilliance.

In return, Felicity offered Hope all manner of well-judged advice about spats at school, the ethics of dissecting a rat, the easy way to get high marks for creative writing.

'And Harry can help with any tricky physics homework,' Felicity said as Hope bit her lip in terror. No one in their right mind would expect Harry to be any good at explaining basic physics but he smiled all the same and said he thought he was supposed to be giving academia a break for a few hours.

'I'm quite good at science,' Hope said boldly, and then, after serving and eating a chocolate dessert she had helped to make, she left the grown-ups to what was always the dull part of the evening, not before raising her eyebrows towards George's wife to indicate that she should extract herself for a few minutes and give her some undivided attention.

Vera saw that Harry was looking at a photograph of Lauren. She liked it when people did that. Much better than them averting their gaze or seeming embarrassed, as Caroline and Stanley seemed to be.

'You never met our Lauren,' she said to Harry. 'She was very talented at drawing.'

Harry nodded approvingly. Talent was something he could relate to. Unlike not having a father, which was not something he could bear to think much about at all.

BOB

He let Rachel drive home without him. He and Pascal walked slowly through the pines and then the lanes and as his blackened-bricked house loomed into view Bob's stride became sluggish. He had been walking long enough to have worked out Rachel had every right to greet him at the door with a loaded shotgun. Or a pan of boiling water. She would leave him, of course. Perhaps his own sister would leave him too.

He set a fresh bowl of water down for the dog and then looked for her. She was sat on their bed, holding the snow leopard tightly against her stomach. Rachel did not often look vulnerable but in that moment she seemed years younger, hurt, almost scared.

'You were my second chance, Bob,' she said, 'and I thought I was yours. I would have done anything to help you get over your grief. When you are quiet I don't try to jolly things up, I let you be what you need to be. I am a good person, Bob, I don't deserve this.'

She was not crying but her voice wavered. She was pale

apart from two small dots of pink indignation high on her pronounced cheekbones. He realised he had not been in love with her before now. Right now, he thought, I think I love her. He was startled. He had thought he would accept his fate passively, as passively as he had accepted their marriage, but he wanted them to survive.

'I'm going to make you even angrier but I have to say something,' he said gently.

Her eyes flashed venomously, she swallowed with an evident gulp of anxiety, but she said nothing.

Gingerly he sat on the bed.

'I've only just this moment realised I love you,' he said. 'You're right, I have been defined by my grief. Andrea was about my grief. I am a mess and I don't have any right to expect you to care any more, but I want you to care.'

Rachel had not been expecting this.

'Why on earth did you marry me, then?' she asked.

'Because that was where we were heading. I was grateful, I suppose; you gave me hours when I didn't brood. I felt lucky instead of cursed. I knew you were beautiful but I didn't feel it. I feel it now, Rachel, so if you want to get revenge you can hurt me really easily.'

She shook her head.

'No, I can't,' she said. 'You've had the worst pain there can be. I can't compete with that. I was stupid to think I mattered to you and I thought, really I did, that you might just disappear one day because the pain was too bad but I never, I never ever thought you'd go off shagging a girl half your age. That is shitty of you, Bob, really fucking shitty.'

There was silence.

'And she's pregnant. Let's really stick the knife into no-kids Rachel, shall we?'

Bob wanted to stroke her hair, place his arm around her, but, sensing imminent physical contact, Rachel squeezed her arms tight against her ribs.

'I'd like you to go, leave the house. Leave me alone. Please.'

Bob was struggling not to openly weep. He felt he was drowning in a disgusting mix of self-pity, fear and desperation. He had no one he could turn to yet he knew Rachel's request was reasonable. And perhaps he needed to leave the house anyway before he unravelled in front of her. His only friend had been Peter, and Peter was still missing. As he thought of Peter, he remembered how George, his son, had filled the space left by his former boss.

Bob wiped his nose, incredulous that only now in this abject state, he was remembering the kindness of his friend Peter, and then George, a young man whose life had been thrown into chaos, who had been the subject of incessant gossip, and had tried to fulfill his father's obligations. And Bob had been an obligation of sorts. Peter had saved Bob and Peter's legacy meant that George had to invite him over, phone him and, when a little older he had driven to see him, when older still had offered advice, only leaving him be when it was clear that Bob was not about to throw himself in front of a train. How easy it would have been for George, getting to grips with his father's company, to have forgotten about Bob when he became self-employed or grown resentful that he had started up alone. Instead, in those in-between years when George was barely a man and Bob was barely existing, the pair would share a pint and talk about the old days.

Now, he did not even know if George would still be with his old company but he found himself booking a taxi to take him there. He had already lost Suki to his wife, even before this crisis, he had no one else to save him other than Peter. Memories of Peter becalmed him. He was light-headed due to skipping the day's meals and wrecking the lives of two women. He began to forget Peter had gone, mainly because he needed him again.

While he waited for the cab, he filled Pascal's other brand-new bowl with food and washed some glasses that were next to the sink. All he took with him when the car arrived were his wallet and his house keys. He patted Pascal's head and wondered if he would see him again.

As he leaned back in his seat, he closed his eyes and imagined a world in which Peter had returned without him knowing it. He recalled Peter's determination to do the right thing. How could such a man vanish? He would be back by now, yes, he would be back. Had he not been so hurt and guilt-ridden already, Bob would not have had the guts to face a back-from-the-grave Peter, or his son, but he was in a twilight world of emotion by now; a crazed man with a machete running towards him would not have given him cause for alarm. He was drained.

It was dark when the taxi dropped him at his old office and most of the staff had headed home, but George was still there, a tall, slender figure, a more handsome version of his father but still bearing a striking resemblance to him.

He stood and shook Bob's limp hand.

'You look awful,' he said. 'Please, sit here.'

George pointed to a sofa against the back wall of his office and Bob fell into it, too full of self-loathing to feel any embarrassment.

'Sorry about this,' Bob said, 'but I thought, your father saved me once, and so did you, and I thought you wouldn't want it to go to waste.'

Bob blurted out the story of his wrecked life, not noticing that George was expensively dressed, that the building was larger and grander than in his day, that George did not recall his name at first. Bob did not notice how busy George was or that deep down George knew he would have to do what his father would have done. George was living every day in honour of a father he had loved and was not sure he was supposed to still love. How do you love the missing?

George left the room and wandered towards the small kitchen his PA used for preparing the hot drinks and simple lunches for him and any guests. She was there, checking to see what was left in the fridge.

'Ah, Miranda, I have a small problem,' he said.

She noted that he seemed flushed and felt an enormous urge to help make things right. She always felt that way, whether the problem was the fact they had run out of milk or a client had been accused of fraud.

Now, once again, her self-imposed rule never to leave the office before 6 p.m. was bearing fruit. Even so, she struggled to not gape as George explained that there was a man in his office who was potentially suicidal and expected George to help him.

Miranda wanted to tell him not to get involved but she was reasonably intuitive and surmised that George was under some sort of obligation or at least believed he was.

'I don't want to take him home, Hannah will –' he paused; he had been about to say something unkind '– well, she will, you know, prefer me not to.'

There seemed to Miranda to be an obvious solution. Mrs Stanning still lived in the family home which, especially with her younger son at university, was a glaringly big enough house to absorb the man on the sofa.

'Would you phone Hannah?' he asked. 'Not with the details, but, you know… Tell her I'll be a bit late.'

He drove Bob to his mother's. There were a few lights on and the kitchen was warmed by the Aga but his mother was not there.

'It's terrible, Peter,' Bob said, shuffling into the kitchen. 'An absolute bloody mess.'

'Peter's not here,' George said gently. 'When did you last eat?' he asked.

Bob shrugged. He was not sure he had even been able to eat breakfast. He had already been nervous that morning about meeting Andrea. Life had become somewhat even less palatable since then.

George opened a tin of chicken soup. He had liked it when he was unwell as a child and then he remembered that sweet tea was supposed help someone in shock and perhaps Bob was in shock.

Bob dunked some bread and ate his soup that way, morosely, his eyes glazed; reflecting a form of trauma.

'What's wrong with me, Peter?' he asked. 'What's the point?'

George worried that his mother might walk in and become upset or indignant at Bob's refusal to accept Peter was not in the house. Actually, his mother might be annoyed that Bob was there in the first place. George felt an enormous responsibility towards his mother but was slightly scared of her. He always had been.

'You're being hard on yourself, Bob,' he said. 'You're not the first bloke to screw around. It happens.'

'But she's pregnant,' Bob said, 'and my wife can't have kids. I might as well have kicked her in the stomach.'

George was out of his depth so he did what he always did in such circumstances and remained quiet while maintaining eye contact.

'She wants an abortion,' Bob hissed.

'Right, and that is bad idea because...?' George paused, wondering if Bob was a Catholic.

'I can't kill another child, I just can't.'

'Ah,' George said. 'Look, you're in a bit of state right now. I'm going to give you one of Mother's sleeping pills and we'll sort this out in the morning.'

He showed Bob the guest room which had an en suite bathroom and a sheepskin rug on the floor next to the bed which made Bob sob uncontrollably.

George knew he was considered mature for his age and he felt old, too, having little in common with his old school friends beyond Barney Browning, who had also lost his father, albeit in the more conventional manner of a fall from a ladder, and taken on the family's building business. This, though, was different. This was raw desperation. Not once had he seen his mother this upset, not even when the policeman had told her she ought to assume the worst. How can he know what the worst is, George had thought, surely the worst is the ignorance? Better than the presumed worst would be finding a body, being able to bury his father.

Limbo was the worst.

It made him almost envy Bob and his catalogue of real, tangible disasters. But Peter had guided Bob out of the depths once and George knew he was here, with Bob, for his father's sake. Just in case he was alive. Just in case he was dead.

George wrote a note for his mother, telling her an old friend of Dad's was sleeping off a trauma and he would pop back early the next morning before she was up and needed to worry about any of it.

Bob stirred before dawn, his head felt heavy and he could not work out where he was for a few minutes. As the events of the day before began curdling in his head, he pulled the blankets over his face and forced himself back to sleep so that when George arrived he was properly in the grips of slumber. George shrugged. He had to get to the office. He tapped on his mother's door but there was no answer. He gently turned the handle and peered inside but the bed was neatly made and no one was there. He would send Miranda over later. It was all he could think to do.

Andrea and Walter braved the morning drizzle. She pretended it was sea spray, it was less unenjoyable that way. The weather kept the shore deserted. A top-heavy woman in a tent of a windcheater lasted ten minutes with her golden retriever and then disappeared. Andrea stared out towards Blackpool but could not see the tower. Neither could she see Robert, the man who had begged her to be here on their beach.

'Maybe his wife murdered him,' she told Walter. 'Or, more probably, he's being a cowardly dickhead.'

She rubbed her belly in a sudden state of panic. It was growing. It was growing and she had done nothing about it. She had not seen a doctor or visited a clinic. She had not confided in a friend or told her parents. She was waiting for Robert to sort it all out and he was nowhere to be seen.

She tilted her face towards the wind, and the rain drifted onto her tongue as she called out his name. It was strangely soothing and she could not be sure if she hated him or hated needing him or simply just missed his company.

LAUREN

She decided it did not count. If Tim made the all the decisions but she was happy with them then that did not count as domineering or bullying or sexist or unthinking or selfish. Tim was controlling, she supposed, but not out of nastiness or even insecurity. He was driven, fearful of empty minutes. The only downside was that his energy and certainty made her feel, now and again, insipid and dull.

He was a man jam-packed with rhetorical questions.

'We'll take Mum to dinner on Sunday, shall we?' was a decision not a debate.

Lauren wondered how long they would last if she really would rather stay in on Sunday but she was content in a gurgling clear-water-stream sort of way to always nod her agreement.

He even said, one Saturday morning, 'Big winter coat. You don't have one, let's get you one today.'

She wondered if that was even normal, for a man to have noticed, let alone want to go shopping. It was as if he had an internal list and if he did not make ticks alongside at least six items every day, he would explode.

Yet if she were to be asked why she loved him, she would say this was the quality that set him apart, made him desirable. He was more demanding of himself than he was of her and there was a fundamental goodness to him. He was not showing off, he simply believed so many things needed to be done.

He was particularly fond of working late enough to warrant going to dinner before reaching home, and as Gregory was similarly dedicated, it meant that Lydia and Lauren made up a regular foursome. Lauren was glad Lydia at least did not work for the agency otherwise the day would bleed into the night without a break from advertising talk.

Gregory held his knife like a pen and tapped the tip of it on the table.

'I was thinking, because I passed by a "missing" poster this morning, about the portfolio you showed us when we first interviewed you,' Gregory said. 'Didn't you have a missing person in that?'

'I did indeed,' Lauren said, 'and he's still missing to this day.'

Lydia, remembering she was a writer and this might be creatively useful, sat up straight.

'I don't know about this, tell me.'

Lauren sighed. She had always felt a little uncomfortable at the way she had exploited the Stanning family misery.

'My dad's boss disappeared when I was, oh, fifteen or something, and it was big news, really big news for my village, and Dad was sort of in the middle of it all even though he knew nothing. I drew a cartoon strip about it and my tutor at art college got excited and it became a running theme through my degree. Which is weird, I know, but on the other hand it is unusual for a man running a successful company to simply vanish.'

'You should find him,' Lydia said casually.

'A lot of people have said that,' Lauren said. 'Maybe you could write a detective series where the sleuth is an artist who only paints crimes and clues.'

'Seriously, though,' Gregory said. 'What clues were there? Are the police still looking for him?'

'I doubt it,' Lauren said. 'He was declared dead; his elder son runs the company now – but it must be odd. I mean his wife must think, deep down, that he could walk back in at any moment.'

'Unless she murdered him,' Lydia said.

'Well, obviously,' Lauren said.

'Did you do any prying?' Tim asked.

'You know, I thought I would, I was tempted. I remember asking the man who owns my parents' favourite Chinese restaurant about it and he said the police hadn't interviewed him about Peter Stanning even though he was, it seems, their best customer, and I thought perhaps the investigation was corrupt or inept or something but then I probably got diverted by what to wear for the next disco.'

'So he ate at the Chinese all the time? Do you think the owner knew something?' Gregory asked.

'I don't know… I mean, he was definitely a regular, he and his wife went there all the time, so it might have been worth the police checking it out.'

There was silence as all four of them briefly pondered the mechanics of tracking down the missing.

'Is it tougher,' Gregory asked, 'to find someone who wants to be missing but is alive or someone who is dead?'

'Someone who wanted to be dead,' added Lydia, 'or someone who was murdered?'

'Most people think there was an accident. No suicide, no murder, no abduction, nothing deliberate at all,' Lauren said, 'and those are the hardest to track.'

'Can I see the stuff you produced for your college degree?' Lydia asked.

'Sure,' Lauren said feeling she had perhaps outgrown it all, 'you'll have to come over for a drink and I'll root it out.'

The evening wore on. Lydia usually started off the evening as a vibrant, engaging creature, keen to clutch Gregory's arm as she argued her point but before coffee came she would turn angry, sometimes even spiteful – or else she would become silent and superior, distracted and bored.

This became Lauren's burden for as soon as the tide turned, Tim would turn to Gregory and dissect the minutiae of office business leaving the women to themselves. Lauren had tried all manner of ruses to improve Lydia's mood and made little progress. It fascinated her, though, the way Gregory seemed not to mind, that he refused to become agitated or embarrassed or weary of her transformation.

'Aren't you ashamed, Lauren,' she said now, hissing, 'of being British?'

'No. Are you?'

'Of course I bloody am,' Lydia said. 'We are the oldest democracy and yet how close are we to having a woman prime minister? No. Where. Near. And yet America with its gun laws and electric fucking chairs finds a way to elect a female president. I tell you, I am embarrassed by that.'

This was a good topic, a meaty topic, but Lydia imbued it with so much venom it became painful.

'Would you rather a bad female president or a good male one?' Lauren asked, stoking the flames but seeing no other option. 'I mean, there was that stroppy Maggie Someone, she was tipped to be PM and she was nowhere near a feminist.'

'It's 1993, Lauren, we should have had two or three women leaders to choose from by now not one big-haired, thin-mouthed lady president.'

They were both silent for a minute as they pictured the female ruler of the free world, a childless fifty-six-year-old blonde who abhorred abortion and had famously shot a bear while camping near Mount Rushmore and was never seen in public without her heirloom pearls.

Betty Weaver was not so much disinterested in women's rights as fearful that to support anything so radical would lose her support among the right of her party who loved her for being so dismissive of the fairer sex.

'It's one big fucking joke,' Lydia said, glaring, as Gregory signalled for the bill.

Lauren nodded but was thinking to herself that for all that was wrong with America's president and indeed with America, it was a country that produced so much that was culturally rich and aesthetically pleasing.

As they climbed the stairs to the flat, she asked Tim if he would be interested in a long holiday in the States. He seemed perplexed and she was not sure if it was the notion of a holiday that unsettled him or the location she had suggested.

The next day Lauren and Tim stood at the foot of the Albert Memorial.

'Do you love London?' Tim asked her. He did not wait for her reply. 'Because people take it for granted. It is full of spectacular beauty and yet we all jet off to Paris or Rome or Venice or New York for romance. It's right here though.'

He gazed up at the monument so lovingly commissioned by Queen Victoria and then across at the Royal Albert Hall. And then at Lauren.

'Are you going all royalist on me?' She smiled.

He tapped her nose.

'I just love London,' he said, trying to sound light-hearted but something was niggling at him, she could tell.

'Are you saying we can't go on holiday?' she asked.

'No!' he said, pouting slightly. 'I'm saying this is the perfect spot to ask a beautiful girl if she will marry me.'

There was silence as Lauren worked through the grammar of what he had just said.

'I mean, Lauren, will you marry me?'

She had both expected it and not expected it at all.

'Oh,' she said. His eyes narrowed. 'Yes, I'd like that very much,' she said and his eyes widened.

They kissed and then laughed.

'But I don't want to honeymoon here,' she said.

'OK,' he said, 'but we'll marry here.' And that was the start of it, a long argument that he had not even anticipated and which she had not anticipated feeling so strongly about. It was as if all the years of being the only daughter her parents nearly lost summoned their own form of energy. She knew what her wedding meant to Bob and Vera. It meant the local church, it meant the local florist, it meant the big hotel near her father's office, it meant their friends, their small family. It meant more to them than it did to her where it all took place and that meant it could not happen in London. And her grandparents would struggle to make it down. The thought of Beryl and Alfie bravely trying upset her. There was something strangely delicate about Alfie, as if he were a cat on its final life, as if he were living on borrowed time, that she was lucky he was still around.

BOB

Miranda almost gagged with pride at being trusted with something of George's that was so personal. He had handed her the key to his mother's house and a potted history of Bob, Peter and George's obligation.

'Mother might not be there, and Bob might not answer the door, but if you could make sure he gets up and dressed and make him a cup of tea and ask him what he'd like to do next. I don't know, maybe you could give him some advice or something. But let him know he can maybe meet me at the weekend to discuss old times, you know, so he feels part of something.'

Bob sat at the huge kitchen table, unshaven, hair tousled, his eyes guilt-ridden and tinged, she thought, with humiliation.

'I'm sorry about this,' he said. Miranda had made him milky cocoa which made him think back to his childhood and the fact he had surely lived more than one man's life.

'I think I'm cursed,' he said. 'I'd rather be dying right now of cancer, than feeling like this.'

There was silence.

'Oh, Christ, I'm sorry, you don't know someone with cancer, do you?' Bob said. He was certain she would. He was having that sort of week.

'No,' Miranda lied. 'I was just thinking about what you should do, how we can all help.'

She liked the sound of that. It made it seem she was part of the Stanning clan. They were all in it together.

'I think you've done more than enough really,' Bob said sheepishly. 'I was… not myself yesterday. I thought I was finding Peter, which was crass of me. I really am terribly sorry.'

And yet, Miranda thought, he stays sitting there, he has not called for a cab or asked about train times. He still needs us.

'Would it help if we were to discuss your options, Bob?' she said, her voice rediscovering its Highland lilt as it tended to do when she was emotional or excited.

Bob ran his fingers slowly through his hair and remembered Peter giving him a list of his options once. It was a list that saved his life, that gave him Rachel, that gave him Andrea and gave him another child. It was sinful, really, that he had risked losing all three. And his sister. And a dog.

'If you have the time, I think I'd like to get things straight in my head before I go anywhere else.'

It took a great deal of effort for Miranda not to beam. She bit her lip and took a deep breath.

'I'm good at taking notes,' she said. 'So we'll be methodical about this. I'm sure it will help.'

'OK. But we'll have to go back to the beginning. Before Lauren… Before my life after Lauren.'

It was an hour that Miranda would never forget. It was an hour in which she felt she could almost touch the pillow made wet by Vera's dying tears. It was an hour in which she remembered her mother shrieking in grief when she was told that her big sister had been hit by a car and killed. It was an hour in which Miranda realised that in that moment her mother had also been hit by a car too, in a way, and that her injury was a loss of a sense of humour. Since Auntie Marie had died Miranda's mother had found nothing very amusing.

'It touches us all,' she said. 'We can't live in this world without grief of some kind.'

Bob sighed.

'I had thought I had come to terms with that,' he said, 'and then I behave like this. She's the same age as my daughter. It's so bloody messy.'

As the sun crept through the kitchen window, causing them both to blink, Miranda had what felt like a brainwave. It was a feeling at first rather than a solid idea and she frowned as she tried to find the words to explain it to Bob.

'When people reach rock bottom,' she said slowly, 'they can find a sort of bravery. They can face anything because it can't get any worse. So I'm thinking, Bob, that you can face your wife and your sister and Andrea and take the blows they give you and, you know, fight your way through because you've been through worse and you can't feel much worse now, can you?'

She was not pleased with her explanation. It sounded a bit like it came from a cheesy play on the radio but Bob was nodding.

'You're right,' he said. 'I have to let them spit at me if it helps them, don't I?'

'Er, maybe,' Miranda said. They were silent for a few moments and then Bob looked up, his eyes shining.

'I think I get it,' he said. 'I am here in this kitchen because it would be an insult to Vera and my daughter if I was to allow my current situation to be the thing that sends me over the edge. Do you see? I kept going then and I owe it to them to keep going now even though I don't want to. I must not hide from my responsibilities. I must not give up.'

Miranda exhaled, trying to hide any signs of triumphalism. She would be able to return to work and report to George that Bob was on the mend.

'Shall I drive you to the office now, Bob,' she said, 'so you can say your goodbyes to George? I can drop you at the station, too, if you like?'

Bob smiled, albeit weakly. He felt weak all over but there was some resolve in him now. He could deflect the pain by telling himself he was suffering for Vera and Lauren. He was about to ask Miranda about train times when he felt his heartbeat rumble in panic. Andrea.

'Christ, I told Andrea I'd meet her.'

He looked at his wrist but his watch was upstairs. Miranda looked at hers, a gift from George for all the overtime she did not mind giving him. She had worked for Peter and she felt a maternal devotion to the son who was in turn devoted to the business his father had started from scratch.

He would not make the beach in time. He would have to put a note through her door.

'Here, I'll help you write it,' Miranda said. She was beginning to feel omniscient.

She found some paper but no envelopes.

'We'll pop this into an envelope at the office and then send you on your way,' she said.

Bob sat motionless, the pen poised nervously.

'Tell the truth. Say you are at a friend's house and he gave you a sleeping pill and you are very sorry indeed and that you will be at the beach… does it have to be the beach?… Then you will be at the beach at ten tomorrow morning and you'll stay there all day if necessary until you see her. So, pack yourself some sandwiches. I can't think of a beach picnic without practically tasting cheese and pickle sandwiches.'

Bob looked at her bemused. Was he supposed to write about cheese and pickle sandwiches? And then he smiled and shook his head and signed his name.

George was in a meeting, the sort he would not normally allow to be interrupted, but his father would not have let Bob leave without a handshake. So neither would he.

'I'm embarrassed, frankly, George, but I want you to know I will be forever in your debt, and in debt to Peter. Thank you. For everything.'

George was pleased to see that Bob was standing straight and sounding sensible rather than something close to suicidal.

'Let's keep in touch, Bob,' George said, and his manner was, Bob realised, effortlessly seductive. This young man, he thought, will go far, and for the first time he noted that he was dressed far better than anyone he had met before, better than any of his clients.

Clients, he thought, when at last on the train, I've probably missed meetings I was supposed to have with them as well. It was a mess but he had not been lying to Miranda. He had no option now other than to plough on and bear the brunt of all the hurt and anger, and there was a refreshing martyr-like sustenance to that fact.

VERA

Their postman used a bicycle and had mail in a satchel and parcels in the basket. He always rang his bell when five yards from the front door. On very hot days she would present him with a glass of ice-cold water. On cold days she would ask if he needed a cup of tea. It took two years before he agreed to one so she did not push it and saved the invitations for when it was particularly bitter and the sky was desperate to produce sleet.

'Wouldn't say no, Mrs Pailing,' he said as he wiped his red nose with chapped fingers.

He produced two brown envelopes addressed to Bob and a white one for Vera.

'I do like a nice handwritten letter, the stamp placed neatly, the address clear as day,' he said.

'How often do people open their mail in front of you, Jack?' Vera asked.

'Oh, my, that is a good question,' he said. 'They often start right away but I make sure to leave straight away. Privacy. Don't blame the messenger but don't *include* the messenger.'

Vera wanted to laugh. Jack was so serious. She ran her fingers along the top of her neat, square letter.

'It could be an invitation,' she said.

'Nope,' he said. 'You pick things like that up. It's not an invitation.'

Vera raised one eyebrow and began to open the envelope. It was clearly not an invitation, it was a letter over one and a half pages, written in blue ink and signed, 'Karen Millington'.

'Oh,' Vera said.

'Ah,' Jack said. 'That is my cue to leave your lovely kitchen, Mrs Pailing.'

'No, please do finish your tea, and well done, you were right. It's not an invitation.'

There was an awkward silence so Vera placed the letter unread on the table and walked over to the window.

'It might snow,' she said. 'What do you do when it snows?'

'I resort to walking,' he said, hastily gulping down his tea. 'Some would call it trudging.'

She watched him cycle down the driveway, heard him deliver one jaunty ring of farewell on his bell and then she turned back to the letter.

She and Karen had drifted apart but in an amicable way. Debbie had been so sweet when Hope was born. Perhaps Karen was writing to tell her that Debbie was to be married.

But Karen was dying.

Her letter tried, at its beginning, to be chatty. She mentioned a fundraiser at the girls' old primary school. But then of how hard it had been to sell the house in The Willows with her sat in a chair, trying to smile through the pain, while yet another young couple wandered through the living room holding property particulars.

'There's hardly anything left of me!' she wrote. 'And there

is so little time left so I wanted you to know I think of you every day, of Lauren every day, and wake every day wishing it had never happened, that I had not been so stupid.

'Please give my love to my god-daughter, who is remembered in my will,

'Yours, with love, Karen Millington.'

Later, when it was dark and the sky was littered with specks of snow, Vera handed Bob the letter. He glanced at the feminine, curved handwriting.

'I don't want to read anything,' he said. 'Summarise for me, darling.'

'I think,' Vera said, frowning, 'we have moved on further than Karen Millington has been able to.'

Bob grunted. He had been quietly glad the families had lost touch. While Vera had been wrapped up with the newborn Hope he had nurtured resentment that the Millingtons had been so reckless. He had opened his front door to them and said 'hello' in his friendliest voice so as not to make them feel any guiltier – while all the time wishing that he could shake them and demand why they'd been so fucking stupid.

'I should see her before...' Vera said quietly.

'Sure,' Bob said, 'but they left The Willows, didn't they?'

'If she's very ill she'll be at the St Agnes Hospice or on a ward at the Burton,' Vera said. 'Anyway, I'll find her.'

Two days later Vera walked through the door of Karen's small, sunny hospital room. Karen blinked her hello. Her voice was reed-like, thin and fragile.

'Debbie wrote the letter for me,' she said. 'I hope you don't mind, I can't even lift a pen any more. But they were my words. It's kind of you to come, Vera.'

Vera kissed her lightly on the forehead.

'I'm glad you got in touch and just so sorry to find you so unwell.'

'Not long now,' Karen said.

Vera sat on the chair next to the bed.

'I want you to know I'm happy, that I don't think about that day all the time,' Vera said. 'I mean, I miss her, of course I do, but I don't think badly of you, not at all. You and Julian, you became family to us.'

'She was a lovely girl,' Karen whispered. 'I think she had a crush on our Simon, you know.'

'No,' Vera said, 'really?'

Karen laughed or at least Vera interpreted it as laughter. It sounded like the last crackle of a dimming fire.

'She was having a really great holiday with us. I need to tell you that. She was so happy.'

'Thank you,' Vera said.

'She would stop and peer at things sometimes,' Karen said. 'What was that about?'

'I'm not sure. I supposed she was a dreamer, an artist, full of imaginings. We took her to the optician but there was nothing wrong with her eyes.'

'I think she saw me like this,' Karen said.

'Whatever do you mean?' Vera asked, but Karen had dozed off.

Vera left the hospice a few minutes before Julian arrived to find his wife's breathing had become shallow and ominous. She died with him holding her hand, and what he hoped was a small smile on her lips.

LAUREN

'I had, to be honest, already imagined the wedding, here, in London, with our London friends, and I most certainly hadn't imagined a church.'

He was not pouting or even moaning. Lauren could tell he was simply struggling at the prospect of losing control of a project.

She did not want to discuss it. She knew if she started to then it would all descend into bartering. What she wanted was for him to agree to back off, to let Vera take control and create a fairy-tale day. Of course it would be Vera's fairy tale but, sometimes, other people's happiness mattered more.

'You are right, Tim, clearly you're right, but this is not about being right, it's about degrees of unhappiness. I believe my mum will be made more unhappy by a London wedding than you will by a Cheshire wedding. We can have a London party separately if you want but there has to be a service and a big dinner up North.'

'I can be unhappy,' he said in a mock-competitive voice and she laughed.

'I'm sorry,' she said. 'You can choose your own best man,' but she already knew he would be picking Gregory, who was at that moment on his way to their flat with Lydia and Patti. Tim had bought champagne and it seemed an odd sort of celebration, to knit together their engagement and the perusal of her 'Missing' art.

She spread it out, propped up along the full length of the skirting board of the living room. Because drawing was her job and her sketches were relentlessly publicly scrutinised, commercially scrutinised, Lauren did not suffer any bashfulness. She felt almost detached from the array of work that came under the 'Peter Stanning is Missing' umbrella.

'I think we can safely say no detective will find this useful,' she said. 'I mean, how can a white square and a Christmas turkey help anyone understand what happened to him?'

'Yeah, but it might help anyone understand why it matters to keep looking,' said Patti. 'I mean, it all looks so sorrowful. To me anyway.'

'There is the excitement of the novelty of it all in the cartoons and then it sinks in and becomes a tragedy,' Lydia said.

Gregory stood apart, nodding seriously.

'You should do something with it. A display or something,' Lydia added, vaguely.

'That's interesting… It should definitely be put somewhere. It's so arresting… And it really makes you think about loss. It tells a story.' Gregory paused. 'Lauren, would it be OK with you of we dedicated a wall in the lobby to this? We can use it to highlight the work of the new missing people charity I saw the other day. Make it the official charity of the company maybe. We are in the heart of London, after all – this is where people come and then go missing.'

Tim frowned. He did not want earnest charity people turning up and pinning posters in his lobby. It would emit the wrong sort of vibe. There was something unsettling about the faces, usually faces in blurred photographs, of people who had disappeared. It allowed the imagination to run wild towards evil. Kidnapping, murder, suicide. And to think, they were here to also toast his and Lauren's engagement.

Perhaps he would now have to toast Peter Stanning. On the other hand, had he not gone missing maybe he and Lauren would never have met given they only shortlisted those who emerged from art college with stellar recommendations. Yes, he thought, I might owe something to this Stanning bloke.

As he poured them all a glass he noticed that Gregory was gazing still at Peter's face, the only traditional portrait in Lauren's collection.

'I am fascinated by this man,' Gregory said. 'People like him just don't vanish. What do you suppose happened?'

Tim was trying to focus on the toast he was about to make and did not welcome the diversion.

'Probably something very dull,' he said.

'Hmm,' Gregory said, 'I think he had squirrelled away money over the years and wanted a new life with a new woman and was a coward about telling anyone.'

'Better not tell Lauren that,' Tim said, 'she is convinced he was the victim of some kind of accident and an honourable man in the wrong place at the wrong time. But now,' and he made a determined effort to seem casual about it when in fact he was feeling this might be the first of many significant toasts, 'it is time for raised glasses.'

Tim had an idea he was regarded as serious and possibly self-important but he hoped his union with Lauren would reflect well on him. I can be funny, he thought, but then thought better of trying.

'I'd been wondering how to cleverly combine Lauren's art with our engagement and it has just struck me that I might never have met the woman who will soon become my wife were it not for the fact she chose to depict the story of missing Peter Stanning which in turn ensured she was one of our picks to interview at JSA and is now part of the gang at Pilot.'

He paused. He knew he was stood in his own home but sounding like he was in the office. He cleared his throat.

'That's me getting too corporate, as always. What I mean is that I am lucky Lauren found a way into my life and perhaps a tiny bit of that is down to a man we will never meet. So please raise your glasses to the love of my life and her art.'

They all clinked their flutes and talk turned to the wedding.

'We're in negotiation,' Tim said when Lydia asked about the venue.

'We're not really in negotiation,' Lauren said and Lydia beamed. She had long suspected wedding plans ruined relationships or at least soured them and here was proof.

Later she asked Lauren if she would call it all off if Tim insisted they marry in London.

'He won't do that,' Lauren said.

'But if he did?'

'Then we wouldn't be able to get married.'

Lydia beamed again, pleased her new friend had some fire in her belly.

'Do you want me to be your bridesmaid?' she asked.

'No,' Lauren said, and Lydia screamed with delighted laughter.

BOB

He went to Andrea's house first and asked the taxi to wait as he posted the short letter. He tried very hard not to run back to the car but he knew he scuttled like a coward.

The front door opened of his big blackened-brick house before the taxi had pulled away. Suki stood there, or rather, he thought, his sister loomed there, larger than before.

'Don't worry,' he said, 'I'm just here to collect clothes and check on my wife. I won't speak to her if she doesn't want to see me.'

'Oh, Bob,' Suki said, and she strode towards him.

Is she going to hit me? Bob thought, not that he would much mind if she did. Instead his sister pulled him into an embrace.

'How could you not come to me? I'm your sister, I love you.'

He was stunned into silence and, confused, he remained, hugging Suki, wondering if he might weep in gratitude. Instead it was Suki who allowed a tear to fall.

'I thought you had, you know, I thought you had...'

He stepped back and held her hand and let her words float down the driveway.

'Just had a bit of thinking to do,' he said. 'Sorry to be dramatic.'

He held her gaze and smiled what he hoped was a smile which conveyed that he was perfectly well aware that this was real drama and he was up to coping with it.

He was surprised to see that Suki smiled back with a hint of her usual impishness.

'I have some ideas of my own,' she said and pulled him inside.

Rachel was out on Rachel's Refuge duty, looking, Suki said, like nothing had happened.

'One minute her eyes are all red and puffy and the next she is composed and beautiful.'

Bob lowered his head.

'That's what makes it worse. She's been through this kind of crap before. I was supposed to be the knight in shining armour, not more of an arsehole than her ex.'

Suki laughed.

'Bobby, Bobby, she was *your* knight, remember?'

'Yeah, well, now I'm scared of her, scared of saying the wrong thing, scared to be here really. She wants me gone.'

'For now she does, but that's understandable. Look, pack a bag and stay at my place. You have to stay with me, I've cleared space for you and made up the sofa bed. With clean sheets and everything.'

As he found a suitcase and began to stuff his clothes into it he wondered why he felt a reluctance to stay with his sister, who was, after all, being understanding and far from accusatory, as he had supposed she would be. And then he reached the answer. Suki lived much further from the beach and he needed the beach. Even though it had been the place where Rachel was humiliated and Andrea driven to despair, he wanted it to be close by. It was the only place since his first dose of pain that he had been at peace.

'Where's Pascal?' he asked, unable to prevent a note of panic.

'Don't worry, she hasn't taken him back to the dogs' home,' Suki said. 'He's with her now.'

'Oh,' Bob said, feeling unaccountably sad. 'Let's go then. Off to Chez Suki.'

'Jesus, it's not a prison,' Suki said. 'Just a bit cluttered.'

Bob followed his sister in his own car. He had never before visited her home. Suki had never suggested it, she was private in that way, despite thinking nothing of turning up unannounced at his house. She lived at the end of a short terrace of pretty cottages that seemed too narrow to form any sort of comfortable dwelling but were very long to compensate. Even so, he was sure he was too big for the place and wondered how whole families coped. It was full of plants and cushions and plenty of art on every wall, some of it crass, some of it intriguing and some of it downright arresting, but what took him most by surprise were the photographs. There was one of Lauren he had not seen before and one of Vera and Lauren and him laughing in the sunshine, his wife's face dappled with shadow, his daughter's hair glistening from playing in the paddling pool. It was such a beautiful image that he forgot, almost, what it meant to him.

'I don't remember you taking this,' he said.

'Did you never wonder where Lauren got her talent from?' Suki said, but Bob had never really thought much about what his sister's talents might be. She had always just been Suki.

'Well, well,' he said, 'but I didn't have you down as sentimental.'

'I'm not. This was just too wonderful to put away.'

'And this?' he said, picking up a photo of Lauren aged about eleven.

'It's fondness, not sentimentality,' Suki said, and she showed him his sofa bed and shrugged when she pointed to the downstairs bathroom.

'All the houses are like this,' she said and asked him what he wanted to drink.

'I don't suppose you have any cocoa?' he asked, astonished that his recuperative cocoa with Miranda had been but a few hours ago. He would send her some flowers although he had a suspicion she was always being sent flowers; she was a problem solver.

He had to settle for warm milk. Suki patted the sunken armchair by the gas fire, before rummaging for a small saucepan.

'Do you want to hear my plan?' she said.

For a moment he thought she was about to tell him about a new carpet or extending her kitchen but he quickly realised that Suki thought she had a means to fix his life.

'I'm exhausted, to be honest, and not sure I will give your plan the attention it deserves.'

Suki scowled good-naturedly.

'Never mind. Later. What are you doing tomorrow?'

Bob wriggled in the armchair.

'I have to be up reasonably early to see Andrea. You know who I mean by Andrea?'

'I do now,' Suki said. 'Rachel didn't say her name. But, well, can we chat before you leave? Please?'

Bob nodded and glanced over at the photograph of his family. His face was in slight shadow, Vera's was partially in shadow but Lauren's face shone brightly, radiantly, so that it seemed she emanated the light rather than being illuminated by it.

'I wonder what she would look like now,' he said, and Suki, so full of surprises today, pulled a tissue from the sleeve of her cardigan, wiped her nose and closed her eyes.

'Beautiful,' she said. 'Simply beautiful.'

LAUREN

She had thought herself plain at twenty but was learning to be more confident, to look in the mirror and approve, to know she needed little if any make-up, to acknowledge she would be an attractive bride.

She had enjoyed enormously asking Tim's half-sister to be the sole bridesmaid. Lottie had scowled at the engagement announcement but when Lauren asked her if the responsibility would be too much for her, she could not bear to turn it down.

'Can I choose my own dress?' she said.

'Naturally. And I'd like you to help me choose mine. It's one of the duties of the bridesmaid,' Lauren said and Lottie's animosity evaporated in the space of five seconds.

'You do realise this is all happening in Cheshire?' Tim said to no one in particular and no one in particular took any umbrage.

'How delightful,' said his stepmother.

'Never been,' said his father. 'Be an adventure.'

'But we'll have a party in London too,' Lauren said, and Tim sighed. He was not sure how he had been quite so outmanoeuvred but a part of him admired his fiancée for being so pleasantly inflexible. He stared at her thinking, for the first time, that he was properly in love. In love with Lauren and not with the idea of being in love. In love enough to be different, to put her first, to make her his priority over anything.

The plans brought Lauren closer again to her parents. The wedding was new territory and the disconnectedness that had become a low irritating hum whenever she saw them disappeared. She did not tell them Tim was reeling from the choice of venue, that he had had to stomach a church – and a church that was in Cheshire – and had suffered a double whammy of incredulity.

Lauren also knew that Tim would not let it show too much in the build-up, and not at all on the day. She had to drag him to the church in the weeks beforehand for the banns to be read and, while Lauren and Tim felt like intruders, Vera and Bob had sat with them comfortably, having visited the church in the months following Lauren's accident and intermittently thereafter. Lauren was surprised at how relaxed her parents were in the church but even more taken aback by how Tim wrapped his arm around her waist and tenderly rubbed her back as the vicar spoke.

They married on a sunny Saturday in May with Bob and Vera clutching hands tightly to ward off tears, sat next to Beryl and Alfie. Lauren made sure to catch the eye of her grandparents and give them a warm lingering smile. Her grandad had suffered two heart attacks in the past few years and much as he pretended he was up for anything, the drive to the church would have been a slog for him. Alfie winked at her, a wink full of all sorts of meanings and she could think of nothing to do but wink back. She did not see him as often as she wanted to but of all the people she knew he was the one she would say, if pressed, she felt most telepathically connected to. With just a smile he could convey he understood how she felt when she struggled to explain herself.

The light careered in through the narrow stained-glass windows so that the dust tingled as prettily as confetti. Everyone inside the small church noticed the shafts of sunlight and sighed at the beauty of it, all except Lauren, who found it fleetingly intrusive, as if someone uninvited had opted to turn up to the ceremony and tried to upstage the bride.

The unease did not last long as the fast-forward button was pressed and all of a sudden she was sat at a long table decorated with roses as her husband stood to speak about his wife. Tim uttered the word 'wife' sixteen times. Everyone chuckled each time he did so. He praised the Cheshire weather, his in-laws, Beryl and Alfie's stoicism and a fine example of long-lasting devotion, his darling half-sister who now loved Lauren more than she did him. What Lauren liked most about his speech and what cemented her commitment to him was that he did not mention Pilot once. He kept it to family, to love, to happiness. And she was happy. The wine flowed, the toasts came and went and Lauren, who had barely eaten a thing, realised too late she might have downed one glass too many. As she gazed across the room, at the finery on display – the pink silks, shiny ties, a tartan waistcoat, a metallic gold shawl – all of it was suddenly pierced by a metal rod that glinted so boldly it put the fashion show to shame.

It mocked her. She felt it had stalked her from the church, and it was daring her to move closer. She stood up and a few guests cheered but she did not hear them. She walked slowly over to the beam, kissing a few cheeks en route. The apparition had landed on the plate in front of Estelle, an old friend of Tim's who she had met only three times before. To peer at it she would need to embrace Estelle which she knew to be odd but the compulsion to get closer was too strong.

Estelle, an angular young woman of high intelligence but low self-esteem who hated her pinched nose, saw the bride walking towards her. She cannot be heading to me, she thought. Why would she be walking to me? I'm probably the least important person in the room – but she *is* looking at me. Do I stand up? If I stand up and she walks straight past me, I'll look a fool. I'm already a fool for thinking she even remembers my name.

But Lauren stroked her shoulder. Yes, she definitely stroked her shoulder, and bent down, which was all wrong. She must stand up for the bride. So Estelle stood up and Lauren hugged her and said, 'I'm so glad you came all the way up here, you're a good friend to Tim,' and Estelle flushed with gratitude and found herself unable to say a single thing as Lauren peered past her neck at the metal beam. It had stopped shimmering now so she peered closer and saw movement inside it so she peered closer still and saw there was a whole new world there, or rather a different wedding, one that had moved on to the dancing and one in which the bride was at least forty and had an entourage of thick-armed bridesmaids clad in hideous mauve.

Tim had watched his wife glide between the tables, had watched her stop to embrace Estelle, and been filled with smug affection. He had been right all along about Lauren. She was special and she loved him enough to hug one of his oldest if dullest friends. He forgot he was in Cheshire, that the food was provincially served, that the non-London women wore too much jewellery on too much décolletage, that he had begun to dread the live music. He took a sip of wine and smiled. He was happy.

Lauren squeezed Estelle's hand and headed back towards her husband feeling light-headed. She had drunk one glass of wine too many and eaten too little and already the vision that had nestled next to Estelle had become something like a figment of her imagination. An hour later and she had forgotten all about it. An hour later she was ignoring her sore knee and jiving to the live band's version of a Rolling Stones song with her father.

'That was nice,' she said sleepily to Tim as she lay in a corny four-poster bed.

'You're nice,' he said, running his fingers along her wedding ring. 'You're so nice I do believe I might develop a soft spot for Cheshire.'

'We have good cheese and fine women,' Lauren said.

'The finest,' he said.

BOB

He looked pale and nervous.

'I feel sick,' he confessed.

Suki made him sit down.

'If I ask you what you want, you'll say you want for none of this to be happening but, Bobby, it is happening and you have to find the best way through it.'

He nodded, unconvinced.

'Hear me out,' Suki said. 'Rachel is so hurt but she doesn't hate you. It's just that she can't have kids and—'

Bob held up his hand.

'I know why this is terrible for her. That's the problem. It's terrible for her, and for Andrea, who doesn't want a baby and can't let her parents know she wants an abortion and it's terrible for me because I can't let another child die.'

His voice began to crack and squeak.

'And I can't even do the right wrong thing and stick with Andrea because she's the same age as Lauren and that's really... so not right, so I'll stay with Rachel and it will be nasty and hurtful and no one can be happy.'

Suki patted his hand and took a deep breath. She had lain in bed the night before thinking of the right words but now she was simply concerned that her brother was capable of listening properly.

'Look, Bobby, it is crap, I'm not going to pretend it isn't, but there is a way through, there has to be. There always is, you know, in the end. Because there are people who love you even when they think they don't. Even when you think they don't. And you need to talk to them, face their pain. Maybe you don't know Andrea as well as you think you do?'

She had so much more to say. She had thought about little else. Her baby brother, who had been such an ordinary chap, was in the middle of an almighty crisis. Another almighty crisis. And she wanted to help; she wanted to help because Bob and his wife were her new life and she had never been so happy. She loved them and needed them. But Bob could not hear anymore, he had to move, be active, face the day.

'We'll talk properly later,' he said. 'I have to go.'

It was a soft, feathery sort of day with wispy clouds and a silent faraway tide. A group of bedraggled men sat with cans of beer, a couple in matching boots walked a German shepherd. Andrea was leaning against a dune, rubbing Walter's chest.

Bob sat next to her.

'I'm so sorry about all of this.'

She said nothing so they sat in silence until she muttered, 'I can't do up the button on my jeans.'

He took a deep breath.

'I stayed with my sister last night and she said we should

talk properly about what you really want. Are you sure, really sure, you want an abortion? Some women can do it and cope fine, just fine, and some struggle, I think.'

He stopped and groaned a little.

'Shit, that sounded dreadful,' he said.

'I'm not exactly looking forward to it,' Andrea said. 'If I'm honest I could have done it easily enough the day I found out but as each day has passed, I've dreaded it more and more. Not sure why, really. Maybe I'm more of a Catholic girl than I knew.'

He held her cheek, tentatively, in his hand.

'I've sort of realised it's a baby. My baby,' Andrea said. 'But I don't want a baby. Tricky, huh?'

He held his breath, the soft light gave her a halo, he could feel something important was about to happen.

Andrea unzipped her coat pocket and pulled out a piece of ruled paper.

'I have some questions,' she said, sounding very young and insecure. It made him feel like a bully.

She swallowed, licked her lips, tasted the salt on them, cleared some gunk from the corner of her eye.

'Do you love your wife?'

'Yes. I know that now. I don't think I truly did before.'

'Will she forgive you?'

'I hope so but I can't be sure.'

'How long will you keep trying to make your marriage work?'

'I don't know. I'd like to think a long time.'

'If Rachel got pregnant, would you keep it?'

'Of course we would.'

Andrea stood up.

'OK,' she said. 'I'll meet you here same time next week.'

Bob stood too, confused but intuitive enough not to pester her about what her questions meant.

VERA

She did not attend the funeral service but laid flowers on Karen's grave and wondered if it was deliberate that Karen had asked to be buried in a different churchyard to where Lauren lay.

Karen's will was simple. Everything was left to her husband and children apart from a savings account she had set up in Hope's name along with a brooch that was encrusted with old but real diamonds.

'You don't have to wear the brooch,' Vera said. 'Just keep it somewhere safe.'

Hope was briefly envied by her classmates who all day-dreamed of distant relatives leaving them castles or horses or a private beach as detailed on a scroll of yellowing paper tied up with a black velvet ribbon.

'She was my godmother,' Hope told them, and those unaware of who their own godparents might be pestered their parents for details.

Vera became quiet and contained. Bob and Hope gave her space. They were used to her withdrawing gently into herself from time to time and she would only spend a couple of days at most in her own sadness.

Bob assumed, correctly, the visit to and death of Karen was the trigger and that his wife was thinking about the terror of their journey to Cornwall that day but Vera was also pondering Karen's question. What was it that Lauren used to see?

She made the beds with vigour to stop herself kicking the doors. How was it that she had never asked Lauren what she saw when she would stoop or stretch in that odd way of hers?

I was waiting until she was older, Vera thought bitterly. But she never became older.

That night she lay next to Bob, her mind racing, the notion swirling that Lauren had known she would die, that she had second sight. It did not bring her any comfort. She climbed out of bed and went into the room next door where there was an overflow wardrobe full of clothes she and Bob rarely wore. She pulled out the long crêpe dress with its silvery woven ribbons. It was such a beautiful dress but she had worn it only for Hope's christening. What a waste.

'You look nice in a silvery silky dress, Mummy,' Lauren had once said. It had spooked Vera at the time but when Lauren died all her words became precious. Vera felt the lump of grief she carried in the pit of her stomach at all times swell dramatically. And with it a bubble of guilt that she had not spoken properly to Lauren about the strange things she'd said. Lauren had been so certain about the dress, so happy, so proud. Vera slumped to the thickly carpeted floor wondering if Lauren had been delivering a message. That it would be OK for her to look pretty even after Lauren was gone. Vera carried the dress to her main wardrobe and hung it on the outside of the door. She would wear it again soon, and again and again.

The next morning was Valentine's Day. Bob had left the house quietly and there was a box of chocolates on the kitchen table with a tiny card that said, '*I love Vera.*'

She smiled. Bob was busy. It was lovely of him to remember. Lauren had, up until the age of ten, always made her parents Valentine's cards. Big bold red hearts, pink hearts made of carefully scrumpled tissue paper, heart-shaped trees and heart-shaped doors.

She walked into the garden. The morning mist had not lifted and as she looked at the glistening sleeve of her rib-knit jumper she wondered if the house was surrounded by something more akin to freezing fog. It was so cold it wasn't cold.

A bell sounded.

'Gracious, Jack,' she said. 'It can't be safe for you to cycle in this.'

'Probably not, Mrs Pailing, but it was supposed to have lifted by now.'

'Well, I insist you come into the kitchen for a warm drink while it does lift,' Vera said.

'That's very kind of you and I won't say no,' Jack said. 'I've no Valentines for you among the post, though,' he chuckled.

'I would hope not,' Vera said and she wondered if Lauren had made a Valentine for Simon, if she really had developed a crush on him as Karen had said.

'Have you lots of Valentines in your post today?' she asked.

'Not as many as you might think,' he said. 'It's more of a hand-delivery thing, I suspect.'

Jack spotted the chocolates on the table and felt a pang of

envy which took him by surprise and caused a deep crimson circle to appear on each of his cheeks.

'It's cocoa weather, isn't it?' Vera said. 'Would you like a warm milky cocoa?'

His cheeks coloured more deeply and he pictured, involuntarily, the two of them sat at the table, their hands touching.

He paused and so Vera nodded towards the window.

'Non-negotiable,' she said.

They did not sit at the table after all but stood looking out at the lack of a view.

'Miserable weather but interesting weather,' Vera said. 'I like that about Britain. It could be mild and sunny by the weekend.'

Jack was tongue-tied. He was smitten and because it had hit him so suddenly he was unprepared and a little frightened.

'Do you have children, Jack?' she asked dreamily.

'Er, no, I'm not married, Mrs Pailing,' he said.

Vera stared down at her mug of cocoa and wondered, not for the first time, whether it was better to have known Lauren, loved her so much and lost her than to have never known her at all. Was Jack happier for a lack of the love of a child? If she was to find out today that Hope had died would she prefer never to have had her?

'I'm pondering big questions, Jack,' she said suddenly. 'Or meaningless ones, depending on your point of view.'

Jack was out of his depth, keen to escape, keen to stay for ever.

'I think it's lifting,' he lied. 'Better be on my way. Letters don't deliver themselves.'

'Please cycle carefully,' Vera said. 'I doubt any letter has ever existed that is worth risking your life for.'

Jack felt a rush of indignation and embarrassment that his career was being belittled and then a surge of gratitude that Vera cared for his safety.

She stood at the door and watched him cycle away, waiting, amused, for a parting tinkle of his bell. He had, if not quite cheered her up, broken her moroseness, and when Bob came home it was to find she had baked him and Hope heart-shaped gingerbread.

LAUREN

For Tim, his wife's keeping of her name was in the same box of mean tricks as the wedding in Cheshire. It was mean in that he had no riposte. Of course, as an only child she had to stay as Lauren Pailing. Of course, he said, but it made no sense at all to Tim. It may be the nineties, but he would have loved to make her Mrs Lewis. The taking of his name would have been the start of a new unit, a proclamation that they were a team.

'What will our kids be called?' he wailed.

He was especially disappointed because of the alliteration. It had all been part of the sense of fate he had when it came to his new wife. If they were to marry, he had thought, after their first date, she would be Lauren Lewis, which suited her much better anyway.

It meant that at work he called her Lauren and at home he called her Mrs Lewis. Far from exasperating her, Lauren was tickled by the inversion.

'I do daydream sometimes of us starting our own firm,' she said. 'Pailing Lewis sounds good, doesn't it?'

He had to agree that it did.

Gregory married Lydia and Lydia, as a not-very-famous-writer, kept her name too. Marriage made no difference, she still sniped at the end of every evening and both Tim and Lauren were relieved when they abruptly moved out of London to Kent which gave Gregory a long commute and the opportunity for post-work dinners diminished.

One late summer's day in 1994 Lauren was told there was a man in reception who wanted to see her. 'Something to do with the Peter Stanning display,' the receptionist said.

Lauren expected, although she had no idea why, to see a policeman. Instead there stood a tall, intelligent-looking man.

'I'm Peter's son. George,' he said, and she flushed.

'I'm sorry,' she said. 'We shouldn't have done this without your permission, should we? I've only just thought of that. I'm really sorry.'

George smiled.

'No, no, I was, literally, just walking past on the way back from a meeting and something made me look through your window. It's good to know Dad is still being thought about, really.'

Lauren looked at her watch and then at George's expensive suit.

'I don't suppose you have time to stay for a coffee, do you?'

'No but yes,' he laughed.

She asked Bella on the desk to find someone to bring them takeaway cappuccinos from the new coffee shop next door. Bella, who had been at Pilot for three weeks, and dreamed of being so efficient she became indispensable, sprinted from her desk, shouted through the coffee-shop door she needed an urgent delivery and sprinted back again before the phone had rung four times.

Lauren and George both glanced quizzically at her then turned their attention to the art project that had so captured Gregory's imagination that it was almost part of Pilot's logo.

'I was really young when I started it, and I wouldn't have carried on, but my college tutor was insistent and we thought it would be good to support a new charity – especially as lots of people come to London and then their families lose touch with them.'

'Yes,' George said. 'It is a lot more common in London than in Cheshire.' He squinted closely at some watercolours, which were framed by tiny bicycle wheels.

'Did you ever meet my mother?' he said. 'Because in that one, you've captured a likeness of when she was much younger.'

'Oh,' Lauren said. 'I suppose I must have seen a photograph.'

George continued to gaze, his brow furrowed.

'Can I ask,' she said, 'is there any news on your dad?'

George shook his head.

'You and I met once when I was about seventeen,' she said. 'But not properly.'

'Probably we did,' George said distractedly.

'Is anyone still looking?' she said.

At this George looked stunned. Lauren wondered if she had been rude but she knew if her father had vanished she would never stop trying to find him. Wouldn't she? When would she give up?

'I call the local police every six months and...' George frowned. 'And I call, but I don't demand anything. He's gone.'

'At the risk of being cheeky, I have heard from my dad that you are madly successful, which means you must have money – so couldn't you pay for someone to help? Do things the police can't do or won't do?'

'Pay who?' George said looking flustered and wondering how this woman had taken ownership of his father's fate, used his disappearance to fuel her artwork, to inspire the hunt for others who go missing.

'A private detective, or someone who specialises in missing persons? I don't know for sure, but there must be an agency that can do things the police can't.'

George stared at the cartoon strip depicting the shock on the faces of his father's colleagues and he felt the floor in front of him fall away. Instinctively Lauren guided him to the chairs in the furthest corner.

'I'm sorry to be so blunt,' she said, 'but I have this sense that if your father was searched for in a... different way, you would find him.'

George did not seem to hear her.

'We haven't buried him,' he said, 'it's weird, but one day I just stopped needing to find him alive. I want to say goodbye to him, that's all.'

Lauren had more she wanted to say but she stopped herself. It was his father. Peter Stanning was a concept to her, to George he was love, loss and unhappiness. It was none of her business what he did next.

'Right,' George said, 'I need to get to my next appointment.' He stood up. 'People have always been shy about speculating in front of us. Even Mum has never suggested what might have happened. What do you think? You must have thought about it when you painted him.'

'Well, my dad, Bob, you know Bob very well, of course. Well, he said years ago that there would have been an accident, maybe a hit and run, or a sudden illness, and he just ended up where he was not to be found easily. Dad was certain Peter would not have done something reckless or vanished on purpose.'

George nodded. 'I agree, of course, but when you don't know for sure you can imagine all sorts of things. It was tiring. It still can be.'

He wanted to add that he sometimes so earnestly wished that his dad would walk into the office and all that had happened was that he had lost his memory. Instead he shook her hand and shouted thank you to Bella, who was already hoping he would be a regular visitor and take her to lunch one day and, now he had bothered to remember her name, had developed a full-blown crush.

The following week a billowing bouquet arrived for Lauren with a note:

'I forgot to say I was moved by your display about Dad, thank you, G.'

Lauren was pleased and relieved and then pondered how flowers were in effect a full stop. To phone him to thank him for them would be odd, a never-ending stream of gratitude. Thank you for saying thank you. So she hoped, simply, their paths would cross again and she fervently hoped, too, he would be proactive about the missing Peter Stanning. On a level that was hardly helpful to anyone, she sensed there was more that was knowable about his disappearance. She peered at the watercolours and the bicycle motif which seemed to be both mocking and encouraging her stance that there was more to come.

BOB

He had an appointment to visit his wife and his dog at his home. The black bricks loomed over him. Should he knock or use his key? He knocked.

Rachel opened the door with an impassive expression. She wore no make-up that he could tell and looked younger and more vulnerable.

He followed her into the kitchen where she pulled two mugs from the cupboard and gestured towards the teabags.

'Yes, please,' he said, instantly convinced he sounded effeminate.

They moved into the living room, where she curled up on the sofa. He sat opposite her, his stomach cramping with nerves.

She narrowed her eyes as he ran his fingers through his hair. She had assumed she would be disgusted by him but she still found him attractive.

'I'm sure you've got some speech rehearsed,' she said, 'but let's get to the point.'

He nodded warily.

'Forget how sorry you are, et cetera,' she said. 'Do you want to come back to me and, if you do, how can you know, let alone expect me to me know, if you will shag around again?'

They were good questions. Excellent questions. Women were good at asking questions.

'I do want to come back. It's not original of me, I know, but sometimes you don't appreciate what you have until it's gone. I drifted into our marriage, if I'm honest. It was a nice drift but it wasn't urgent. And now it is. I don't want to drift in the other direction. I want you and I want to make you happy and for us to be in love.'

Rachel allowed him to see her smile.

'And part two?'

'The answer is in part one. If you allow it, I'll be properly married to you, not accidentally married to you.'

They sat in silence. She closed her eyes. He could smell her perfume, always the same perfume, daringly masculine.

'And there is a girl who is pregnant,' Rachel said cautiously, as if the words were too sharp, too painful to pronounce properly. 'What happens there?'

'I'm not sure I know the words to explain how sorry I am and how angry I am with myself. She is the same age Lauren would have been.' He exhaled noisily. 'And I'm having a problem with another child dying. I think she might not have an abortion. I'm not sure.'

Rachel sat up straight and leaned forward.

'That implies you want a relationship with the child,' she said and she could feel bile forming at the back of her throat.

Bob looked at the ceiling, then at the rug on the floor, then spotted a small spider's web above the curtain rail.

'I want you,' he said.

LAUREN

She had read a feature about couples falling apart because of a failure to conceive.

'You do know we can't just decide *"oh next summer or next autumn we will have a baby"*,' she said.

'Hmm?' he said as they had, he thought, been in the middle of discussing whether they really wanted to be involved in a campaign to advertise cider.

'I mean, we can't even assume we can *have* children.'

'Right,' he said puzzled as he had indeed assumed that they would have children exactly when they chose to have them. 'Can you do a test, then, to see if we can?'

'Sure,' she said, 'the test is coming off the pill and getting pregnant.'

'Oh,' he said. 'Well, let's do that then.'

They both laughed and then hugged and then ended up in bed.

'You'll probably be pregnant now,' Tim said.

'No doubt about it,' she said. 'I'm sure me even considering not taking my pill tonight is enough.'

She was almost right. Three months later they were staring at a pregnancy paddle.

'My, oh my, I'm virile,' he said only half joking. He had somehow found himself almost thirty and was worried he might be slowing down.

'Let's buy a house. With a garden. And a paddling pool,' he said.

'Let's,' she said and they embarked on the busiest few months of their lives, with the agency thriving and the house-hunting exhausting and the pregnancy daunting. Lauren suffered more headaches than normal but her doctor was unconcerned so she stopped even mentioning it.

She felt she had been on a conveyor belt. Find a nice job, marry the boss, have a child together. In her final few months of pregnancy however she had slid from the conveyor belt and sat and contemplated her grown-up world, finding that it afforded her such warmth that her eyes would fill with tears of gratitude. She would watch Tim lug the groceries into the kitchen, unpack and start to prepare them both supper, see how he picked up the pepper grinder and then replace it knowing she was not keen on the stuff. She noted how he would read books on diet during pregnancy and look at her not as the beached whale she thought herself to be but just as desirable as before.

He sprouted a few grey hairs, grew a moustache then immediately shaved it off, dumped his new aftershave in the bin when she said her hormones hated it.

'I think you're getting sexier with old age and new-found responsibility,' she told him one evening.

Tim stood up, loomed over her and licked her from her chin to her forehead.

It was, she thought, the craziest thing she had ever seen him do and it filled her with nervous excitement. They were becoming better together, she was loving him more, wanting him more.

They found a pretty semi-detached house with a courtyard garden close to Richmond, which was inadvertently close to Tim's mother, and as they reminded her of her promise to babysit she hastily detailed the demands of her rep company and her current run in an Alan Ayckbourn.

'I think she's pleased,' Tim said in mock dismay. 'But I guess being a grandmother hinders her forty-something persona.'

In the last weeks Lauren could barely walk such was the pressure on her knee, and it made her sob with the indignity of it.

'I want to stroll through the park with you,' she grimaced, 'not wait for you to come home with treats like I'm a house-bound pet.'

'We're nearly there,' Tim said and he really did feel they had run a marathon and were in the final half-mile stretch. He was by turns panicked and proud and bemused. He exchanged contracts on the Richmond house when his wife was eight and half months pregnant, which seemed to him to be either astonishingly efficient or appallingly foolhardy depending on how well Lauren had slept the night before.

He hatched a plan for all the packing to be done while Lauren was in hospital and for him to drive her and the baby to their new home straight from the ward. He was much more exhausted than he knew but filled with the energy of responsibility and love.

'I did have my doubts,' Bob said to Vera, 'but he's made a first-rate husband for our Lauren.'

The climb down the stairs to reach the car for the drive to hospital would have been comical but for Lauren's tears.

Tim wanted to call an ambulance but Lauren shrieked she would kill him if he did, so he rang Gregory, who dashed over from the office and between them they half carried her to street level. Gregory, sweating into his no longer crisp white shirt, waved them off self-consciously but neither Tim nor Lauren were watching.

With every push Lauren's head hurt. The contractions were but a distraction. The instructions from the midwife were confusing; she could hear monitors beeping but her vision was blurred. She thought she could see slivers of shimmering light falling from the ceiling. They were bright enough to hurt her eyes.

'Tim,' she said. 'Tim.'

She wanted to tell him she loved him more than ever, that she could not imagine anyone loved their husband more than she loved him but the words were trapped in her throat. Have I told him I love him? she wondered. Have I ever told him? I can't remember.

Tim stepped back as they transferred her to an operating theatre. *She's not pushing*, they told him. He held her hand and wiped her brow and wondered why her eyes were rolling.

'You have a baby daughter,' someone said.

'Did you hear that, my love?' he said, but her eyes were glazed.

He trembled a little. No one had told him quite how scary childbirth would be. His poor wife was barely aware of what was happening. She was exhausted. He vowed to spoil her rotten over the coming weeks. He vowed to make her a cup of tea the moment he got her home to their new house, into which their belongings were being unloaded that very minute.

'We have a baby girl,' he told her gently as someone ushered him firmly out of the room.

For some time, Tim sat, alone, in a pastel-coloured windowless cubby-hole. There were flowers in a vase and a box of tissues on a small table.

If he'd had more experience of hospitals, he might have been more worried.

BOB

The sensation, he decided, was most similar to how he felt when waiting for his exam results. Had he worked hard enough, would he get lucky? Andrea asked him if Rachel was likely to try again with him.

'I really think so,' he said. 'She's worried, though, about the baby.'

'How come?'

Bob frowned.

'If I'm honest I think she is simply, if understandably, jealous.'

Andrea nodded and frowned too. They sat in silence. It began to rain. Bob helped her to her feet.

'Ask her if she wants me to get rid of it,' she said.

Bob did as he was told.

Rachel slammed her mug down in irritation.

'What sort of a question is that?'

He looked down at the floor.

'Let me hold you,' he said and, he gathered her into his arms, pressing her head into his neck, rubbing her back.

'I love you, I love you,' he said softly and as he did so he realised what Andrea's question had meant.

'We could have a baby after all,' he said, ignoring the way her body tensed. 'I am an idiot and deserve all the pain in the world, but you don't deserve it and neither does Andrea really and certainly not the baby. There is a baby that needs us.'

He braced himself for a punch to the stomach or slap across the face. Neither came. Instead, Rachel was silently weeping, making his shirt damp with her tears.

'I always wanted a child,' she said, but she sounded only mildly bitter.

This could work, Bob thought to himself. This could work.

Suki climbed into her car and nearly dropped her keys. She was in a state of near feverish excitement. The more she turned her idea over in her head, the more perfect a solution it seemed.

She would take the baby.

It would mean no abortion, no pain for Bob, no guilt for Rachel, and she would have a child. Perhaps not for long. Andrea might come back for it one day or Rachel might come to love it and take it to her and Bob's home, but that was far ahead. A solution was needed right now and she had found it. She struggled not to break the speed limit. She struggled to recall a time when she had been so excited.

Andrea was understandably nervous about walking into the blackened-brick house and Rachel was understandably pro-prietorial about her being there but it was better than meeting at the beach, and preferable to meeting in a café.

Bob had thought through what he would say in such acute

detail that he shook with nerves as Andrea sat at the kitchen table. Rachel, politely, asked her what she wanted to drink.

'Really weak tea and a biscuit, please. I'm queasy all the time.'

'Of course,' Rachel said, wondering if she sounded sympathetic or sarcastic given that she was not yet sure herself. If pushed she would say she felt sympathy. She was always brewing tea for young women in trouble. She wanted to feel sympathetic. She wanted herself free of a jealousy that if left to its own devices could ruin more than just her marriage. She was, after all, the grown-up. Andrea was young, inexperienced, but she was about to make a big sacrifice. Rachel had to cling to that, not her own insecurities.

To Bob's astonishment, Rachel led the discussion.

She spoke of Lauren, of how she and Bob had met while he was grieving, that he had been a father, then he wasn't.

'In most ways, Bob and I don't matter,' she said. 'You and the baby are what matter. But perhaps this way the child can be with its father who will love it and...' Here Rachel swallowed and breathed in. 'And I will love your baby too.'

Andrea made to speak but Rachel held up her hand.

'Please, let me just say this: I am hurt. But I am already hurting less. And you don't know me, Andrea, but I would not offer to adopt your baby if I didn't know I could be a good mother. A really good mother. I meet lots of young women who find themselves in unexpected circumstances. I only ever want to help them. You can trust me.'

'And you have to trust me too,' Andrea said. 'I didn't want this; I like Bob, but he loves you, and I really don't want to have a child now. I think I could be happy giving it to you both.'

There was silence and both women looked at Bob, who ran his hands through his hair and smiled weakly.

'We'll make it work,' he said softly as they all heard a car screech to halt in the driveway.

Bob and Rachel opened the door together, smiling bravely.

'You'll never guess, Suki,' Rachel said, her eyes damp, 'but we've found a way. I think we are adopting the baby.'

For an almost imperceptible second, Suki's face fell and she looked more middle-aged spinster than the daring vibrant woman she had felt seconds earlier.

'This is unconventional,' Rachel said as they drove to Andrea's home.

'It's really hard for her parents,' Bob said, 'so let's put them first, just this one time, darling. It will be worth it, I promise.'

Andrea opened the door in dungarees that accentuated her bump.

There was a plate of plain, chocolate and pink wafer biscuits on the coffee table and cups and saucers that were clearly not in use every day.

'Mum, Dad, this is—' Andrea was about to say Robert and Rachel but decided it was best to keep it formal. 'This is Mr and Mrs Pailing.'

They shook hands, Bob and Rachel bending slightly to reach Andrea's father, who remained in his voluminous armchair, Walter back at his feet having enthusiastically greeted Bob.

'I'll make the tea,' Andrea said neutrally.

'Please, take a seat,' said her mother.

Rachel noted that the mother was wearing a small gold

crucifix pendant and instinctively smoothed out her skirt to better cover her knees.

There was an awkward silence during which Bob cleared his throat but did not speak.

'Thank you for having us over,' Rachel said at last, wondering why she felt guilty, why she felt the need to make this work.

'It was very important we meet,' Andrea's father said.

'Yes, yes, very important,' Bob said. 'Thank you.'

Andrea carried in the teapot and placed it on the table next to a copy of the *Daily Express* which had a photograph of a Spice Girl on the front page. Her mother stared at it as if it had been Bob and Rachel who had brought the newspaper with them.

'Best to let the tea brew for a few more seconds,' she said.

Andrea remained standing, surveying the scene. She sighed.

'Look, this is really weird,' she said, 'and we don't have to pretend that it isn't but neither do we all have to be cross with one another. Mrs Pailing has every right to be angry with me and Mum, Dad, you have every right to be angry with Mr, well, with Robert. But I don't have to be angry with him. I'm old enough to have known better and I knew what I was doing.'

'I'll pour, shall I?' said her mother, avoiding eye contact with everyone.

Andrea sat down with another sigh. She had thought through her options in such detail that she was almost bored of the whole thing. She turned to Robert and Rachel.

'Mum and Dad don't believe in abortion and that has rubbed off on me, I guess.'

She turned to her parents.

'As I've told you, Robert had a daughter who died and he has trouble with my having an abortion too.'

'Well, it's too late for one now,' her mother said sharply.

'Yes,' Andrea said patiently. 'But I don't want a child now. I was hoping, when Dad is a bit better, to go to college, maybe part-time with a job, leave home – and you and Dad can't take on a baby. So.'

She looked across to Robert but then changed her mind and caught the eye of Rachel.

'Andrea thought it was worth considering if we should bring up the baby,' Rachel said softly. 'And we have given it a lot thought, a lot of soul-searching. I can't have children and Bob lost both his first wife and daughter so this could be a blessing.'

Rachel stared down at her skirt. Had she really just called it a blessing? It was that damned crucifix.

Andrea's mother frowned. She had hoped that Andrea's boyfriend would offer them a large up-front sum so she could give up work and look after the baby and she had steeled herself to argue that he should, but Rachel's plight and self-sacrifice made her doubt her rights in the matter.

'Whose child would it be?' said Andrea's dad.

'It probably can't work unless it is theirs, Dad,' Andrea said. 'They have suggested they adopt and help fund my education and keep me informed as to the baby's progress. I'm happy with that.'

Her parents were speechless. It all sounded immoral and dreadful but sensible at the same time.

'But it's our grandchild,' said her father.

'That's partly why we are here,' Bob said. 'It is of course your grandchild. We can't do this if you are unhappy. It's a good solution but only if everyone is on board.'

'Oh,' said her father, feeling cornered. 'It's a right mess, if you ask me,' but he sounded resigned.

They all stood and shook hands again and Rachel gave Andrea a hug, something which surprised them both, and as he sat in the car Bob smiled to himself. He had not once had to say it was his child too, but it was his child and he would work as hard as he possibly could to make sure Rachel felt it was hers as well.

'It'll be tricky, my love,' he said, 'but it will also be amazing. I love you.'

Rachel exhaled. 'I must love you too, I guess. Or be the biggest fool in the North of England. Or both.'

He grasped hold of her hand. 'Thank you,' he said and his eyes welled up in gratitude. 'Thank you.'

From her bedroom window Andrea watched them leave. She had run out of tears and she clung instead to the idea that, both morally and practically, she was right. She was right. And her child – her child would be loved.

PART THREE

LAUREN

'Mu-um,' said a voice. 'Mummeee, what you doing?'

Lauren thought it a good question. Her mind was wrapped in damp cotton wool, she had dribbled onto the towel under her face. Her back was sore.

She lifted her head and blinked into the sunlight. 'Why do I let myself do that?' she mumbled. 'I always fall asleep and then feel dreadful when I wake up, usually sunburnt.'

She fiddled automatically with her bikini top. 'Christ, what time is it?' she wondered. 'What day is it?'

She could sense someone was staring at her and turned her head to see a little boy dressed as Spiderman scowling at her.

'You're boring, Mummy, when you lie down,' he said.

Lauren had no idea who this child was but felt an over-whelming urge to cuddle him. She held out her arms and he sighed and ran to her.

'You're Toby,' she said.

'No, I'm Spiderman,' he said crossly as he ran back inside the house.

As soon as he disappeared from view Lauren became

anxious. She was certain she was supposed to be somewhere else. She sat on the sun lounger in a state of utter confusion. The garden was familiar, her bikini was familiar but who was she? I've had a stroke, she thought. Yes, and I was in hospital.

She clutched her head. She could remember pain, searing pain but aside from her sun-sleep grogginess there was no pain at all now. She involuntarily stretched out her legs. He knee was fine, just fine and very slowly she recalled being carried down the stairs, being told to push. She remembered beams of light mocking her. She remembered that if it was a girl they were thinking maybe Amber and if it was a boy maybe Joe. Definitely not Toby. When did they decide upon Toby?

She felt an overwhelming urge to sob creep up on her and the tears flowed. She knew they were tears of loss but she was not sure what it was that had gone. She put her face in the towel as her body shook from weeping.

'Hey, what's all this?' said a gentle, Northern-accented voice, and she felt an arm enclose her tightly. She leaned into him. His smell was comforting, sexy, a part of her, and it made her feel brave enough to put down the towel and look at him.

He was handsome and shirtless and trying to appear concerned but his eyes were smiling.

'Don't laugh,' she said. 'I've had a stroke.'

There was a second's pause and then he burst out laughing.

'You should be banned from sunbathing, Mrs M,' he said. 'You're always either in a strop afterwards or a right tizzy.'

'I am?' she said, thinking this was good news. Pretty soon she would be back to normal, then.

He placed the towel around her shoulders.

'I am running you a bath,' he said. 'That usually does the trick.'

As she lay there amid masses of bubbles, the boy burst in, ripped off his costume, climbed into the tub and began clapping so that the bubbles splattered and landed in her hair.

'Toby,' she said. 'Toby's a nice name.'

'Mummy's a nice name,' he said.

'No room for me then,' the man said, and Toby shook his head sombrely.

'Feeling OK?' the man asked.

'I think so.' But really, Lauren reflected with alarm, she still couldn't be sure who he was. Or who she was, for that matter.

'Hey, you already sound much happier,' he smiled.

Lauren wondered if her stroke diagnosis was wrong, perhaps she had suffered a nervous breakdown and that's why he'd said 'happier' and not 'better'. She knew which was their bedroom and what clothes she would find there. There was a card stuck onto the side of her dressing-table mirror written in silver ink. It was an invitation to a christening addressed to Mr and Mrs Simon Millington.

The name sounded familiar. 'Simon Millington,' she said out loud not realising he was in the doorway. 'Simon. Simon Millington. Millington. Milling... Debbie Millington. Oh my God, I'm married to Debbie's big brother.'

He coughed. 'You're worrying me,' he said. She jumped.

'I'm fine,' she lied. 'Well. I'm fine, but I feel there is something bad happening and my brain has gone all sluggish.'

'There's nothing bad here,' Simon said. 'We are together and we are happy and Toby is happy and healthy and a superhero.' He paused, trying to find an explanation. 'Perhaps Mum being in hospital, that's worrying you?' He cocked his head to the side. This was their life and it was a good sort of life. She did not look ill to him, she looked the same.

She nodded. 'Yes, I was in a hospital,' she said hesitantly, and he nodded encouragingly because she looked so uncertain

At that moment she saw the dressing table and its array of family photographs, which included a girl, older than Toby although very like him.

'Rosie,' she said, and at that moment a tomboy burst through the door, her hair bedraggled.

'The rope-swing broke,' she said, 'and Chris fell in the nettles.'

Simon laughed and told her there would be hot water in an hour or so for a bath or she could shower straight away. Lauren sank onto the bed. She had married Simon after becoming pregnant with Rosie, who was clearly a daddy's girl, and then they had had Toby. Like a photograph in a developing tray she felt her personal history bloom. She remembered Simon kissing her for the first time and how mad she had been for finding him so unexpectedly attractive. She remembered how annoyed her parents had been when she said she could not go to art college, that she was getting married and having a baby, and how quickly their anger had dissolved in the face of Simon's adoration of their only child.

We are happy, she thought. I can tell, I can feel it, we are happy – so why am I so scared?

She stayed in the bedroom while elsewhere she could hear the hustle and bustle of normal family life. There was a clattering in the kitchen and cartoons blared from a TV and then in bounded Rosie, who announced they would be eating in the garden 'like the French'.

Lauren sat quietly gleaning what she could from the conversation. As soon as one fact was established she discovered it blossomed into other solid memories. She taught art at a sixth-form college and, once a week, at a community centre. Simon ran a thriving motorcycle garage and showroom which sold new bikes, second-hand bikes and did repairs. It was much easier for her to recall Bob and Vera, now Granny and Grandpa, but she assumed that was because she had spent more of her life with them.

Later that evening she sat on the sofa with Simon.

'You can see Doctor Haines on Monday,' he said. 'Maybe you should have a scan or something.'

She nodded. The day had improved but still she was fearful.

'I feel half empty,' she said, 'like there's a big secret you're not telling me.'

'Nope,' he said. 'No secrets here. What you see is what you get. Oh, and I love you.'

She slept better than she had expected, drained from the heat, the disorientation and the dread, but also soothed by being loved so much. Toby woke her the next morning by bouncing on her tummy.

'Oh, no, the baby,' she groaned and that was the start of it, a gnawing realisation that she was definitely supposed to be here…

But, also, to be somewhere else.

TIM

He phoned Bob and Vera's house but he reached their ansaphone. He was not ready for that. Perhaps they were on their way to London. He did not leave a message and then worried he should have done. His mother was holding his daughter. She had pulled out of her production. He was touched but also scared. If his mother was putting him first then it must be bad, really bad.

His mother was watching his every move with a beady make-up-free eye. He was in shock and she was waiting for the collapse.

'Let's go to my flat,' she said. 'It's cosy for the baby and cool enough for us on a hot day and I can look after you both for a bit.'

'I can't leave Lauren,' he said.

She did not have an adequate answer to that so she left the pastel room and asked a passing nurse if anyone could help her do or say the right thing, and then her voice trailed off as she spied, scuttling towards her, Lauren's parents. She had chatted to them amiably enough at the wedding and had joked about seeing them again when they were all grandparents.

'We couldn't wait for the call,' Vera said. 'Is that the baby?'

Beatrice stood open-mouthed in shock and Bob and Vera looked at her puzzled.

'Tim tried to phone,' she said. 'It's a girl.'

Vera scooped the baby out of Bea's arms and shed a tear of joy but Bob felt uncomfortable.

'Please, come in here,' Bea said solemnly.

They walked in to find Tim slumped, rocking, moaning with his head on his knees.

Bea gently took back the baby as Vera started to gurgle the way someone being slowly poisoned might gasp at air and lose their voice.

'I'm so sorry,' Bea said knowing now that nothing else need to be said for them to understand the terribleness of what had happened.

'Where is she?' Bob said.

'I'm not sure, Bob, I'm trying to get some information. Tim won't leave the hospital.'

It was, Bea noted, a tableau worthy of any play as they stood in varying states of despair and ignorance. And silence. Later she would say the silence could have lasted for ten seconds or it could have been minutes but it was suddenly punctured by Vera screaming the scream of all bereft mothers. It was piercing and agonising and forced Bea to leave the room again whereupon she shouted in the clearest of stage voices into the corridor, 'Get us some fucking help. The mother of this baby is dead.'

It caused complete strangers to burst into tears, husbands to shield their pregnant wives, nurses to stop in their tracks and porters to frown in confusion. It also prompted help and apologies for the delay in providing practical advice and information, if not for the actual death.

Tim was led away. Thirty minutes later, he returned to retrieve Bob and Vera. The goodbyes to Lauren were long and only ended when Vera collapsed, her legs buckling in grief, her mind incapable of absorbing how a day of excited anticipation had turned into this nightmare.

Bea arranged for taxis and took them all to her flat. Tim and Lauren's new home was full of boxes, some unpacked, and her flat was not big enough for more than Tim and the baby, so she phoned around and found a hotel room nearby for Lauren's parents although she was not at all sure how she would usher them out of her flat when the time came for bed.

The flat's buzzer sounded and a nurse, on her way home after her shift, handed over a steriliser, bottles, some powdered milk, and the tiniest nappies, which Bea placed on her low glass coffee table in the middle of her lounge and then abruptly ran into her bedroom so she could weep and swear in private.

'What did Lauren want to call a baby girl, Tim?' Bob asked in a voice that he hoped sounded strong but wavered under his lack of control. 'We kept asking and she kept saying neither of you had decided.'

'She liked Amber, that was in pole position as we drove to the hospital,' Tim said as if recalling the events of last year, not the day before.

'Oh, Amber is nice,' Vera said. 'Does she look like an Amber, Bob, do you think?'

'She looks like a Lauren,' he said.

LAUREN

She dropped by the pharmacy on the way to the doctors' surgery. She did not want to make a fuss about it with the doctor, she wanted quiet confirmation, that was all.

'A what?' asked the young girl on the till.

Lauren blushed. She did not want to shout it out.

'A pregnancy test, you know, a home pregnancy kit.'

The girl eyed her suspiciously and went behind the sharp white wall where the pharmacist was bustling. She returned, pleased with herself.

'We don't stock them and the chemist says no one does. He's not heard of them anyway.'

'Oh,' Lauren said, and she suddenly felt a wave of panic that brought daubs of sweat to her forehead.

The girl softened.

'You're registered at the doctors', aren't you? I've seen you here before, so just go there like everyone else?'

Lauren nodded, feeling stupid. Why had she been so sure she could buy a pregnancy testing kit over the counter? As she walked out of the pharmacy she caught sight of the post office that doubled as a sweet shop and had an urge to buy licorice allsorts. They were her cheer-me-up sweets. She could smell them, see them, the gaudy blue and garish pinks of them, and yet no one in the post office had ever heard of them. She had to settle for barley sugar. But I didn't want barley sugar, she grumbled to herself. What I really wanted was a pregnancy test.

Dr Haines was on holiday, which meant that Lauren found herself sat opposite Dr Buckingham who was popular with the over-eighties but whom everyone else hoped to avoid.

'I've never heard anything quite like it,' he said with a marked lack of curiosity.

'No, well, could you send me for a scan or some tests or something?' she said.

'You'll have to go to London,' he said. 'Might take a while for the appointment to come through. But there's a psychiatrist in Chester who could see you quicker.'

Lauren knew better than to argue with him. Dr Haines would be back soon.

'Please, put me the on the waiting list for the scan,' she said. 'I don't need a psychiatrist, thank you. And can *you* arrange a pregnancy test?'

Dr Buckingham frowned.

'You have two children, Mrs Millington,' he said. 'Surely you can tell without an expensive test?'

Lauren wanted to yell and ask what was wrong with people today, but thought better of it. She was the one with the problem. She knew that much.

She walked out to her car, holding the car keys as if they were precious stones. She could drive. She knew she could drive and yet it seemed to her as if she should not be allowed to. Simon had the children so she decided, on a whim, to drive to her parents'.

It was a bad idea. The main lane looked familiar but she could not find the turning to the cul-de sacs that led to her old road. She slowed and wound down the window.

'Could you tell me where The Willows is, please?' she shouted to a mother pushing a pram. The woman shook her head.

'Ashcroft Road?'

The woman shrugged and said sorry. Lauren turned the car around and drove slowly along the lane and at last saw a track where the road should have been. She parked the car and walked along it until she reached a metal gate behind which there was a field full of sheep.

It was peculiar and yet she was not upset. The memory had been sharp and was now fading. Her parents lived on the other side of the farm. Of course they did. But she did not drive over, just in case. At least now, with Simon and the children, she felt secure. When she arrived home, he was ready to leave to get to the garage.

It was the school holidays. She and the children were to be together all day and for a few seconds she felt helpless. What does anyone do with two children for a whole day? she wondered.

'You OK, love?' Simon said. 'I can get home early if you need me to.'

He noticed the slight panic in her eyes. 'Tell you what, I'll come home for lunch,' he said.

'Yes, please, thank you,' she said, relieved.

She watched him rev the bike and drive away. Rosie tugged at her arms.

'Mum, you're acting weird,' she said unsympathetically.

'I love you,' Lauren said. It was all she was sure about. Her daughter grimaced and ran upstairs to her room but not before turning to glare at her mother.

'And your voice is weird too, it's a bit posh. I don't like it.'

'Oh,' Lauren said. 'I'm sorry, darling.'

'There, just like that. Posh.' And then the bedroom door slammed shut.

Toby was watching an old Elvis Presley film, which seemed to her an odd thing for a four-year-old to be doing, but he liked the songs and the dancing so she left him to it while she toured the small kitchen. She found a fridge stacked full of food and in a flash remembered the trip to the supermarket, the overladen trolley, Toby grabbing chocolates, Rosie moaning about how boring it was.

It all felt like she was on a juddering conveyor belt, one step behind everyone and then suddenly up to speed only to fall behind again. Without thinking she made Simon a cheese and pickle barm cake and she was pleased she had not had to think about it but less pleased that when she did she doubted she had ever made one before. She filled the kettle and stood next to it while it boiled. It took so long she began to flick the switch on and off in annoyance, finally snapping and throwing the entire contraption into the sink. The lid sprang open and some water splashed up onto her arm. It did not scald her, the water was merely tepid.

'And what's the kettle ever done to you?' Simon asked as he stood, trying to appear relaxed, at the kitchen door.

His wife's eyes were smarting in anger.

'It takes so bloody long to boil. It's ridiculous,' she said, and he gave a her hug, aware that perhaps the kettle was not all that was frustrating her.

They sat at the small kitchen table while the children ate on a rug on the small lawn.

'I went to see Mum and Dad this morning,' she said, meaning to explain to him that she had tried to find them but forgotten where they were and that perhaps she had some neurological disorder, but Simon laughed before she could find the right words.

'And how could you do that when they are in St Ives?' he said.

'Oh, they'd never go there,' she said.

Simon shook his head.

'I think you fell off the sun lounger and bumped your head. You really are all mixed-up about stuff. When's your scan?'

She pulled a daft face. 'It was Dr Buckingham.'

'Say no more. We'll chase it up with Dr Haines.' He paused. 'Just out of interest, why would Bob and Vera not go to St Ives?'

'Because of…' She rubbed her knee but her knee was fine. 'I thought we didn't like it for some reason.'

'They've been going ever since we were kids. We all love the place, you know that. Mum was cross her operation kept her away this time. Don't you remember Vera promising they'd all go back late September or spring to cheer her up?'

'Yes, yes, I remember now. It's like all my memories are stuck for a few seconds and then burst free but only one at a time. I'm sorry. I'm not doing it on purpose. I remember the big things properly, like I love you and the children, but I don't understand why I thought Mum and Dad lived somewhere else.'

She did not tell him that the somewhere else did not even exist. When she closed her eyes she could see, as if through an early-morning mist, the willow trees, the Squeezy Bottle war, the Christmas lights, her sheepskin rug. Maybe they were all part of her parents' other house, but she doubted it.

'Are you dizzy, do you feel ill?' he said.

'No, I feel better than I've ever felt, even with the sunburn on my shoulders. It's just my memory that's wonky. And, Simon, do I sound a bit posh?'

Simon tilted his head to one side.

'Not posh really, a bit different, yes. But only a bit.' And then he changed the subject. He had no idea what was going on and the more they talked about it, the stranger, to him, it seemed to get.

Dr Haines was swift to act but the scans revealed no evidence of trauma or disorder. Dr Haines also noted that Lauren was disappointed rather than relieved. He wrote down the name of a therapist he had once used for a rape victim.

'Please, go and chat, have a few sessions with her. You can tell her anything without being judged. It might help talking it through in confidence with a stranger who has heard about all sorts of problems and won't be cynical or shocked.'

He paused. 'Actually, I insist that you go. You seem very distracted to me.'

She nodded miserably. She was becoming tired of all the surprises in her life. Tomorrow her parents would be back from Cornwall and she was afraid of how desperately she wanted to see them. Their devotion to her had been stifling over the years but now she yearned for their unconditional love, yearned to be with people she had always known, who had always been there.

BOB

'But you don't believe in God,' he said.

'It doesn't matter,' Rachel said. 'It's a way of telling our friends this is our child, our new life. It is symbolic.'

There was a small church christening and a slightly larger gathering for drinks back home. Bob was astonished to discover that his clients had become his friends and they arrived bearing gifts for his son. Andrea had asked his middle name be Grant, after her father who, three weeks before the birth, had suffered another stroke and was still in hospital trapped in 1969.

That meant Rachel had full control of his first name and she had picked Jevin for no other reason it seemed than she liked the rhythm of Jevin Grant Pailing. Bob would have liked to have called his son Peter. As the years had passed, the dignity and loyalty of his boss became increasingly clear. Peter had saved him. Peter deserved to be remembered but Bob could not deny that Rachel was right, that Peter Pailing sounded like a character from a nursery rhyme while Jevan Pailing had an intriguing statesmanlike air to him.

'He'll be famous or important,' she said.

'Or an accountant like his dad,' Bob said.

They had reached the point where he could say something like that and not risk hurting her. They had swiftly moved to a place where he was in charge of the nature of their new son and she was in charge of the nurture.

Suki had never had the chance to tell Bob of her plan and never would. They had not needed her and for the first time she felt herself to be a spinster doomed to be looking at families from the outside. She was proud of her brother's new family, that he had held it together, but she had to convince herself she far preferred to help look after the peeved Pascal than the gorgeous Jevin.

It was not all plain sailing. Bob would find Rachel gazing at the sleeping baby wistfully and knew his wife was either wishing she had given birth to him or torturing herself that Andrea would appear unannounced.

Bob was less worried about Andrea. She had told him she was sure she had done the right thing and they had all agreed that she should send letters and postcards to her son about her life to form a Birth Mother Box so that when he was old enough he could have all his questions answered and not feel rejected.

They told no one what had happened and most of their small number of friends and acquaintances decided Rachel and Bob had adopted the child of a woman from Rachel's Refuge.

The stayed in most evenings, tired and even happy as they watched film videos. The whirr and clunk as yet another VHS tape was pushed into their machine became a punctuation point of their life. It meant supper was over, the baby was in his cot and they could finish their wine with *Rain Man* or *The Accidental Tourist* or a Hitchcock classic with Pascal dozing on the thick rug beside them. Sometimes, when a character had an affair, Rachel would stiffen, Bob would stroke her hand and she would relax.

The entire arrangement existed on the premise he would never again hurt her and they were starting over from scratch. This meant he could not dwell on Lauren and Vera so now and again he would shed a tear, just with Suki, and when Beryl died, Rachel stayed at home with Jevin while Suki and her brother attended the funeral.

Andrea addressed letters to Jevin within letters to Rachel and Bob which was thoughtful of her, he thought. It meant their baby's letters could remain unopened and private but they did not need to worry about what was in them. Andrea stayed put for a few months until it was clear her father was stable, if still in hospital, and then, on funds provided by Bob, took a course in French, which she had been good at in school, and then found a studio flat to rent in Paris where she, with some irony, found a small job as a dog walker.

Bob wanted to know if all the dogs in Paris were called Pascal but the deal was that any communication would only be about Jevin and come only from Rachel, who hoped to hear soon that Andrea had fallen in love. But Andrea's unwritten rule was to keep her private life private.

LAUREN

They arrived with boxes of clotted cream fudge and Rosie and Toby hugged them tightly, so Lauren felt less self-conscious about doing the same.

'A moustache, Dad?' she said, laughing. Bob pouted.

'You've liked it well enough the past six months,' he said.

'I forgot all about it,' Lauren said lightly.

'I wish I could,' Vera said, and from that moment Lauren felt her parents were much more feisty than she'd been, deep down, expecting.

She had been in need of some cosseting but none was forthcoming. Neither she nor Simon wanted to burden them with details of the trips to doctors but Lauren felt even if they had told them the whole sorry tale they would not have been overly concerned.

'You'll never believe it, darling,' Vera said, 'but Ben turned up with a girl in tow. We were speechless, your dad and I, and we spent the whole day trying to act natural but looking right muppets.'

Bob and Vera laughed conspiratorially, Lauren smiled and

waited for her memory to click into gear. Ben. She waited. Ben. And then Ben filled her head. Baby Ben, who she thought of as her own darling possession, whose pram she had struggled to push, whose hair she had decorated with daisies. Boisterous Ben who had run around with plastic guns and burst into her bedroom demanding ransoms and treasure. Ball-mad Ben who had discovered rugby and cricket and whose sporting escapades would mean she never saw her father at weekends, and the Ben she had left at home when she married Simon, and the Bright Ben who went to university and never spoke of any girlfriends and who now it seemed had one.

'Is she nice?' Lauren asked, surprised by how protective she felt.

'A bit quiet, very pretty, seems to adore him though.'

'Who wouldn't?' Lauren said, and she saw that Simon's expression was a mixture of relief and pride that she had not said anything to unnerve her parents.

'Feeling better?' he said when they had gone.

She wanted to say that she was but, really, all that had changed was that she was coping better with the mechanism of delayed memory. The dark cloud of elsewhere was, if any-thing, becoming more doom-laden and she was desperately disappointed by how casual her parents had been. They had not even intuitively noticed their daughter's displacement.

'I'm still not quite there,' she said, and he nodded, convinced that before long all the peculiarity of the past weeks would be forgotten, a funny story to tell at his thirtieth birthday party.

Simon abruptly stood up, left the room, and returned with a box wrapped in bright shiny paper.

'A little pressie,' he said.

Lauren ripped at the paper, laughing. He had bought her a new kettle.

'We don't have to do this,' Simon said. 'if it makes you uncomfortable.'

She punched him playfully in his stomach.

'Don't be daft, I'm looking forward to it.'

She wasn't, of course. There was the usual issue of delayed memory but also a nagging fear that something bad was going to happen.

Vera and Bob hosted it. Their converted barn was ideal for parties and somehow Karen and Julian bore no resentment at how the Pailings had become increasingly well off while they had stagnated and remained in the same semi-detached house where once the two families had briefly shared a party line to keep the phone bill down.

The bunting declared 'Simon is 30' and his friend Matt was turning DJ for the evening, having hired a turntable and a stock of mostly dated dance and rock singles. Matt had a friend who acted as lackey, silently carrying records, bringing Matt drinks, fiddling with the electrics. Lauren thought he looked familiar, there was something sad and small and brow-beaten about him and she pictured him, suddenly, as being bullied at school even though she had no idea who he might be.

As soon as it turned nine o'clock, Vera and Bob would take Rosie and Toby to Simon and Lauren's home and babysit, and Simon's parents would leave too, allowing the evening to turn to drunken revelry.

'I won't drink too much,' she told Simon.

'Oh, come on, you love a drink at a party,' he said.

'Do I?' she wondered.

Simon pushed Matt from the microphone.

'Before they leave, I want you all to raise a toast to my parents for being the best ever, and especially my mum, who probably should be lying down after her operation not trying to dance to Roxy Music.'

'Karen and Julian!' everyone shouted.

'And I want you toast the best-ever in-laws for handing over their wonderful home.'

'Vera and Bob!' everyone shouted.

Lauren watched them leave as Ben and his girlfriend arrived.

Ben, she thought. Do I love you the way all sisters love brothers in that they have to love them – because I really don't know why I do love you.

She grabbed a glass of wine to take her mind off it. One ought to be OK. The glitter ball, also hired by Matt, threw patterns onto the walls and across people's faces. Five blokes began pogo dancing to Nirvana while their wives and girl-friends shrieked in laughter. Debbie pulled Lauren onto the makeshift dancefloor.

'I can't, my knee will hurt,' Lauren said.

'What?' Debbie shouted. 'What did you do to your knee?'

Lauren stared at her feet, which were in high heels, and then stared at Debbie. A miniature laser display, Matt's *pièce de resistance*, began as he played the Electric Light Orchestra.

Blue and green beams of light were spinning through the dancers' bodies. Simon's forehead was covered in beads of sweat as he leaped about. She knew everyone there, not instantly perhaps, but pretty quickly. She could reel off their names if she had to and state one interesting fact about each one. There was Kelvin, clutching a tankard of bitter, who loved rugby league so much he had married the plainest and dumpiest of girls because her father had played for St Helens and was happy to drive north and east to watch the least attractive of games. There was Wendy, in high white boots and a miniskirt, who had found herself pregnant with twins at seventeen and managed to never tell a soul who the father was. She knew them all and felt varying degrees of warmth towards them, but from a distance that was impossible to explain.

She smiled at her husband and twisted her hips to show she was having the fun she wished she was having and then a beam of light bounced off the glitter ball like a javelin being thrown and she tensed at the memory of slivers of light through which she used to see things she was not supposed to see. But it was not a memory, not a normal memory. It was old and dark and forbidden and felt as if surrounded by a forcefield that had been temporarily weakened but would rise up again leaving her confused. She clung while she could to the sensation of otherness. She had been somewhere else, lived somewhere else and that explained, without really explaining anything, why she was remembering things so slowly and differently.

As Phil Collins began singing about two hearts, the memory ebbed.

Humans cannot have two hearts, she thought, but I think I have.

Simon grabbed her by the waist.

'That's my girl,' he said.

'That's my boy,' she said. 'Happy birthday, handsome.'

And although they danced and friends pointed at how in

237

love they still were, Lauren was not lost in the moment. The only way she could describe it, if anyone asked, which they did not, was that feeling she had had when Rosie was a newborn and she and Simon had left her with Lauren's parents and she had known she was supposed to enjoy the freedom from feeding and changing nappies but could not stop fretting at the separation. Yes, she was separated from something or someone – and it was hurting her.

She parked the car on the verge and stood before an attractive stone cottage that had the date 1840 engraved on the stone lintel. The door was opened by a woman in her fifties who wore being in middle age well. She was graceful and her eyes possessed a piercing intelligent kindness.

'Please, call me Miriam,' she said as she led Lauren to her consulting room which was an elegant study and furnished so beautifully it reminded Lauren of places she had not been.

Miriam cleared her throat, smiled, and explained the basics to her newest client. She stressed the confidentiality, that she had listened to many and varied experiences, and that Lauren must not worry about sounding silly or sad or threatened or worried.

'Honestly, my dear, you can tell me anything. This is a safe place.'

Lauren nodded, grateful for the chance to try to gather her thoughts without having to worry about worrying Simon or the children or her parents. Hopefully there were hundreds of people who had her problem, or she hoped at least that Miriam had helped someone in a similar predicament before.

'I do have a note from Dr Haines that confirms you are

in fine physical shape, that you have no head trauma but you have suffered disorientation and memory loss. Bear with me, but if you could tell me in your own words when it began and in what circumstances, please.'

Lauren sighed. Miriam had a soothing manner. It was easy to relate what had happened, to tell her that half of her was missing

'Do you have any sense of what or where the other half is?' Miriam asked.

Lauren placed her hands in front of her mouth and rubbed her nose. She no longer felt soothed.

'In another place. It feels dark and I don't want to think about it. I can't process it but I can't shake it off.'

'Is it getting darker or bigger as the days pass?'

Lauren shivered.

'Yes,' she whispered. 'I think someone needs me.'

Miriam had not lied to her patient. She was not shocked but she was perplexed. Lauren was exhibiting all the symptoms of someone who had experienced a deeply disturbing incident – a rape or assault or bereavement or traumatic external event such as a bomb blast or a shooting – and was refusing to recall it, knowing the pain that would follow. But there was no evidence of such an event and in any case most of the detail was peculiar. Lauren might well want her parents to live somewhere else if she had been attacked in the family home, but again, there was no evidence to support this.

She knew she was heading towards encouraging Lauren to access the other place. It had to be confronted if she was to recover but Miriam was reluctant to let a patient become that vulnerable with so little information. On the plus side, the case would be one to present at her annual conference. Perhaps she would submit a paper.

On Lauren's next visit, Miriam asked her to lie on the couch and Lauren told her how, that morning, while looking through a photo album with Toby and Rosie, there had been a picture of Lauren aged about nine, the same age as Rosie, looking a lot like Rosie, building a snowman with Ben and Debbie.

It made her think of a time when she had regularly run across a spoon-shaped road to play with Debbie, but Simon had already mentioned how her family had lived next door to the semi-detached house that his parents still lived in.

'I can't think why I would remember such an unimportant thing so differently. I mean, what's the point of that? Why would my brain do that?'

Miriam had no idea.

She stood at the door as Lauren climbed into her car. There was something in the way she found her keys and opened the car door that unsettled Miriam. It was like watching someone who had never before seen a car, let alone drive one, trying to seem comfortable with owning one. She made a note to ask Lauren about her driving test but otherwise her notebook was full of exclamation marks, question marks and cross-references that would be of little use to the patient but made Miriam feel a bit better about handling a case that she suspected could become too tricky for her.

The phone rang. It was Bob.

'Hello, darling,' he said. 'Just checking about next Saturday and whether you are bringing the kids. I don't think you should; apart from anything, they'll be bored and fidgety, don't you think?'

Saturday. She paused, waiting for her brain to play catch-up. Saturday. Nothing stirred.

'Saturday, Dad?'

'Oh, my, I did mention it, didn't I? The service for Peter Stanning. It would be his fiftieth birthday so there is a memorial sort of service in the church for him.'

For the first time since waking up on the sun lounger, Lauren felt no sense of disconnection. Peter Stanning was still missing. It was about the only thing that felt solid, non-contradictory, ordinary. She scowled at her selfishness, that she was, in effect, celebrating that a perfectly pleasant and harmless man had probably died a lonely death.

'Of course, of course, but I don't think you did mention it. Simon's mum is still in hospital and I can't ask his dad so maybe Debbie can watch the children. Or Simon might not want to go. What time is the service?'

Bob went into the detail while Lauren recalled the way the village had been gripped, how she had turned the mystery into an art project. There had been other church services but none for a few years now. She was sure they were well attended because people liked to take a peep at the reclusive Mrs Stanning, forever rumoured to be engaged but who never did remarry, who was from titled stock, some said, although no one really knew for sure. The cold facts of it were that she never shopped in the local store or drank in the local pub nor appeared at the local hairdresser's. The warmer facts were that if anyone in the village was ever ill, she would send over her homemade jam or bake a cake for them. She did not take them in person, but still, she made an effort to be kind.

And she had not sold the house, that too was in her favour. It made her appear sentimental. Some people would say she was still hopeful Peter would turn up one day and she wanted to be there when he did. Others would speculate that the large house with its land and stables for her horses was too lovely to dispense with. One or two others would suggest she had buried her husband on the land and needed to stay put to prevent a property developer from one day digging up his corpse. But, as Bob would argue, the police would have searched for signs of disturbed soil or new flagstones at the time. Mrs Stanning was never a suspect, not really. She did not need the money.

Simon was disconcerted by Lauren's enthusiasm for the service.

'Do you want me to go?' he said. 'I mean, it might be easier if I stay with the kids.'

She hardly heard him. The more she thought about Peter the happier she felt. This was perhaps the start of belonging and the end of unsettling isolation.

The church was three quarters full and bursting with flowers. There had been a wedding earlier in the day and the bride had insisted the memorial attendees share in her joy, given that the event was not supposed to be sad but a celebration of a man's life.

George stood to speak and Lauren nodded enthusiastically. She knew George at once. She did not wonder at the length of his hair or even which son he might be. She knew him. She recognised him instantly. It was a remarkable feeling and, elated, she felt she might break into song earlier than the service wanted her to.

The late-afternoon sun illuminated the simple stained-glass windows, making the church feel almost cosy and not at all its cold formal normal self. Lauren looked over her shoulder and too late realised she was looking for herself. This was not something she had ever done before or heard of anyone else doing but it was the knee-jerk response to the almost suffocating sense of déjà vu she was experiencing. Yes, she knew this church, but she had the overwhelming sensation that she had cried and loved and loved again and disappeared there. She looked down at the heavy grey flagstones and breathed in slowly and deeply and knew she did not want to lift her head, to see the stained light.

There was shuffling and a low murmur as Mrs Stanning stood to address them all. She had never done so before.

She was impeccably dressed in a cream suit and pale pink silk shirt. Her jewellery glinted as she cleared her throat.

'I just want to thank you all for keeping Peter, my husband and George and Harry's father, in your thoughts. We miss him every day, and today, his fiftieth birthday, we would have planned a party, done nice things together, maybe,' she smiled, 'had an extra party, and we can't do that. Many of you will have lost loved ones, I know, but while we know we have to accept Peter has gone forever, part of us will always hope for a miracle. Knowing you care and perhaps wish for a miracle too, helps such a great deal.'

There was an appreciative gentle hum and then a group of choir boys sang 'Ecce Panis Angelorum' which the order of service informed her meant 'Behold the Bread of Angels' and had been a piece Peter Stanning had once heard in a church in southern Italy and rather liked. It moved her deeply and as it drew to a close the sunlight pierced its way across the nave and spread into a fan of narrow sunbeams. Lauren gasped. The pews around her began to spin and the music became a shriek of pain. She clutched at her seat and closed her eyes determined not to faint and spoil the service. Slowly the sounds returned to normal and she risked opening her eyes. The sun was behind clouds and the church was almost monochrome as a result. She breathed a sigh of relief and wondered if she had eaten too little at lunch or if the weight of a sluggish memory was starting to make her weak.

As the vicar led them in prayer, Vera turned to smile at her daughter and Lauren noticed, for the first time, a tiny mole on her left cheek. The smell of the church with its excess of flowers prompted images of her mother in a hat, trying not to cry, of her father in a shiny silver tie, a white rose in his lapel. Her heart opened with happy memories, of Simon placing the ring on her finger, of the very same vicar beaming as if he had engineered their love. Lauren smiled. It had been such a strangely beautiful day, she was too young to be walking down the aisle but by the time she did so everyone connected to her and Simon was sure it was the right thing to do and both sets of parents had been true to their word, helping with childcare so that she could attend college part-time and then go to work.

For the first time since falling asleep in the sun she felt at peace and she wished Simon had accompanied her after all so she could link his arm and lean on his shoulder and tell him everything was all right, that the déjà vu was not sinister but a mark of the depth of their love.

Bob squeezed her hand as the last hymn was sung and the

sun reappeared to light up the church and Mrs Stanning's jewellery. At that moment Lauren's heart unfurled. She frowned in astonishment. This was not déjà vu at all, it was an almost physical sensation, akin to discovering she really did have two hearts and double the amount of love she thought possible. It was similar to how she had felt when Toby was born, how instantly she felt herself capable of a double dose of love for two children where she had been concerned she would find her love for her daughter diluted by the new arrival.

This, though, was much stronger. Her heart was so swollen that it needed to open a second set of double doors and through them she did not so much see as feel another wedding. The same church, her parents the same or almost the same, and a curiously familiar soreness in her knee, a sense of being older, more mature, the same vicar, and there, turning his head to peek at her, another groom, less handsome but intelligent and intense.

And then George tapped her arm. She had been ignoring his presence by her side for several seconds.

'You look pale,' he said. She knew then she had to speak to him, alone. First, she would have to work out why.

'I'm fine, thank you. Really lovely service.'

George moved on. After all, he barely knew her.

Miriam had drawn the curtains against the sun. It was a cloudless late-August day, Toby and Rosie were with Lauren's parents and Lauren was fearful that talking about her memories was not quite the unburdening she had hoped for.

'That is very common,' Miriam said. 'As we make progress, the pain increases and it feels as if we are making it worse, but it is a journey and it often hurts to get there and find a place where you can be content again.'

Lauren was, briefly, irritated by Miriam's serenity and wondered what it would take to make her break down or throw her out.

'Well, I had a dreadful time in church. No, actually, it was great for a while, I had no problems at all. I felt normal and in tune with everything and then it all went weird, much weirder than it has before.'

'That's good news, Lauren, we have to be patient, and you must tell me every detail.'

Lauren was not sure this was possible.

'I don't think the words exist to explain what happened. I've never read about it or felt anything like it. And, if you want me to be honest with you in all this, then I have to tell you that I'm not even sure this is an emotional thing that is happening to me. It feels external, not internal.'

Miriam nodded, paused, and suggested that Lauren sit in the armchair, that they chat more informally.

'I'll make us some tea.'

'Thanks,' Lauren said, and as she waited and waited, because it seemed there was no quick way to have a cup of tea, she scoured the room hungrily. It was so impeccably furnished. Antique chairs, intriguing tiny sculptures, elegantly framed paintings. It smelled of expensive furniture polish and there was a crack in the deep red velvet curtains which allowed through a gentle sunbeam that hit a small polished mahogany table.

Miriam arrived back to find Lauren peering at the sunbeam close up and sliding her fingers through it.

Looking at her, Miriam felt as if she were holding a newborn chick she could kill if she held it too tightly or too loosely.

'I once had a patient who killed herself,' she said. 'I was much less experienced back then and did not grasp that the obvious problem is not always the one that matters.'

'What went wrong?' Lauren asked.

'I encouraged her to open up about abuse she had suffered as a child but she had been so heavily schooled by her abuser that she was the one who was disgusting and to blame that she found the telling of it too much to bear. I gave up work after that until my husband, my very wise, late husband, said that I should carry on in order to make her death mean something, that I should learn from my mistakes and use what had happened to be a better therapist. I tell you this because I want you to know I do not ever think I know it all or that I can anticipate an outcome. I am here only to offer an objective, sympathetic ear, to guide you to finding out why you feel as you do. If it gets messy or complicated or bizarre I don't want you to stop trying because you think I will judge you or not believe you. All that matters to me is that you participate more happily in life when you leave me than when you arrived.'

Lauren fiddled with her wedding ring.

'I don't know what is happening to me. I don't know what are important clues and what are dreams or fears. I could spend half an hour telling you something that will not help at all.'

'OK, that's a fair point. Let me ask a few questions instead. Since you woke up in the garden what has been the most frightening thing to have happened, the most frightened you have felt?'

'Oh,' Lauren said. 'I'm not sure I've felt frightened at all really. Maybe in the church when I thought I might faint and everything was spinning.'

'Do you know why you felt poorly?'

'The sun came out,' she blurted.

'The sun?' Miriam asked.

'Yes. The church was full of sunbeams.'

TIM

He took the baby and would not let go of her even though Vera was desperate to hold her. It was not that he was ignorant of the grief of others, but he knew if he handed her over then he would begin to sob and he did not want to do that here in the Cheshire church where he and Lauren had been married.

His half-sister had insisted she be allowed to address the congregation and she stood up in an expensive black coatdress that her mother had bought specially.

'I wasn't very nice to Lauren when I met her because I was jealous. I thought she would take Tim away from me. But Lauren was such a lovely person that she put up with me and was kind and then asked me to be her one and only bridesmaid. She was...'

Lottie made the mistake, at this moment, of glancing at the coffin and realising for the first time that Lauren's body was actually inside it. A dead body. Lauren's dead body. Maybe it was a funny colour, maybe her eyes were wide open, maybe a cockroach was crawling across her face. She gasped for air, unable to speak any more and her mother rushed to be by her side.

'Lottie wanted to say how much she and all Tim's family loved Lauren, how blessed we all feel to have had her in our lives,' she said and then guided her daughter, not back to her seat, but out of the church. She closed the heavy door behind her but the congregation inside could hear the muffled howls of Lottie's despair. She had only just comprehended the finality of it all and all she could do was scream.

The vicar felt he was losing control of the service. Not that this occasion could in any way be a good one. He had seen her parents pray in thanks that she had survived her accident in Cornwall; he had conducted her wedding ceremony; and now there was a motherless two-week-old baby in the front row and a teenager outside who had broken down. He looked at the card in front of him and saw that an Estelle McGinty was due to read a poem.

'Estelle will now read "But Not Forgotten" by Dorothy Parker,' he said which only made his sense of unravelling worse. There were plenty of religious poems they could have chosen, he thought. And here was a young woman, the same age as Lauren, with a crystal-clear voice about to reduce anyone left still composed to snivelling wrecks.

Estelle, so touched by Lauren's embrace at the wedding, had begged Tim to be allowed to speak. She had practised the poem over so many hours that the church could have burst into flames and she would not have lost her place or her intonation.

'*You still will see me, small and white,*' Estelle recited.
'*And smiling, in the secret night.*
'*And feel my arms about you when*
the day comes fluttering back again.'

Vera unleashed a wail of pain and buried her head in Bob's chest. The organist played an errant note before even the first hymn had been announced and Debbie fled the church, her brother Simon wondering if he was supposed to go with her given she had persuaded him she needed him there in the first place. Only Alfie, frail but sitting bolt upright, did not flinch, and the vicar noted that he had a peaceful, faraway look in his eyes, an expression he would often see on the face of his more elderly parishioners when they contemplated their mortality and the existence of Heaven.

Tim had written what he would have said if capable of speaking and had asked a humbled Gregory to deliver his words for him. Tim stood, still holding his newborn daughter, in front of the snivelling crowd.

'My friend Gregory will speak now,' he said. He was clearly hoping to add one more sentence but his legs were wobbling so he sat down.

'Tim has written a letter to Lauren which it is my privilege to read to you all,' Gregory said.

There was the sound of rustling as the congregation prepared for the worst. Women looked in their handbags for extra tissues, men patted their breast pockets. Tim stroked the velvet cheek of his sleeping child. Lydia sat up straight, feeling like a drama teacher who had coached a pupil through a difficult part of a play just as the live performance beckoned.

George Stanning, at the back of the church, lowered his head. He had not had the chance to tell Lauren his news nor thank her for her part in it.

'My darling beautiful Lauren,' Gregory said. Lydia had told him he had to find a balance. He knew he would remain composed if he read Tim's words in a monotone, as if listing the ingredients on the back of a jar of mustard, but Lydia, the writer, had insisted he find a way to add more light and shade to avoid insulting Tim and Lauren's parents. He took a deep breath. He would try, but the second he felt his voice crack, he would return to autopilot.

'I saw your art before I saw you and I expected you to be a little arrogant given you were so talented. But you were modest and sweet, a listener, unaware of how clever you were and unaware of how attractive you were. Even so, I found it tough to ask you out and you always maintained I never really did. I remember thinking, if this goes badly, I'll pretend it was a business meeting.'

Gregory paused and those who knew Tim well laughed gently.

'We fell in love. We were married in this church and I gasped when I saw you walking down this aisle with Bob. You were even more beautiful when you fell pregnant with Amber and I want to promise you that our daughter will be loved as you were loved by Bob and Vera. I miss you. I love you.'

There was, briefly, the silence of breath being held as Gregory slowly sat down next to Lydia who only just stopped herself giving him the thumbs-up.

The rest of the service passed in a haze for most. The hotel that had hosted Lauren and Tim's wedding breakfast served food and drink and at last Vera could hold Amber. Tim spoke to everyone there, thanking them for their condolences, before leaving with his immediate family and Vera and Bob and Suki for the interment. Amber came too. It became Tim's style of parenting. Wherever he went, his daughter came too. He worked from home as much as possible, and when unable to, his mother or a babysitter would bring her along to lunch.

Vera and Bob travelled down every Tuesday, stayed in the new spare room, and left every Thursday. George valued Bob at work but offered him a part-time role which he grasped with gratitude. George would have liked to discuss his father's disappearance with Bob, but decided to bide his time. He had waited so long already, he thought, that waiting a little longer did not really matter.

LAUREN

Lauren could not sleep for worrying at her lack of empathy with Miriam. The poor woman had counselled someone who had killed themselves and she had lost her husband. Have I become so self-absorbed and selfish? she thought.

'Are you awake?' Simon said.

'Yes. Why are you awake?'

'I was thinking about your staff meeting next week. You should tell them you had a virus and you're fine but it left you a bit drained, that way if you forget something they won't be mad.'

She wanted to say that was funny because she had forgotten all about the staff meeting but decided it would be inappropriate.

'Thank you, that's a good idea. I'm awake because this whole thing has stopped me being a good person. Your mum, for example, I haven't been to see her in hospital. Can we all go tomorrow?'

'I told her you had a virus and wouldn't be allowed in. But yes, she'd love that. The kids will last five minutes then get bored but we can take it in turns to take them to the vending machine or something.'

The next day, Karen, Simon's mum, was sat in an armchair by the side of her bed, a loose black cardigan over her long cream nightdress. As the children ran to hug her – 'Gently now,' shouted Simon – Lauren froze.

She remembered vividly seeing Karen sat in a chair, frail and thin and deathly many years before. She realised with horror that she must have seen her as she was now.

'Oh, Lauren,' Karen said, 'surely I don't look that ill.'

Lauren dashed forward to embrace her mother-in-law.

'Of course not,' she said, 'I was just reminded of a childhood memory that was confusing me.'

Lauren made a concerted effort to be cheerful and chatty but her heart was not in it.

On the way home, Simon wondered if they should go away for the night together to mark the end of summer and she knew he was grasping at ways to have his wife back to normal.

'Am I very different?' she asked as the children counted red cars versus blue cars.

'No,' he said lightly, 'but you are worrying about things, and that does upset me, of course it does.'

He dropped her at the bottom of Miriam's road. It was not unusual, she now recalled, for her to walk the last few miles of any car ride home, so she did not even have to lie about the need to visit Miriam. She was half an hour early for their next appointment but decided a stroll along the lanes nearby might be therapeutic. There was something liberating about the simple act of going for a walk; the ease with which her limbs worked. Each step was a delight, like walking on pavements padded with foam.

Miriam was busy at her desk plotting ways to decipher Lauren's problems. She made a list of possible avenues of enquiry and had, in bold letters, the word 'SUNBEAMS'. She would have to tread carefully there. She traced back over her notes and realised she had failed to pursue how content Lauren had initially felt in the church, how she said she had belonged there. Sometimes the more productive course is the less obvious one, she thought.

Lauren arrived promptly and Miriam poured her a glass of iced water and slowly it emerged that the Stannings had needed no introduction. She had remembered them instantly.

'And can you think back to when you had met George before?'

'I took Rosie in when she was born so Dad could show off his new granddaughter and George was still getting to grips with the company. Poor bloke, he had to grow up fast. I took Toby in as a baby too but I don't think I saw him that day.'

Both women knew this was an incomplete answer. Lauren would not have felt an urge to speak to George if she had only met him once, nine years earlier.

'And I had used the disappearance of his father in an art project at college so I probably felt closer to him than I was,' she added, hoping this would satisfy Miriam. It didn't.

'I can't get past a block,' she sighed. 'It's like there is a window but there are big rolling black clouds blocking the view, warning me off.'

Lauren stared at the patterns in the tasteful flock wallpaper. These sessions were becoming more a case of cat and mouse than a means of regaining her equanimity. She was deliberately not telling Miriam all that she had felt, not because she wanted to lie or deceive her but because the self-defence mechanism was too strong.

'I'm a bit scared, Miriam,' she said, 'that to get through the clouds will be so painful or shocking or hurtful that I might die or something. I'm sure you're right that it is usually best to confront such things but I'm not convinced. I might have to just accept the weird way I live now. I'm sorry, but I don't think this is working.'

Miriam admired her honesty. Most clients who backed off did so via letter. The least she could do was be honest in return.

'I understand, really I do, and I have no point of reference for your symptoms. I can't reassure you that I have been through the same scenario with someone else and it all worked out for the best. We'll take a break. I'll keep doing research and maybe we can meet again. When you are ready.'

They shook hands and Miriam noticed, as Lauren left, that she walked away with a slight limp that she corrected within a few seconds. In that moment, Miriam wondered if it really was counselling Lauren needed or a private detective, but the thought passed and she went back to her books to prepare for the visit of an eighteen-year-old boy who had developed a shyness so chronic he could not start the university course his parents were so proud he had qualified for. She looked at the clock. He might not turn up. Sometimes she felt quite worthless.

TIM

It turned out just as Bella had predicted. There was a long queue of women hoping to be appointed Tim's nanny and housekeeper. He had used agency staff on an hour-by-hour basis at first but soon it became clear that everyone, and most of all his daughter, would benefit if just one person could be relied upon.

'They'll all think they'll end up marrying him,' Bella said from behind her sleek reception desk in the ad agency to anyone who would listen, as if such romantic-fiction-style thoughts were beneath her.

To Bella's astonishment, Tim handed her a sheaf of CVs one morning.

'Bella,' he said, 'do me the biggest favour and look through these and tell me which ones catch your eye for good and bad reasons.'

She was almost paralysed by the unexpected responsibility and many a visitor to Pilot that day had to cough three times to be noticed by her. She photocopied every application and used highlighter pens to draw Tim's attention to the salient points and then divided the CVs into three piles of: Yes, Maybe and No.

That evening Tim looked through Bella's rejections first to check she was on a similar wavelength and not prioritising hair colour or likely regional accents and, having agreed with her objections, turned his attention to the best of Bella's bunch.

There were just two he decided it was worth meeting; just two he could bear to meet.

Emily and Moirin.

Emily arrived by train from Devon and was young and smiley with a buttery complexion and a round, open, innocent face. She had a folder full of certificates that confirmed her competence in skills ranging from hygiene in the kitchen to kiddies' arts and crafts, the latter being something Bella had highlighted; knowing that Tim would prefer a nanny who could bring out the artistic side of artistic Lauren's child.

He liked her instantly, the way she kept looking almost greedily at Amber, the way she nodded eagerly, happily. He wondered if his sadness would poison her.

'I ought to stress what might be seen as negatives to the job,' he said. 'There's still a lot of grief and pain in this house. You'll have to put up with all sorts of relatives grabbing hold of Amber, leaving you to sort the washing and the boring stuff. On a practical level, the house really isn't big enough and I have yet to tell my in-laws that if I hire a nanny they'll have nowhere to sleep. Which might make you feel awkward, I don't know.'

Emily nodded and asked to see the nursery.

'I'll move in here when your in-laws stay,' she said. 'If you're happy to get a camp bed for me. All it takes is changing some bed linen and I can do that while they hold the baby.'

He laughed.

'Well, I'm seeing one more applicant tomorrow,' he said, 'so I'll call you in a few days.'

Moirin arrived by train from north London, her long black hair in a plait, her white skin blistered by fading acne.

'I won't lie to you, Mr Lewis,' she said, 'but I'm desperate to leave home where I've been looking after five brothers and sisters, for all my life, it seems like, and I need the peace and quiet of one beautiful baby, a living wage and a beautiful home like yours is.'

Her Irish brogue was faint but mesmeric. Moirin was streetwise, practical and probably liked a nip of whiskey, he thought. He looked at her resumé. Bella had highlighted the fact that her mother had died eleven years earlier.

'Won't you be needed still at home?' he asked. 'I'm after someone to live in and do just about everything.'

'You'll be giving me a day off, though, won't you?'

He had not thought about this.

'Oh, yes, of course, we can work that out to suit both parties.'

'To answer your question, of course they'll be needing me at home but they're not having me. They can fend for themselves these days, they just take advantage of my accommodating nature.'

He repeated what he had told Emily about Bob and Vera staying over and the lack of space.

'You haven't seen my house, Mr Lewis. This is a palace. We'll all fit in just fine, trust me.'

When she had gone he bit his lip. He had thought Emily was perfect but now he could see how Moirin's experience should not be ignored.

He took Bella out for a coffee and explained what had happened.

'Great girls, both of them, but I'm at a loss how to decide,' he said.

Bella stirred her drink, her hands shaking at the magnitude of the task.

'Let's say you have to leave for a business meeting and you'll be back late tonight and you have to phone one of them right now to help out. Who do you ring first? Which one does your gut trust?'

'Good question,' he said. 'But Moirin lives closer so that's not fair.'

'Then I know who you should hire,' Bella said, her eyes sparkling.

'You do?'

'Of course. You wouldn't have qualified your answer if you thought Moirin was the one.'

'Ah,' he said. 'Bella, what are you doing spending all day on reception? You are a genius.'

When he introduced Emily to Bob and Vera he felt far more nervous than when Lauren had introduced him to them. He saw how Vera cradled Amber that bit more tightly, how Bob scrutinised Emily's face for signs of stupidity or callousness. But then Emily surprised all of them.

'I hope you don't mind but my mum is in the car downstairs and wants to meet you all, you know, seeing as how I'll be living here.'

Suddenly it was Bob and Vera who felt under the microscope; it was Tim who hoped to be deemed of solid enough character for Emily's mother to sanction the deal.

Emily's mother Brenda was just as buttery-skinned as her daughter but shorter and rounder and reminded Vera of the covers of the Beatrix Potter books that were still on Lauren's bookshelf in their home.

'Emily was so pleased to get the job,' Brenda said, as if she were less sure, less pleased, and Vera instantly knew why. She would not have wanted Lauren, at nineteen, to be surrounded by the bereaved day in and day out.

Vera did not know what to say so made the ultimate gesture and handed Amber to Brenda, who cooed appropriately and then handed her over to Emily, who beamed but instantly gave her back to Vera and said she would make them all tea.

Bob watched this all unfold with a sense of déjà vu which he could not explain so shrugged it off in order to engage properly with the conversation which, gradually, flowed more easily as Tim realised Brenda had every right to ask about bathrooms and privacy.

When Amber needed a nappy change, Emily whisked her off and Vera nodded appreciatively.

'That's a lovely daughter you have there,' Vera said, and neither she nor Bob nor Tim felt the weight of the words; and neither she nor Bob nor Tim felt tearful.

BOB

It was as decent a life as Bob could have hoped for. Rachel occasionally became withdrawn but she never actually raised the subject of his infidelity. A whole year passed without a letter from Andrea, who never asked Bob for more money. He had given her as generous a lump sum as he could muster and she had no intention of bleeding him dry.

When Jevin was three and a half a letter did come for him inside the usual envelope addressed to Mr and Mrs Pailing. A few words on a postcard told them she was happy in Paris and grateful that Jevin had the home he deserved.

They read the card together. It was as much as Rachel could have hoped for although a dark part of her now and again half hoped Andrea would be found dead in the Seine, just to avoid the potential for a scene one day. Rachel adored their son more than she had ever dreamed she could and when she gazed at him she saw only glimpses of Bob and nothing much of Andrea at all. The brusqueness of the note was a sign of a young woman who had moved on. Of a woman unlikely to turn back and turn their lives upside down.

VERA

The day came when Hope was older than her big sister had been. Vera had expected the world to change as a consequence, and kept thinking of the phrase 'nature abhors a vacuum'.

Maybe nature abhors little sisters being older than their big sisters, she thought. It also made her think of whether Lauren was aware of her family. What was Heaven, after all? It could be a place that had a window onto the world through which the dead could keep an eye on them, but that sounded cruel, like being in a prison, so she hoped it was nothing of the sort.

For all her grief and the certainty she had that but for Hope she would have killed herself, Vera had no real sense of Lauren by her side. She knew that the breeze that seemed to smell of her or the rustling branches that sounded like her were figments of her own imagination, that it felt plausible only because she needed it to feel plausible. If Lauren still existed, it was in a place she was incapable of understanding.

When Hope was older than Lauren by six days and Vera was still mulling over what impact that would have on Hope and on her own bereavement something terrible did happen. Hope's classmate did not turn up for school, and the teacher told them it was because her brother had been knocked off his motorbike and killed. The teacher had paused, Hope said, as if hiding something and that was when the whispering began. Daisy's brother had been decapitated.

As she told her mother the news, Hope, who sounded as if she were relating the gory details of a B movie, burst into tears the way only thirteen-year-olds can and Vera, full of foreboding, held her tight.

Vera knew the call would come, and sure enough two weeks after the funeral, the school nurse phoned her up. Would Vera meet with Mrs Talbot?

'I don't know Mrs Talbot,' Vera said.

'Yes, yes, but you are the only person I know among the parents, Mrs Pailing, who has lost a child in a road accident. I think she could really do with some help.'

Vera wanted to shout that there had been no one to help her other than Bob and then pinched her own arm in punishment.

'Of course,' she said. 'Would you be kind enough to arrange how and when?'

She told Bob about the phone call later that evening after he had spent fifteen minutes stroking Hope's hair and telling her to think of ways to be kind to Daisy rather than dwelling on the macabre detail that seemed to gain new levels of gruesomeness with each passing school day.

'That's very nice of you,' he said, 'but you know it might be tough, really tough.'

'I know,' she said, 'but I don't believe I have any choice.'

Mrs Talbot was divorced. Mrs Talbot had been told, by her

ex-husband, that it was her fault their son had died. Why had she let him ride his bike when it had been raining?

Vera had suffered guilt, oh, she knew that feeling all too well. Why had she let Lauren go away without her? Had she been more protective, Lauren would still be here. But Bob had never blamed her. No one had blamed Vera but Vera, and that was bad enough. She tried to imagine how she would have felt if Bob had accused her of neglect.

For the first time, Vera properly accepted that although she had believed her grief to be the deepest of all grief, it could have been worse.

Mrs Talbot looked awful. Her eyes were red-rimmed and puffy and, for reasons Vera could not fathom, her hair was soaking wet on a sunny day. The kitchen was untidy and smelled of old bacon fat. Where were her friends, her relatives? Someone should have been keeping things tidy, keeping things ticking over, keeping an eye on this vulnerable woman.

Vera had assumed she would be asked about how she coped, how long it took her to smile again, how often she thought about her dead daughter. Instead, she saw that she needed to assume the role of a social worker. This woman did not need to be told that grief ebbs and flows and time heals the worst of it. This woman needed practical help.

'Who will be here this evening?' she asked. 'Just you and Daisy or is there someone else popping by?'

Mrs Talbot, too distressed and disorientated to tell Vera to call her Connie, looked alarmed.

'I'm not expecting anyone else,' she said. 'I want David to come home, that's all I want.'

'Were you expecting me?' Vera asked.

'Oh, yes, the school nurse said you knew. She said you wouldn't expect a cup of tea and some bloody chocolate digestives and all the gory details.'

Vera stroked her hand.

'How would you feel about me coming back later with the car and taking you and Daisy home with me and letting someone spring clean the house, but not touch David's room at all, so you can get some sleep and Daisy can be with a friend.'

Mrs Talbot sat in silence, staring at the calendar on the wall showing the month before. Time had stopped when David had stopped.

'I loved David more,' she said. 'I loved him too much and look at us now. Who bought David his motorbike? It wasn't me. I blame Colin but say nothing and he blames me and tells everyone it's my fault.'

She turned to Vera. 'It is my fault, isn't it?'

Vera did not know this woman and saw a grief that was different to hers but a desperation that she recalled all too well.

'It will take time, but one day you will understand that it is not your fault, and one day you will be able to smile again, enjoy a walk, a film, the grades Daisy gets at school. But it takes time, and I'd like to help now, while it's raw and terrible.'

Mrs Talbot looked directly at Vera.

'I'm so tired,' she said. 'Some help would be good.'

Bob gawped.

'Here? Stay with us here?' he said.

'Why ever not?' Vera said breezily. 'I had you and then we had Hope. She not only has no husband but the one she *did* have is blaming her for the accident.'

267

Bob wanted to say that his home was his refuge after a long day at work, and he could do without tiptoeing around a wailing mother and her daughter, but as he considered an acceptable way to phrase it, Hope said how much she liked Daisy and wanted to help her.

'Right, it seems to be decided, then,' he said, 'but, please, allow me some say in when it's time for them to leave.'

Vera kissed him on the cheek. 'Of course, my love,' she said and winked at her daughter.

Hope enjoyed the planning, she enjoyed her mother asking her opinion. Should Daisy share her mother's room or share with Hope? Was Daisy a fussy eater? Was Daisy struggling to concentrate at school?

Vera collected them the next evening. Daisy looked like a young girl being evacuated to a safe haven in wartime, while Mrs Talbot looked like she had just seen a bomb destroy an entire city. They stood awkwardly beside their suitcases, Daisy still in her deep burgundy school uniform. Vera felt a wave of energetic empathy. She would make them better; she would heal their wounds and send them back home ready to face the next stage of their lives.

Mrs Talbot was put in the formal guest room with its en suite bathroom, and Vera suggested she have a long soak in the bath and maybe some cocoa or warm milk and then sleep as long as she could, knowing Vera and Hope would make sure Daisy got to school on time.

'Thank you,' she said, 'only I have to wake up again, don't I?'

'It will get better, really. I was like you, I understand completely, but I also know that I kept going for Hope and you will keep going for Daisy.'

'They all say that,' Mrs Talbot hissed.

'But they are guessing,' Vera said. 'I know.'

The next day she found a company that would, for a rather steep fee, rigorously clean and tidy Mrs Talbot's house. Vera let the cleaners in and pointed out David's bedroom and told them not to even open the door.

By supper time Mrs Talbot had dressed and even combed her hair, which was dry. Daisy had told Vera that her mum liked salmon so they ate salmon with buttered new potatoes and peas and string beans. Vera made a big bread and butter pudding in case Bob was still hungry.

They talked about school and homework and Bob wondered if they had heard about John Smith, of the Labour Party, and how his survival from a heart attack would gain him short-term sympathy but probably mean he would have to stand down to avoid claims he was too weak to be the party's leader.

Hope glared at him.

'Who cares, Dad?' she said.

'Sorry, I'm sure,' said Bob while trying to smile conspiratorially at Mrs Talbot.

'David was a Communist,' she said flatly.

'Right,' Bob said. 'I think all young men are Communists, probably, at some point.'

'Well, he'll always be one now,' she said.

'Hmm,' Vera said. 'Actually, we know nothing about David and we'd love to hear what he was like, if you can bear it.'

A tear rolled down Mrs Talbot's cheek. Daisy swallowed a piece of salmon.

'I really loved my big brother,' she said. 'He made me listen to some weird music but some of it was great and he was funny and...' she trailed off. She had learned that she could say the wrong thing so easily.

'He sounds lovely,' Vera said, and Bob nodded along, mostly feeling perplexed at how adroitly his wife was handling what seemed to him to be the most awkward of situations.

In bed that night she clung to him and said: 'We're saving a family; that has to be worth a little bit of inconvenience.'

I'm wrapped round her little finger, Bob thought, and I live in a world of loss.

LAUREN

She had once read a novel in which the protagonist found happiness by being with the two women he loved. He did not divorce his wife because he loved his wife. He did not leave his lover because he loved her too. And as both women were so deeply loved neither grew suspicious that there could possibly be another love. It was a dreadful book but, now, it rang true.

She was happier for accepting that she had another life. She did not yet know what was in it. She had fragments, crystal clear flashes of faces and feelings, but also an innate sense that she would soon form the complete picture. She was happy for about three days. Happy that the wave of loss had not engulfed her. Happy she had survived the event she had been evading, happy that she had left Miriam before churning up her own insides even more. She had a weird condition, that's all and so what if she had other loves and other homes, she knew she loved Simon, loved her children. It would be fine.

But she knew it would not last, that she would have to close her eyes and let the memories form a narrative and after that... she had no idea. While the image of another man waiting to marry her inside the church was one she tried not to dwell on, Lauren was eager to think about the Stannings. She felt she could help them, and they could help her. She just didn't know how.

VERA

Vera heard the kerfuffle of Jack's bike. Was she imagining it or had it become noisier over the years? She opened the door to say good morning and as he gawped she unconsciously dabbed at the corner of her mouth in case there was toothpaste sticking to her lips.

'You look different today,' he blurted out.

'Guests,' she replied, and she tried not to smile as Jack's cheeks pinkened as they tended to no matter what she said.

Mrs Talbot was unloading the dishwasher.

'Oh no need,' Vera said.

Mrs Talbot smiled at her.

'There is every need,' she said. 'I feel less of a zombie today and that is thanks to you. And Daisy is so happy here, I think she feels safe. I hadn't thought about it until this morning but to lose your big brother who was the one who protected you must make a young girl feel so, you know, vulnerable.'

Vera tried very, very hard not to feel triumphant. She had been sure she could help this poor family and here was Mrs Talbot, her eyes free of the glaze of panicked grief, able to communicate. Still, it had been a week and she knew Bob wanted his home back.

'Do you fancy driving over with me to your house after lunch?' Vera asked. 'I want to see how well it's been spruced up before you move back in.'

She noted a slight narrowing of Mrs Talbot's eyes but then she cleared her throat.

'Thank you, yes, let's do that,' Mrs Talbot said.

Her hand shook as she unlocked the front door and Vera felt a spasm of guilt.

Mrs Talbot stood in the small hallway and looked at the stair carpet which had that perky freshly shampooed look to it. She summoned a small smile.

'Seems wrong to walk on it,' she said and Vera laughed.

'Probably feels lovely barefoot,' she said.

Vera offered to put the kettle on as Mrs Talbot took off her shoes and walked upstairs. Vera knew where she was going. She was gone a long time.

Vera took off her shoes and cautiously climbed up to the first floor. One door was slightly open so she knocked gently before entering.

Mrs Talbot was sat on her son's messy bed, one of his T-shirts pressed against her face. She looked up.

'You see this in films,' she told Vera. 'Mothers sitting on the bed, hoping the child's smell is still there. Did you do this?'

'Oh yes,' Vera said. 'I found it hard to leave the home we all shared but one day it felt the right thing to do.'

'He was thinking of moving out,' Mrs Talbot said. 'And I thought that would break my heart.' She snorted. 'I'd no idea, had I?'

'Come and see the kitchen,' Vera said gently and Mrs Talbot stood, her eyes glazed once more.

They sat and drank tea, Vera washed up the cups and then they left. Vera did not have the heart to suggest Mrs Talbot stay behind and once back home she cheered up a little and chopped onions and carrots and even hummed a Frank Sinatra tune. As Daisy and Hope burst through to door she smiled and asked what their new French teacher was like. It all felt so normal apart from the fact that they barely knew the woman.

The girls sat in their shared bedroom, revising as Madame Morel had told them there would be a test the next day, while Mrs Talbot stirred a melting stock cube.

'I doubt she's really French, the new teacher,' Vera said.

'It is peaceful here,' Mrs Talbot said. 'Like a haven.'

'I'm glad you feel at ease,' Vera said. 'What you are going through is, apart from everything else, exhausting.'

'And look at Daisy,' Mrs Talbot said. 'It's like you've performed a miracle.'

The next morning saw the house surrounded by mist and late autumn sunshine. It was beautiful.

'Let's go for a wander,' Vera suggested.

'Is all this yours?' Mrs Talbot asked as they meandered through damp grass and old roses.

Vera would have been embarrassed but she knew as well as anyone that if you lose a child, someone's wealth or good fortune is neither impressive nor intimidating.

'We haven't been here that long,' she said. 'But I have grown fond of the place.'

'It's a beautiful place to bring up your daughter,' Mrs Talbot said as a sluggish squirrel peered at them from behind an ancient tree stump.

Vera was about to say she supposed Hope would find it a dreadfully dull place by the time she was sixteen but thought twice about conjuring images of teenagers having fun, dressing up for parties, discovering cider, the opposite sex and riding motorbikes.

Bob did not allow himself to even imagine it would be just the three of them at supper but he was pleasantly surprised by Mrs Talbot's demeanour and how she beamed when Daisy said something amusing or when Hope playfully squeezed her daughter's arm.

'It's the anniversary of when we met tomorrow,' he told the table and then turning to Mrs Talbot said, 'I hope you don't mind if I steal my wife for lunch.'

'You have a nice time, you two,' Mrs Talbot said.

'We don't normally do midweek lunch and we don't normally celebrate the day we met,' Vera said as they sat in a quiet, expensive dining room of a newly refurbished pub, the hazy early November sunshine illuminating the polished unscarred wooden tables.

'I was feeling selfish, I wanted you all to myself and I wouldn't feel comfortable leaving Hope alone with Daisy and her mother,' he said. 'I know that sounds uncharitable or mistrustful but well, I just wouldn't.'

They ate profiteroles they did not really want but could not resist because they were covered in warm chocolate sauce, and then Bob said he would have to pop back to the office but could drop Vera home first.

'I'd like to come along,' she said. 'Say hello to George if he's in.'

George was in Manchester buying up yet another failing but potentially profitable firm so Vera pottered around in her husband's office, checking for dust, peering out of the window.

'OK,' Bob said, 'let's go home.'

They kissed and Vera, emotional having drunk two glasses of wine so early in the day, felt weepy at how lucky and unlucky her life with Bob had been.

'We didn't toast Lauren,' she said. 'And Lauren was why we got married quicker than we planned.'

He squeezed her hand. He knew better than to offer an explanation. They had forgotten to make any sort of toast. That was all.

The house was quiet and still and they wondered if Mrs Talbot might be in bed. Eventually they noticed a letter propped up on the mantelpiece of the large, slightly formal living room.

'*Thank you,*' it read. '*Daisy is so happy here. I'm sorry for all the trouble this will cause but I want to be with my son, Connie Talbot.*'

'Jeez,' Bob said. 'Does she expect us to keep Daisy here indefinitely?'

'I don't know,' Vera said. 'I'd have thought it would be easier for her to be at home with Daisy than alone, sitting in her son's bedroom all day.'

Bob ran his fingers through his hair.

'I suppose we let Daisy stay another few nights, then, or something,' he said doubtfully.

'I suppose,' Vera said. 'I know it's been odd but we've helped them and I'm not sure it is entirely healthy for a girl of Daisy's age to be holed up with only a grieving mother to keep her company. Her father sounds unreliable at best, damaging at worst.'

Bob grunted then patted the large sofa.

'Foot rub?' he said and she giggled as she took off her thin cotton socks but then as a fat blackbird swooped by, narrowly avoiding collision, she went to the picture window from which she could see at the very edge of the view a bright red scarf billowing in the breeze a quarter of a way up an old sycamore tree.

She turned the key in the pretty brass lock, opened the door and ran barefoot towards the scarf, not feeling the scratch of the twigs and dead leaves until she saw what she feared she would see. Mrs Talbot swinging from the branch of a tree, a stepladder on its side and an awful aura of peace.

LAUREN

She was not pregnant after all. She was not relieved, she was not sad. She was perplexed. She had no mysterious memories of other versions of Rosie and Toby, but as her breasts ached as if filling with love, if not milk, the black clouds rolled in, taunting her. She felt like someone with a fear of flying might feel when passing through security, a point of no return. She needed to be with someone who would not be hurt when she started to panic.

She knocked on Miriam's door and took a deep breath.

'I need to piece things together and I think I could do that here with you but I am really worried that you might diagnose me as deranged or schizophrenic. I'm not. I know that I'm not but I need to be able to trust you.'

Miriam, delighted to see the intriguing Lauren again, shuffled some papers on her desk to buy her some time, then told her she would be honest with her and not refer her to anyone else without her permission.

Lauren looked her in the eye. She really liked Miriam but then Miriam would be bad at her job if she was the sort that people took a dislike to.

'Let me tell you what has happened to bring me here,' she said, 'and if you feel you can't fall in with me on it then I'll leave.'

Miriam needed to know so she nodded.

Lauren sat in the armchair and calmly explained the way her heart had expanded like a rosebud rapidly unfurling to allow her to love more people than those in her current life.

'I wish I could express it better but I feel I have landed here from somewhere else,' she said. 'And that is why my memory lags behind. This is not the only life I have been living. And I think that I might be about to remember the bits I don't want to remember.'

Miriam felt her pulse quicken. She had listened to only one other patient in her career who had, effectively, been exciting, and that had been a mouse of a woman called Tina who had witnessed her aunt murder her baby and allowed that to stop her having children of her own. The aunt was arrested at the age of fifty-eight, thanks to Tina's evidence prompting a new investigation. Thanks to Miriam's teasing out of the dreadful details. Lauren was different, Lauren was in charge now. Lauren simply needed Miriam to listen, to prompt, to guide, to perhaps console, and because of the power shift Miriam was briefly at a loss to know how to start.

'How would you like to start?' she asked.

'Well, that I don't know,' Lauren said. 'I was hoping you'd find a way to help me piece it together.'

Miriam turned the page of her A4 notepad and stared at the blank space. At the top she wrote: *Lauren is born.*

'What is your first memory?' she asked. 'Are you in a cot or a pram or a playground?'

Lauren closed her eyes.

'I remember being sat on a sheepskin rug and drawing. I used to draw a lot. I remember being a bit lonely. I remember how pretty I thought my mother was and I missed her when she went to work in the dress shop.'

Lauren sat up half in a panic and half in exhilaration.

'Now that's interesting,' she said. 'I really do remember the shop but I also remember there not being a shop and I also remember it not being a boutique but it being a dentist's reception.'

Miriam felt her jaw slacken. She was out of her depth.

'Shall we try to pin this down, then?' she said. 'Did your mother work when you were little?'

Lauren knitted her fingers together. 'Yes, no and yes,' she said.

'But that's three memories,' Miriam said.

'Yes, I've missed my real mum for a long time,' Lauren said, and she felt herself floating like a kite, hoping the string would stay firm in the buffeting wind.

Miriam made some notes.

'You recall a mother who worked in a boutique, a mother who did not work and a mother who worked with a dentist?'

'That sounds daft,' Lauren said. 'My mother is Vera and has always been Vera but somewhere along the way she became a bit less pretty and I had to start again, loving the one who was less wonderful, and recently I've had to love the Vera who is a bit more practical and dotes on Ben and worked on Saturday mornings at the dentist's reception until my brother was born.'

Neither woman spoke for a few seconds and then Lauren frowned.

'I remember I saw other versions of my mum but I didn't know them. It used to upset Mum when I mentioned them so I stopped telling her even though I was letting her know that she was the prettiest and the nicest.'

Miriam gazed about her study and her eyes settled on a painting of a jug of water containing some fading bluebells placed on a small mahogany table. The artist was unknown but she was often mesmerised by the image. It was at least two hundred years old and yet could have been painted in that very study a week earlier. Sometimes the light was exactly the same.

'How is this making you feel?' she asked Lauren. 'Is it distressing?'

Lauren's eyes were shining almost feverishly.

'No,' she said louder than she meant to. 'It's liberating.'

'Shall we continue?' Miriam asked, and Lauren nodded, so Miriam composed her thoughts.

'I think I have to ask you *how* you saw other versions of your mother. Did you have dreams?'

'No, not dreams,' Lauren tilted her head to one side and felt herself propelled through a set of old-fashioned double doors where she could see herself sat in front of a sunbeam.

'I remember it now. There were threads, thick threads like sunbeams, and I could peer through them and see people I knew, people I didn't know, and I knew I couldn't mention these beams because when I had done it upset everyone and my friend Debbie called me names. It was my secret.'

'Do you see them still?'

'No, I lost them.'

'When you woke up in the garden a few months ago?'

'No, I had an accident when I was thirteen and…' Lauren's bottom lip began to tremble. 'Only I didn't have an accident. I'm sorry, I'm confused.'

'Did you hurt your leg in the accident?'

'Yes, yes, and I keep on being surprised I can wear any shoes that I like.' She smiled weakly. 'I feel a little less liberated right now. Sorry.'

Miriam allowed half a minute to elapse. Her patient had shifted from being elated to exhaustedly confused. Miriam wrote down '*How many lives has Lauren lived?*' and underlined it.

'We can stop now,' she said 'but my feeling is that we should try to keep things chronological and slow and not jump ahead to big events like your accident. Let's see how the accident fits in later. At home, when you are up to it, why don't you write down as much of your childhood as you can – you know, birthdays, holidays, the big memories – up until, say, aged twelve, and then we can go from there next time.'

As Lauren drove away she wondered if she had found an ally or if she was being patronised. She was relieved too, though, that they would take it slowly. Miriam was patient and logical and she needed that. She understood that she missed her mother, the adoring one, the prettiest one, the one she supposed would miss Lauren so much that the pain would be unbearable.

'And I miss someone else,' she said to herself softly, because why else did she have this gaping hole in her blossoming, huge heart.

The writing was hard, so Lauren sketched. She sketched a young slim and tall Vera, a Vera without a mole anywhere on her face, a Vera with a touch of designer flair to her outfits. By the time she returned to Miriam's serene house, she had a reasonably clear idea of the childhood that felt most real. It was a childhood full of the people she knew now but the detail was either marginally altered, as in the case of the disappointing Christmas decorations, or dramatically so, as in the lack of a close called The Willows. And there was a sort of buffer between the two, another childhood that mirrored the first but was indistinct. She tried to draw the Vera from that one but it was impossible to catch hold of the image for long enough.

'I had no idea you were so talented,' Miriam said as she looked at the sketches. 'Who are they?' she asked, pointing to the drawing of two impish little boys. 'They lived in my cul-de-sac,' Lauren said shyly for it was strange, was it not, to refer to a street that did not even exist and was, right now, full of sheep.

Miriam smiled encouragingly as she listened to Lauren's peculiar and fragmented childhood illustrated by mysterious sketches in which her mother's face sometimes had a mole on it and sometimes did not.

'. . . And then I moved into a house, I fell in love, I think, and I got a really good job.'

'In London?'

'Yes, in London. Charlotte Street.'

Miriam was breathless. The other life was flowing from Lauren's lips so matter-of-factly and causing her no distress at all. And it sounded genuine, real, normal. In fact, having got to know Lauren, Miriam thought this London life would have suited her much better than her provincial one.

'I know Charlotte Street,' Miriam said. 'It's between tube stations.'

'Yes, we were nearer to Goodge Street,' Lauren said so naturally that had Miriam been in court and sworn in she would have had to say Lauren was telling the truth.

'Life sounds good,' Miriam said, knowing it could not be good, not really, or else why was Lauren here as a patient.

'I can feel lots of happiness,' Lauren said. 'Here and in London.'

Miriam kept writing, kept waiting.

'And then Tim asked me out and I moved in and he asked me to marry him.'

Miriam stopped writing.

'Did you love Tim? Do you love Tim?'

'Well, I did marry him,' Lauren laughed. 'You're thinking I'm a bonkers bigamist but it's not like that. It's a whole other life, not a secret life lived at the same time.'

'No, I understand that at least,' Miriam said in her gentlest voice. She was increasingly sure that something painful was on the horizon, that Lauren did not know what was coming, that she, Miriam, would have to be alert and reassuring.

There was so much detail missing but Miriam resisted the temptation to slow Lauren down. There would be time for the detail later.

'Two hearts,' Lauren said shaking her head and smiling. 'Madness, but there you go.'

Miriam made a note: '*Only two hearts? Might be three.*'

'I can't believe how easy it is to see some of the chronology now,' Lauren said. 'It was a like a jigsaw puzzle dropped on the floor but I can feel the rhythm of it now. I think you have the knack, Miriam, of letting people find their story.'

'Good, good,' Miriam said. 'So, you married Tim.'

'Yes, I sort of saw my wedding to him when I was in the church for the service for Peter Stanning. It was the same church and I feel a bit guilty about that but I'm not sure why.'

Miriam wanted to know whether the guilt was attached to Tim or Simon or the church but she remained silent.

'Anyway, I kept working and George came to see me but I have no idea why that is significant or indeed why he would be with me in London or why I remember it so clearly but I do. And I'm pregnant and we have a ridiculous dash to the hospital because I can't walk and—'

Lauren's eyes widened and she began to tremble. She held her hand out to Miriam, who took it and held it firmly.

'It hurt so much,' Lauren said. 'I couldn't push properly, every push felt like I was taking a hammer to my own head.'

Miriam noticed a bead of sweat on Lauren's forehead but could not note it down because Lauren was clinging tightly to her hand.

She sank back. 'My baby,' she said. 'I never saw my baby.'

TIM

If he had been asked whether being a widower had slowed him down at work, Tim would have denied it with good reason. With one less salary, one larger mortgage and a live-in au pair to fund, he felt he had to raise his game.

Pilot was expanding rapidly and new staff kept arriving, which only served to create more expansion. Tim tried to sit in for most of the recruitment interviews.

'If we gave you the power to change one thing about the firm,' he asked a slim young man with slicked-back hair, no stubble and a Greek surname with eight syllables, 'what would you do?'

The young man knew that the wrong answer was to say that Pilot was perfect but the right answer was not to state that something fundamental needed to change. So he alighted on the building's reception and how the display about missing people was too prominent and could dampen the mood of sensitive prospective clients.

'Did it dampen your mood?' Tim asked.

'No, not all,' he said.

'You're not overly sensitive then?'

'Er, no,' he said, wondering if he had missed the memo which said that the new vibe in advertising was to be charitable and soppy.

As always, Tim confided in Bella when an interview was over.

'Was I a bit harsh on him?' he asked.

'Not at all,' Bella said. 'We wouldn't want him here if he thought Lauren's display was upsetting or inappropriate.'

'Quite,' Tim said as Emily arrived with Amber so that all three of them could go for a walk, eat a sandwich on a park bench or use the baby-friendly pasta place. If Tim had longer than half an hour to spare he would tell Emily to leave Amber with him so she could go shopping or have some baby-free time otherwise he used their time to catch up on domestic issues such as teething, crawling and whether Emily should enrol in the new water-babies class at the local pool. There were other fathers at Pilot and none of them met their babies or toddlers for lunch, but none of them thought Tim was in any way peculiar.

When Tim returned to the office that afternoon, a tiny piece of egg white on his lapel, Bella was gazing adoringly at a tall man in the lobby whom Tim vaguely recognised.

He introduced himself as George Stanning and pointed at Lauren's artwork.

'I wanted to let you know that your wife urged me to investigate my father's disappearance, she was most insistent in fact, and after a few false starts, I am making progress and I would have liked very much to let Lauren know about it but as that, sadly, is not possible, I wanted you to know how grateful I am that she cared enough to, well, nag me about it, really.'

Tim exhaled. He had braced himself for bad news, although that George might be the one to bring it was absurd.

'Great, I mean, thank you. Have you found out what happened to your father then?'

'Not exactly, but I think I know what needs to be done to at least know why he vanished.'

'Right,' Tim said. 'Good luck and, really, do keep in touch. For Lauren's sake.'

After George had left, Tim stood in front of the display. A man had disappeared when Lauren was fifteen and inspired her to draw and paint so engagingly about the despair and the mystery that he had ended up interviewing her for a job. From behind her desk, Bella watched surreptitiously and guessed almost exactly what was going through his head.

When he turned round she made eye contact.

'If you were George… or someone like George, and I asked you on a date, would you automatically think I was cheap or odd, or would you think, good on her for taking the initiative?'

'And did you ask him or someone like him on a date? That kind of affects how I answer you,' he said.

'No, of course not but I'm wondering, you know, if I should have done. He's probably got a fiancée or something. Has he?'

'Heck, I don't know, Bella, but if he gets in touch again, I'll find out for you and to answer your question: ask him to go for a coffee. Just a coffee.'

Bella blushed, wondering if by 'a date', Tim thought she

had meant full-blown sex after a drunken night on the town. There was, though, no elegant way to deny it if he had, so she smiled her most demure smile and handed him a package to take upstairs to Gregory.

LAUREN

There was a box of tissues on Miriam's desk but Lauren's agony was dry-eyed.

'I need to know my baby is well,' she said. 'I have to know. It's *my* baby. Maybe she died with me. Maybe it's a boy and he was starved of oxygen and he's in hospital and alone and—'

'Or maybe you didn't die,' Miriam said.

Lauren stopped summoning terrible images of what might have happened and looked at Miriam.

'Why would you say that?' she said.

'Because this is unprecedented and we don't know what it means. And you remember *this* life and you remember *that* life so why assume they can't keep running together as they used to?'

For a moment Lauren was filled with a sad joyousness that somewhere she and her baby were snuggling on a sofa, wrapped in warm blankets, healthy and happy and bonding beautifully. Then she clenched her teeth. She knew in the pit of her soul that her baby did not have its mother.

Lauren was drained now, tired of the complexity and the simplicity. Tired of knowing she was alone in the knowing. Mournful that her baby, if alive, would never know her.

'I didn't choose any of this. It is what happens to us, that's all.'

Miriam was baffled, entranced and concerned. She hardly slept that night, and the next morning she opened her diary to find out when she would be able to spend a day in London.

'It might be unethical,' she said to the ghost of her dead husband, 'but I doubt it and, anyway, I don't care. I'm going.'

Lauren popped over two evenings later. It was not a scheduled appointment but Miriam was beyond the point where she was going to maintain normal boundaries.

'Obviously, I can't keep using you just to handle my millions of yet-to-reach memories but I feel safe here when I do try to piece things together. At home I feel guilty about it. They all need me and I'm not going to get back into the swing of it all properly if part of me is dwelling on my other world. If I know it's OK to come here, it makes it easier.'

Miriam made them tea, which to Lauren still seemed to take for ever, and then, out of self-interest and with a frisson of excitement, she asked Lauren if she wanted to pin down any detail to the broad brush of her other life story.

'Yes, that might help, I'm not sure.'

Miriam started a fresh page in her notepad and milked Lauren for information about her London job and her London homes and the following Monday Miriam took the train to London Euston. She had two hours in which to visit several streets before meeting her sister, a solicitor, for a late lunch.

She knocked on the door of an address Lauren had summoned in Paddington as the place where she first fell in love. A young woman answered.

'I'm terribly sorry to disturb you but I'm looking for Kat, Amy or Luke or a Jeffers,' Miriam said.

The woman looked blank and shook her head.

'How long ago did they live here?' she asked.

'Ah, yes a few years now, it's a long shot, I know.'

'Say the names again.'

Miriam repeated them and the girl frowned.

'Step inside a minute, there's some old letters in one of the drawers in Callum's room. I'll get them and you can take a look.'

'That's really very kind of you,' Miriam said as the girl loped upstairs. There was some scuffling and scraping and then she returned with a few old, unopened bills and a couple of envelopes with the address neatly handwritten.

One of the personal letters was addressed to a Luke. The rest were of no interest.

'Would you mind if I took this? It's really quite ancient and I know his family.'

The girl shrugged. 'Don't see why not,' she said, and Miriam felt a tremor of triumphalism.

She caught a taxi to Charlotte Street where Lauren had first worked and found the agency, still called JSA, if, she thought to herself, the phrase 'still called' was appropriate. She asked them about Pilot but nobody had heard the name. She asked them if they knew a Tim Lewis and the receptionist shook her head but a big-boned woman in big shoes who was passing overheard her.

'Tim used to work here, we overlapped for about a year, and I think he joined Saatchi and then went solo maybe.'

'Can I just clarify that is Tim Lewis and not another Tim?' Miriam said.

'Yeah, Tim Lewis.'

'Have you any idea how I might find him?' Miriam said.

The woman turned to the receptionist.

'Put her through to Ped, he'll know.'

Miriam found herself on the receptionist's phone asking Ped if he knew where she could find Tim Lewis.

'Sure, he's with MVL over in Golden Square.'

Miriam thanked him and then walked to Golden Square, enjoying the fact that although she had not been in the capital for two years, she knew the way.

The offices of MVL were small, very shiny and minimalist.

'I don't suppose you have a company brochure, do you?' she asked the woman in a bright red shift dress who was sat on a cream leather chair behind a glass table.

'A brochure?' she said incredulously. And Miriam could see it was a stupid question to ask in a lobby that was completely clutter free. However, the receptionist turned to a black oak filing cabinet and pulled out a glossy postcard that had eight images on the front and one of them was of the three founder members.

'Which one is Tim Lewis?' Miriam asked.

The girl squinted.

'The dude with the blue tie,' she said.

Miriam placed the postcard in her handbag just as Miss Marple would have done, she thought, thanked the red shift girl and turned on her heels to join her sister at the pancake house they had been using for their once-in-a-blue-moon lunches for the past twenty years.

What Miriam liked most about meeting with her sister was that they never dwelled on how long it had been since they last saw each other and could dive into conversation the way two sisters might had they been in the habit of meeting once a fortnight.

'I've been sleuthing,' Miriam said.

'I've been helping couples get divorced,' Samantha said. 'But as I've been doing that for most of my professional life, let's get to the nitty gritty of your new career.'

Miriam laughed. 'I've lost the plot, I think,' she said. 'I have a patient who believes she has landed in a new life, boom, and, because I think I believe her, I've been double checking her story.'

'And?' Samantha said.

'And it still rings true.'

'And?'

'And, yes, "and" is a good point to raise because I don't know if it is best to let her know there is evidence she is telling the truth or to try to guide her away from dwelling on it.'

'I thought you thought that all patients should face up to the truth and that your job was to help them through the difficulties of that because once they had unshackled themselves of the guilt or the pain or whatever they could live properly.'

Miriam felt a surge of love for a sister who had not only listened for all these years but also understood.

'You're right, of course, but if I believe her then she doesn't need me, she needs a detective or a scientist or a hybrid scientist-PI.'

'Nonsense,' Samantha said. 'It doesn't matter what the problem is, your role is the same; to make the journey to sanity or happiness smoother. You got room for a maple syrup pancake?'

'No, you have room and I say I don't and then I order a banana and chocolate sauce one at the last minute.'

They toasted tradition and smiled and Miriam produced the glossy postcard from Golden Square.

'She thinks she was married to him, the one in the blue tie.'

Samantha took out her reading glasses and, to Miriam's bemusement, groaned.

'I'm representing him in his divorce,' she said matter-of-factly. 'And his wife definitely doesn't live up North.'

'You're not serious?' Miriam said.

'Oh, I've conquered the advertising world,' Samantha said. 'They all come to my firm now.'

'I really like this room,' Lauren said. 'It's incredibly peaceful and elegant.'

'And it reminds you of somewhere,' Miriam said.

'I have lots of that in my life right now,' Lauren sighed, 'the things I should know well are strange and the strange things are familiar.'

Miriam felt sick with nerves. Under her A4 pad was the shiny postcard and the letter addressed to Luke.

'Officially, Lauren,' she said, 'our sessions come to an end today.'

Lauren's eyes widened.

'Don't worry, they have hardly been run-of-the-mill sessions, but I'd like us to see each other as friends, or at least for you to see me as someone who can help you through this, so I need to officially sign you off.'

Lauren was deeply touched.

'I would like that enormously,' she said.

'Good, good,' Miriam said, playing for time.

Lauren smiled, waiting for Miriam to ask how she had been. Miriam fiddled with her papers.

'I went to London last week to see my sister and I– ' she coughed 'and I tried to track down bits of your London life.'

Lauren frowned.

'I don't understand, it doesn't exist here,' she said.

'But it does, my dear,' Miriam said and she pulled out the letter addressed to Luke.

'He doesn't live there any more, but he did live there and he left behind this letter. I thought it might help. I might be wrong.'

Lauren ran her finger across the address and remembered, hazily, how frustrated Luke had been about the way his mother wrote to him about his father.

'I won't open it,' she said. 'Not now.'

'Of course,' Miriam said, 'but the postmark is almost four years ago so there's no harm if you do.'

Lauren breathed in deeply. 'Did you find anything else?'

Miriam slid the postcard out from under her notepad, unable to prevent her cheeks from flushing pink.

'I didn't speak to Tim but I think I found his office and this tiny picture of him.'

Lauren gasped and devoured the images on the card.

'Yes, that looks like him, the one in the blue tie,' she said. 'What does it mean?'

'It means I believe you,' Miriam said.

The next morning her pillow was wet. She had wept in her sleep, dreaming of the baby she had not met. She was glad Miriam believed her but the letter and the postcard had acted like a spoon stirring up her memories, mixing them, confusing her.

Simon had woken in the night and felt the tears silently seeping into his wife's pillow and felt helpless and unable to broach the subject the next morning.

On her way home from the college where she did find some respite as she enjoyed the teaching so much, she called in to her father's office.

'Hello, darling,' Bob said. 'Everything all right?'

'Yes, yes, I was just wondering about your work, Dad, and if this is still the head office?'

'Yes, although we have a presence, as the directors like to put it, in most cities now.'

'And does George have an office here?'

'Of course, it's in the new annexe, very plush.'

'Can I see the new annexe?' she asked.

'I don't see why not,' Bob said, 'although it really isn't all that interesting.'

Bob used his passkey to gain entrance, and a woman, clearly more significant than a receptionist, beamed at them both.

'Just showing my daughter the new building, Miranda,' he said.

'Is George in?' Lauren asked, trying to sound nonchalant.

'Actually, he is – which is a rare thing these days,' Miranda said.

'Do you think I could just pop in? For one minute?'

Both Bob and Miranda were puzzled but she knew how much George valued Bob so she nodded.

'Let me just check,' she said, and she did that light knowing tap the best assistants know how to execute and opened the door to George's office.

'Go straight in,' she said.

George stood immediately and decided to kiss Lauren's cheek before indicating that she sit in the chair the other side of his desk.

She sat down tentatively.

'Right,' she said. 'This is hard for me, and possibly rude of me, but I have to say something just in case you can help. I'm not holding out much hope but...'

George smiled. 'Fire away,' he said.

'I've been having a tough time of late, feeling like I don't belong here, and for some reason you and your family and what you have been through are the settled parts of my memory. And I wondered if you had any idea why that might be?'

George blinked.

'Well, I wasn't expecting that,' he said. He looked at the clock above her head. 'Do you think you could explain more within the next ten minutes?'

'Only if you promise not to tell anyone.'

'Deal,' he said, half amused, half perturbed.

Lauren had practised what she would say if allowed and so she calmly told him about waking up disorientated, the eventual acceptance of another life, and the fact that she felt no memory lag or confusion when it came to George and his father.

'And I feel there is something important I should tell you that isn't about all this and I wasn't going to speak to you until I had worked out what it was but then I thought maybe if we do speak it will trigger the reason.'

George tapped his fingers together.

'I have to make a few calls I can't put off but, look, I'm here on Friday. Do you fancy lunch?'

She would have to lie to the college about a doctor's appointment but she didn't care.

'Would you really do that for me?' she asked.

He smiled.

'Miranda let you into my office and she has never yet made the wrong call.'

Bob had gone back to his own desk.

'What was all that about?' he asked her.

'I'll fill you in later, Dad,' she said, with not a clue how she would manage to do that.

VERA

True to his nasty nature, Colin Talbot sought to sue the Pailings for contributory negligence. True to the hypocrisy in his soul he was, at the same time, content to allow Bob and Vera to care for Daisy. The social worker was aghast and agitated but astute enough to see that living alongside Hope was the best place for a young girl who really ought to have been more morose but somehow summoned a sweet smile each time they met.

Vera was kind and attentive around the girls but withdrawn the rest of the time.

'How could I not see what was coming?' she pleaded with Bob every evening, and her thoughts were clogged by attempting to interpret Mrs Talbot's logic. Hope had saved Vera so why had Daisy not saved Mrs Talbot? Grief, it seemed, had many guises.

Struggling to sleep, Vera sat in front of Lauren's box of drawings. It occurred to her that if there was a place in Lauren's mind for a life in which they had owned a dog then perhaps there was a place where David had not owned a motorbike.

Mrs Talbot thought she was meeting David in heaven but perhaps she was meeting him right here but not quite here. A here where her son was alive and well. It was a fleeting thought and the next morning she had forgotten it altogether.

One thing that was clear to Vera was that Mrs Talbot had believed Daisy to be safe with her and so she decided she would fight to make sure Daisy could become a member of their family.

Vera had the sycamore felled and a cherry tree planted in its stead. One day she would tell Daisy about everything. One day she expected Daisy to ask her why her mother did not love her enough, why her mother chose to be with David, but Daisy, it seemed, had accepted she was less important a long time ago and it helped that she knew first hand just how adorable and adored her brother had been.

Mr Talbot had banned the Pailings from his wife's funeral but they had held a small service in their garden, which Daisy pronounced the more beautiful of the two events. Their home was altogether sunnier for the addition of Daisy, whose flair for the arts complemented Hope's mathematical strengths and they each urged the other towards better grades in their weaker subjects at GCSE.

Not once did Mr Talbot visit Daisy in her new home, not once did Daisy seek to discuss the fact her father had a new wife and a new baby and had given her up without even a hint of the fight Bob and Vera had feared from him. Bob preferred to think of Mr Talbot as irreparably damaged by the death of his son but Vera had made up her mind the first time she had heard about him that he was 'a nasty piece of work'.

The years passed. So fond did they all become of Daisy that

when George and Felicity's son was born, they gave him the name Oliver Peter David Stanning. His christening was the only time any of them had seen Daisy properly and completely sob and upon being told why, the vicar felt a surge in the goodness still abounding in the world and that his church still had a place for selfless love.

And then one day the two girls appeared together in the still slightly too formal living room and announced they wanted to attend boarding school together for their A level years and Vera and Bob both gawped in astonishment and slight terror but neither shifted the blame to Daisy nor lamented her influence on Hope. They dropped them off, fees paid for both by Bob, at the grand granite edifice that would be their home from home and Vera was almost too disbelieving to weep, but weep she did as they drove home, and she was amused to discover that some of the tears were shed for how much she would miss Daisy.

She turned to her husband and was surprised to see that he was smiling.

'Bob?' she said.

'I know how you feel about Connie's death,' he said 'but, my love, just think what you've given Daisy.'

Vera pushed her head back into the car seat and closed her eyes. She had given Daisy a sister, which meant she had given Hope a sister.

She opened her eyes and gazed at the sky ahead and, instead of feeling she had let Lauren down, she felt she had honoured her and a small swathe of what had been a steady grief was, in that moment, swept away.

She turned again to Bob and this time it was her turn to smile.

TIM

He found a rhythm to life. He worked long hours but was amenable to a drink before heading home. He spent all Saturday with Amber, and Sundays would find him invited to family meals with Bea or at his father's house, where Lottie could be relied upon to dote upon his daughter.

Vera and Bob still travelled down but usually stayed just the one night and, as all they had in common, apart from Amber, was the tragedy of Lauren, there was little in the way of revelry when they sat down for some food after Amber was in bed.

'Your boss was in my office the other day, Bob,' Tim said. 'He was looking at Lauren's display and it made me think, I'm not sure you've ever seen it, have you?'

It was all he could do to stop Vera and Bob leaping into a taxi there and then but they turned up at noon the next day with Emily and Amber.

'Do people ever just come in to look at this display?' Vera asked Bella. 'I mean, people who have no meetings here.'

'One or two, not too many because it's a bit obvious we are a business and not a gallery, but it is an amazing display, isn't it?'

'What a nice girl,' Vera said as they travelled back up North. 'Do you think Tim will ever remarry? Do you think we would cope if he did?'

Bob mulled it over. 'I think we would see more of Amber if he did. It's the way these things work, I'm sure.'

LAUREN

To her surprise, George said they should meet at the newly opened American Diner. Even more surprising was the delight he took in explaining the menu and how delicious the various relishes were to accompany burgers that could be cooked to order.

'You can even have a medium-rare one,' he said. 'And the milkshakes are amazing.'

Men, she thought, no matter how successful, are still boys, and she noted how he gazed at the giant juke box and she guessed he was imagining a world in which he was an American college boy at Harvard, bunking off class, about to drive off in a cherry-red Chevrolet.

'You are so nice to spare me some time, George,' she said.

'It's good to get a break, chat to someone different,' he said.

'You might wish you hadn't bothered,' she said. 'This feels like when you see someone off the telly in the street and you think you know them and stupidly smile at them and say hi and then realise they have never seen you before. I feel I know you or ought to know you and I also feel safe in your company. And that must sound very awkward. But I want to be honest.'

'OK,' George mumbled. 'Fire away.'

The waitress took their order, which cheered up George, and then she leaned back, aware that to lean forward was to act conspiratorially. Leaning forward was what weirdos did in film about ghosts.

'I've slipped into this world after dying in another one and everything is supposed to be so similar that I don't notice but everything is different so I do notice and it's really, really, confusing and upsetting and draining, actually, but your father's disappearance is exactly the same and you seem exactly the same. Except I knew you a bit better before. You came to see me in London. I worked in London. I can't recall what we talked about though. I'm hoping by sitting here I do remember.'

The milkshakes arrived. George took a slurp.

'Did you work for me in London?' he asked so placidly that Lauren chuckled.

'No, I worked in advertising. With a man I ended up marrying.'

'Not Simon, then.'

'No, not Simon.' She took the postcard out of her bag. 'I married him,' she said. 'The one in the blue tie.'

'So he exists, here?'

'It looks that way,' she said.

'Maybe you did some advertising for me?' George said.

'Maybe,' she said.

Their burgers arrived along with a tray of multi-coloured relishes.

It was a relief that George was so calm – and worrying. She wondered if he was humouring her as a favour to her father. Or, possibly, he was bored.

George chewed thoughtfully.

'If I came to see you in London *there* but not here, then not everything is the same about me, is it?' he said.

'True,' she said, 'but it feels the same. I'm not conflicted with you.'

'Well, it's an interesting puzzle,' he said, looking at his watch. 'I'm picking my brother up from the station.' George suddenly froze then frowned. 'Do you know Harry, my brother?'

'No, not at all,' she said.

'Do you know what he does?'

'Nope, although Dad has mentioned that he's extremely bright, a scientist, I think he said.'

'A physicist,' George said. 'Was at Cambridge, now at Imperial College. He stopped studying for a bit when Dad went missing and I made a promise to, well, to Dad, I suppose, to make sure he didn't go off the rails. Sometimes I think I went too far. All he does is research. He's obsessed.'

'OK,' Lauren said.

'You should come with me to the station.'

'I should?'

'Yes, I think you should.'

She followed in her car and waited in it while George collected his brother. Once Harry was in the passenger seat, George tapped on her window.

'Follow us to The Hare,' he said.

The pub was a five-minute drive away and had a pretty beer garden overflowing with dahlias even more colourful than the diner's relishes. While George bought some shandy for himself, lemonade for her and a pint of bitter for his brother, Harry looked intently at Lauren.

'George says you've had an experience of another world,' he said flatly.

'Yes,' she said defiantly. 'Why does he think we should meet?'

'It's an area of interest to me,' he said, 'although not in the terms George explained.'

'I don't understand,' she said.

'Well, there is a many-worlds interpretation that helps to explain the randomness of our universe. People tend to think of this in terms of parallel universes. You can, for example, be alive in one and dead in another. At least, George says that's what you think has happened to you.'

Lauren felt the blood drain from her face.

'Are you telling me I might be in a real world now and was in a real world before? That these things can really happen. Scientifically?'

'I'm not telling you anything,' Harry said. 'George thinks you needed to meet me, that you knowing the possibility of many worlds might explain your predicament.'

George placed the drinks on the small rickety table.

'I might not have explained your experience to Harry very well,' he said. 'Tell him in more detail.'

Lauren had begun to flag but was energised by the prospect of a non-psychological reason for her new life.

She told Harry what she told Miriam and as she reached the point at which she died in labour and had not been able to set eyes on her baby, her eyes welled up with the kind of tears that she hoped she would never need to shed over Rosie and Toby.

George nodded sympathetically.

Harry, dry-eyed, took a sip of beer.

'Are there any measurable differences?' he asked.

'Everything's different,' she said.

'But that is your perception. Is there anything physically different?'

'Oh,' she said and mulled this over. 'You mean I should think like a scientist?'

'If that helps,' he said.

She closed her eyes and rubbed them hard. She was desperate to maintain Harry's interest. For the first time since the sunbathing episode she did not feel like an outsider.

She thought so hard that George and Harry began their own conversation about their mother, the flat that George had bought Harry so he could continue his research without worrying about money, the driving test that Harry kept forgetting to take.

'The kettles,' she said, loudly, interrupting them.

The brothers looked at her, half amused.

'It takes much longer to make a cup of tea here.'

Harry sat up straight.

'Kettles are not all the same, maybe you've been using a slow one,' he said.

'No, Simon bought me a new one and it's just as slow and everyone who makes one in whatever home takes for ever. It's maddening.'

'Have you timed the comparison?' Harry said.

'Timed it?' she said. 'Timed it? I didn't know I was going to die and land here in the land that kettles forgot, so, no, I never timed it. But I know it's significantly slower. Significantly.'

George guffawed. 'This is, well, it's crazy,' he said.

'It's intriguing,' Harry said. 'Anything else?'

'Fish live in trees,' she pouted, and even Harry smiled.

'Actually, I hadn't really thought about it until now, but I haven't seen any cats here at all.'

'What's a cat?' George said, and Lauren delved into her bag, produced a notebook and pencil and drew an everyday domestic moggy sat on the outline of an armchair to offer perspective. She knew she was not being humoured. She had spent one of her lifetimes in a world without cats so of course neither Harry nor George would know what one looked like.

'That's a cat,' she said.

'Looks like a giant hamster,' George said and she giggled. Her life was quite maddening but here, in the beer garden, she was able to clutch at both her worlds and feel rational about it.

As they stood to leave, Lauren not caring that her fictitious doctor's appointment had overrun, George spoke to her softly, out of Harry's earshot.

'If Dad hadn't left us, Harry might not be so consumed by his studies and so clever about these multi-worlds so maybe that's why, somehow, you needed to see me?'

'Maybe,' she said, 'that has a certain crazy logic to it, but there's something else. I feel it. It's something for you.'

TIM

'My son-in-law says you've seen the artwork our Lauren made about your father,' Bob said.

'Yes,' George said. 'I've been wanting to talk to you about it but wasn't sure when would be an appropriate time.'

'I like talking about Lauren,' Bob said. 'She was very talented, you know.'

'Very,' George said. 'Actually, she told me something, or rather she urged me to do something to find out what happened to Dad.'

'Really?'

'Yes and she was right. I've made all this money and you don't need a degree in psychology to know I'm motivated to protect my mother and brother in light of what happened to us, to keep expanding the company, and for what? What really? I'm not sure Mum needs any more money, not really. I'm glad I've been able to make sure Harry can study but, as Lauren pointed out, why hadn't I used my success, all the resources available to me, to find out what happened?'

Bob listened intently. Any new story or fresh insight about his only child was welcome.

'And so I have employed someone to do what he calls forensic investigation, and he concluded that were some loose ends.'

'That's good, isn't it?' Bob said.

'Yes. Yes and no,' George said. 'A lot of it is personal stuff. I don't want to go into detail but I do want you to know that I am grateful to Lauren for prodding me into action and I wish I could tell her so.'

'There's so much to regret,' Bob sighed, and the two men awkwardly embraced.

Dylan Stenson was a wiry man with round glasses, a police background and a knack of re-reading files until they produced a nugget of new information. He was expensive but produced a daily report for his clients so they could see they were getting their money's worth. Dylan Stenson had even gleaned that Mr Yee had not been interviewed by the investigating officer. There was nothing Mr Yee could offer that was very helpful but it told Dylan Stenson that those searching for the missing Peter Stanning had not been sufficiently thorough. It was not entirely insignificant, he thought, that Peter had dined regularly at Mr Yee's with his wife but, in the months before he went missing, he had dined alone. There would be other holes, some much more gaping, and Dylan Stenson had borrowed Mr Yee's treasured grey scrapbook, leaving Mr Yee to feel that, at last, someone was taking the case seriously.

'She counted the bicycles,' he told the detective.

'Who did?' Dylan Stenson asked sharply, but his tone softened when he realised it was the woman who had, in a roundabout way, made sure of his big fat fee for the current case. He would have counted the bikes too if they were still in the shed but they had all been taken to the tip. If only she was still alive. No one, he thought, counts bikes for no reason.

Dylan Stenson had reached the end of the first phase of his investigation and sat down with George to give him his summary.

'I have been through all the witness statements and collected my own where necessary and the only conclusion I can draw is that your mother needs to agree to a full and frank interview.'

George swallowed hard. 'You're not suggesting—'

'Absolutely not,' he said, 'but there are inconsistencies and gaps and I believe, having weighed up all the evidence, that Mrs Stanning must have spoken to your father before he left that evening.'

'But, why? Why would she not tell us that?' George said.

'I did warn you, Mr Stanning, that I often unearth truths that people find hard to accept. I do not want to offer empty conjecture but let me give you an example of a possible reason. Let us suppose your parents had a row. And then your father goes missing. Many wives would want that to remain private. They might think their children would blame them for the disappearance and so decide to say that nothing happened.'

'But if that's what happened, it won't tell us where my father is,' George said.

'You'd be surprised,' Dylan Stenson said, 'what the truth can yield.'

On his way home he called in at Mr Yee's once more. He wanted to know if Lauren had said anything about the number of bikes.

Mr Yee sat down gingerly and rubbed at his temples. He so wanted to help.

'Maybe she say eleven?'

LAUREN

George was busy in the intimidating manner of all successful businessmen and Harry returned to his research. They promised, though, to make time to see her again when Harry was next up to see his mother. Lauren was relieved. There had been something so soothing about the way Harry nonchalantly explained the possible existence of other worlds. He could not offer a reason as to how she had slipped into this one but he at least accepted that her other life could have existed.

She told Miriam, who issued a deep sigh.

'You sound happier,' she said.

'I feel less bonkers,' Lauren said. 'But in a way, it's wounding, you know, to think that somewhere else I really am dead, that I died on the cusp of becoming a mother.'

Both women were silent as they dwelled upon the notion of being dead somewhere else.

'Perhaps this Harry would know better than me but if you are dead in this other world then you can't go back and you need to embrace the fact you have a shot at another life. You have to try to focus on this life, Lauren. It's not inconceivable that the more you try the faster the memories will kick in and soon you'll feel you belong.'

Miriam could not quite believe she was having this conversation and yet it seemed the only way forward.

'But it's like I'm lying to Simon every day. He's so lovely, so patient and I can't tell him what happened. I love him, really I do, but there's this itch to escape.'

'Right, right, OK. You need to accept that there is nowhere you can escape to. If you went to London and sought out Tim he would not know you. In fact, he is in the middle of a divorce to another woman. We know that to be a fact. This is your life now and, slowly, slowly but surely, you will lose that itch.'

Miriam felt triumphant. They had worked through a puzzle and there was a path ahead.

'You can see me any time. We'll get you through this,' she said. 'Now, would you like a cup of tea?'

'No,' Lauren groaned. 'Can we go for a walk instead?'

They strolled like mother and daughter down to the stream. It was quiet enough to hear it gurgling and Lauren experienced a glimpse of peace. She took Luke's still unopened letter out of her bag, ripped it to shreds and threw it into the water.

'Symbolic,' she said.

'Well done,' Miriam said.

That evening Lauren commandeered the tiny dining room that had no dining table and was used for toy storage.

'I'm going to paint here,' she told Simon and the children and, as all three of them were to varying degrees a little wary of Lauren since the sunbathing incident, they all nodded enthusiastically.

It became a form of connection to her lost life. She thought of every piece of artwork as Her Other Past, and as she flung russet reds onto a canvas she at last remembered the small exhibition that George had seen and how she had told him to spend his money on finding the truth.

She wondered if he had found the truth there and if he would find it here. She was certain the truth would be the same in both worlds, that perhaps Peter Stanning's truth was the only complete constant, for it was the only element of her life that felt exactly the same to her.

Only while painting could she be calm in comparing her lives. The sudden realisation that she had not seen any cats was a worry to her. There might be many things missing from this world, so many that it was a poor version, a weaker version, one that no one would choose if given the option. It was hard, though, to recall things that had gone missing. It would be easier to recognise things that were here right now that had not been with her before but it seemed to Lauren that in this world there was less, not more, of everything. It was a world with less energy, less sparkle. It was a world with flat light and repetitive sunsets; one that needed her art.

They met in The Hare and sat round a small table in a small alcove as the rain swirled against the small leaded window. Harry had brought Lauren a sheaf of papers about Many Worlds. There was an essay about Hugh Everett III, who, Harry said, was the physicist who had seized upon the concept of multiple universes to explain the contradiction in the way particles behave at the micro and macro level of reality.

'It was the fifties and he was ahead of his time and so he

was ridiculed,' Harry said. 'But there are many physicists who now think that his is the right approach.'

He pointed to a drawing of a rabbit in a box.

'Have you heard of Shrödinger's Rabbit?' he asked.

'I think so,' Lauren said, as she peered at the picture of the animal sitting alongside a bottle of poison.

'Well, Mr Everett gave us the option of the rabbit being alive in one world and dead in another instead of being both alive and dead inside the box.'

Lauren could barely breath. She was proof.

'What happened to Everett?' George asked.

'He died relatively young having turned to drink,' Harry said. 'We scientists like a good pint,' he added, sipping from his tankard.

'This really helps,' Lauren said, astonished but grateful. 'I mean, it's complicated, of course, but the fact that it's science, that it's worthy of research, well, it helps. Thank you.'

Harry smiled and George beamed, proud, as usual, of his younger brother.

'In return, I have something to tell you,' she said, shyly, wanting to forget about her dead self, wanting to give something back. 'You know I told you that you came to see me in London?'

'If you insist,' George said, laughing.

'Well, I remember now what happened. You were moved by pictures I had produced about your father's disappearance and I told you to spend your money on finding out what happened and you started to investigate, I'm sure of it, and I think you should do that here. You should spend all it takes to find out.'

'I call the police every six months or so,' he said a little sullenly.

'No, you need to be proactive. Hire someone. Hire the best. Hire someone who will look at the smallest detail.'

Later, in her mini-studio, Lauren sought to express the notion of being both alive and dead and she acknowledged that to be happy she had to accept she was not trapped in a box, feeling both alive and dead, but that she was Everett's rabbit and alive in this place even if dead in another.

At Lauren's invitation, Miriam drove over to look at her art.

'It's called *Another Life*,' Lauren said, half expecting Miriam to scold her for clinging to her other world. Miriam, though, understood perfectly that the paintings were a necessary outlet.

The older woman was almost overwhelmed.

'This is remarkable, Lauren,' she said. 'This has to be exhibited.'

'Really?' Lauren said, although deep down she knew she had produced something powerful and beautiful, but not necessarily because she was talented. She did not think herself overly gifted but there was something lacking in the light in this life that she brought to her paintings. Through her art she could express some of what she was missing, let people see light they had not seen before.

Miriam stood before the self-portrait and saw a woman in mourning but not in despair. It was the sort of painting anyone could stare at for hours and remain undecided at just how much of it contained hope and how much of it expressed sorrow. Beyond that it was, simply, a very fine piece of art that played with light and shade and hinted at complicated unseen windows. It was art that spoke of a land where the light was more beautiful.

Miriam knew a gallery owner in Chester and convinced him to make a big deal of Lauren's work.

'She's a complete unknown,' he said.

'So imagine the kudos of being the one to first exhibit her,' Miriam said.

Miriam enjoyed herself enormously, ringing up old friends, drumming up people to attend so that come six one warm June Thursday evening Lauren, Miriam, Simon, Bob and Vera were nervously stood among the art, the rows of wine glasses, hoping that someone, anyone, would turn up to view it. By six-thirty, the gallery was humming, glasses were clinking and sales were made. The self-portrait was not for sale for the simple reason that Rosie had stood in front of it, holding her mother's hand, and told her she was the prettiest mum she had ever seen.

Simon thought it was pretentious tosh, the way people stood in front of a canvas uttering words such as 'warmth' and 'depth' and 'passion', but he could see the art was a cut above competent, that he was married to someone with a special talent and it gave him a shiver of pride to see his name attached to it all.

Another Life – Lauren Millington. It was a huge success. Soon there was chat of a second exhibition and the possibility of taking it to London.

'What do you think?' she asked Simon. 'I was considering asking to have my hours cut down at college so I can do this properly but I'll understand if you think that's too risky.'

'It's made you happy and it's made you some money. Go for it, sweetheart,' he said.

Two summers later she was in Swallow Street off Piccadilly

amid yet more wine glasses and even more admirers. Tim walked past and glanced at the single piece in the window which he liked but he was running late and was not, in any case, on the guest list. He told himself he would take another look later in the week but he never did. He remembered the name though when she was mentioned in a magazine article about the highlights of the art scene in London that summer of 1999.

The years flew by but Simon never forgot about the day his wife woke up with a gap in her memory. He was never entirely sure they were as happy as everyone said they must be and he quietly blamed that summer's afternoon, but because Lauren never mentioned it these days, neither did he.

They bought a house which was, perhaps coincidentally, just a five-minute walk from Miriam's home. It was an old rambling affair with an acre of land, a large garage and a separate building in which Lauren painted and sometimes, but not very often, wept for everything she had left behind.

The light in her paintings was almost always a source of delight to the critics and a source of anguish to her. Lauren wanted to capture something of the intrigue held by a shaft of sunlight but it induced a deep sense of melancholy whenever she tried.

Simon spent hours on his bikes and could sometimes be seen stood stock-still, oily rag in hand, gazing towards his wife's studio, wondering why he felt alone even when they made love.

Rosie kept her hair short and played hockey ferociously to county standard. Toby developed a passion for food and by thirteen would at weekends be the one to prepare the family meal. As Vera and Bob lavished praised on Toby's culinary talents Lauren recalled the way they had been devoted to Ben as she grew up and she would wonder at how she had rarely suffered any jealousy. The comparison with being an only child was not something she dwelled upon and instead she funnelled the differences into her paintings.

Simon's mother slowly wasted away and his father was pounced upon by the newly divorced Sylvia Ainscough, who whisked him off for months at a time for cruises on the Mediterranean.

The more Miriam knew about Lauren the more convinced she became that her young friend had lived more than one other life. Indeed, Lauren would speak fondly of the Vera who was that bit more attractive than the ones that followed but it seemed to suit Lauren to only think in terms of one extra world and so Miriam did not push the point and instead waited patiently to be shown a painting clearly alluding to a third path.

Ben married the girlfriend and then left her shortly afterwards, an event that did remarkably little to make waves in the lives of the Pailings or the Millingtons. Rosie went to university in Leeds, then became a sports teacher. Toby attended catering college and flitted from hotel to restaurant to hotel until, in desperation to secure his happiness, his parents and grandparents helped him to buy his own restaurant in Chester which was dutifully frequented by George whenever he had need to eat there.

Lauren let her hair remain the white type of grey it wanted to be and it suited her. She remembered that Debbie had called her Ghostie Girl but not this Debbie, the one who had moved away to Birmingham and had three grandchildren.

'I'd like to see the world on my bike,' Simon said one evening. 'Before I'm too old.'

'You're too old now,' Lauren said, but she had sensed the end was coming and this was a nice way to part.

'I might not come back,' he said. 'I mean, I might break down in the desert or be murdered in Pakistan. So. Will you tell me now what happened to you?'

In that moment she felt closer to him than she ever had. All her internal wrestling with another life had taken its toll on her patient, caring husband.

'I would have told you and I only didn't because I love you and I didn't want you to think I was mad or that I didn't love you. It's a hard thing to explain but if you really can be open-minded...'

Simon grunted that of course he could.

'When I woke up that day in the garden I truly believe I had just died in another world. There are other worlds, lots of scientists think that is possible and I know it is possible. They run in parallel and I used to, in my other life, even, I think, be able to see them.'

She paused as she could see he was unnerved.

'I can handle what you are saying,' he said, 'but not how calm you are about it.'

'I've had a long time to get used to it,' she said softly, 'but it hurt at first because I was about to give birth and I never saw the baby. I'll never know if it was a boy or a girl or if it died with me.'

'So you were married in this other place?'

'Yes, but not instead of to you. I was always here, it's just that the Lauren from there came here too and we mingled.'

She paused. She had grown so used to absorbing her other, London life that she needed to let Simon digest the notion that his wife was an amalgam. Lauren ran her fingers through his hair, knowing he had not had the marriage he deserved and yet he had never been bitter, never threatened to leave her.

'You mingled,' he said flatly, gently pulling her hands away from him.

'Shall I stop talking?' she said.

He shook his head.

'Keep going.'

'I strongly believe this happens to everyone but the lives are so similar that people rarely even sense they lived somewhere else. It's a way of living perhaps until the right age or the time we are supposed to go. Miriam's friend Gareth is an actuary and he says I will probably live until my early eighties. That's when I will properly die. I believe. It's what I believe, Simon, and it *is* peculiar, it's madness, so I couldn't tell you.'

He sniffed and frowned and sniffed again.

'No more peculiar than most religions,' he said. But it was too late. He had lost her years ago and now he wanted some time to himself.

'Maybe you'll miss me,' she said. 'I won't go anywhere. I'll be here when you get back.'

'I've been missing you a long time,' he said, and walked back out to his garage.

She watched him disappear behind the huge wooden doors and realised then how much she had taken him for granted. He had been a solid presence when she was fractured and flimsy and lost and now he had found out she was partly married to someone else. His reward for asking her for so little in return was to discover she had never been entirely his. He deserved to travel, he deserved time alone, but the thought of him speeding down dirt roads frustrated by how his romantic life had been half strangled frightened her. This was the mood in which men are reckless and crash, not caring if they live or die.

Lauren pushed open the doors. She wanted to hold him tightly to tell him she loved him with her all her heart, but she could not say it. Her heart was not all his. She was unfaithful without being unfaithful. She was a translucent sort of wife, a woman who was supposed to be dead.

He looked up at her, his expression was kind if perplexed.

'I love you more than you know,' she said, 'more than I have been able to show you.'

'Thank you,' he said but he quickly looked down at his prized motorbike. He would leave soon. She could tell.

Sometimes she pondered how the only person she could truly relax with, even if she rarely saw him, was George Stanning. She could look George full in the eye.

BOB

He was at his happiest playing cricket on the beach. Fortunately, it was something he and Jevin did as often as they could. Even when his shoulder began to ache with the twinges of early arthritis, Bob kept on bowling the tennis ball and Jevin kept on smacking it over his head with Pascal acting as fielder. On warm days Rachel would bring a rug and sit and watch. Sometimes she would act as wicket keeper but only if Suki had tagged along and joined in too. Afterwards they would look as healthy as any family could, all rosy-cheeked and cleansed by the salty sandy air, and Jevin would march to the weekends-only ice-cream van and order everyone's favourite treat which was in his mind set in stone, and had Suki wanted to try another flavour of ice lolly she was not given the chance.

As the rain cleared, leaving only a biting wind Jevin, aged seven, appeared with the frisbee he had been given at Christmas.

'Come on, Dad,' he said.

Rachel rolled her eyes good-naturedly as Bob heaved himself out of his chair.

'It's too cold for Paz,' she said but Bob had already wrapped the dog in its little waistcoat and they were off to the shore.

They were rewarded by an intense silvery sky as the black clouds rolled away to sea, and Jevin loved the way the air was so cold he could almost bite it.

A woman in her late twenties wearing a bobble hat stood on top of a sand dune and watched as the three of them leaped about, rarely catching the frisbee but laughing at each attempt.

Bob eventually felt they were being watched and looked inland. He knew it was Andrea straight away. He waved in acknowledgement but politely, hoping it was clear he did not want her to join them. This was not how it should be done. Not without Rachel. Andrea did not move towards them. She stayed, watching for five more minutes, and then left the beach altogether. She never saw Jevin again and wrote him a final letter in which she told him he had the best possible parents who she knew loved him more than any child could hope to be loved and so her own love for him meant she was happy to leave it be.

'One day,' she wrote, 'you might want to search for me. I won't make it hard for you but please enjoy the life you are blessed with.'

To Bob and Rachel she simply wrote:

'It has occurred to me that you might wonder when I'll pop round or start interfering. I want you to know that I won't. Jevin Grant has a wonderful life and I do not see how me turning up will improve it. I wish all of you every happiness. A.'

Bob reflected that there had been a time when being wished happiness was a hopeless sentiment, but as he read again Andrea's message he acknowledged that he had found it. He could laugh with his son wholeheartedly. He could stroke Rachel's cheek without guilt. His daughter was gone but she had enriched his life, a life she would have wanted him to have, and sometimes, when Jevin brought home a good report from school or told a funny story, Bob saw a twinkle in his eyes that had once belonged Lauren.

TIM

George was in reception again.

He remembered Bella's name. She flushed as she called up to Tim's office.

'Almost just passing,' George said as he shook Tim's hand.

'Good to see you,' Tim said and he meant it. It was a different sort of connection to Lauren.

'We've made some progress in trying to find out what happened to my dad and, given Lauren's role in that, I just wanted to tell you. I'm even told we might find him; his body, I mean.'

'Lauren would have been so pleased,' Tim said. 'Look, when I'm next taking my daughter up to Bob's house, we must grab a pint or something. If your wife will allow it?'

'Not hitched,' George said.

They shook hands again and George smiled at Bella as he left. Tim raised his eyebrows dramatically and mouthed the word 'single'.

She jumped up from her chair and ran out into the street.

'George,' she said, breathlessly. 'Could you squeeze in time to go for a coffee next time you are passing here?'

'Sure,' George said, 'but we've already agreed to go for a pint when Tim's next up North.'

Bella stared at him vacantly.

'I meant a coffee with me,' she said, her eyes turned towards the pavement.

'Oh,' he said. 'Yes, of course, how nice.' And then he climbed into the taxi wondering what on earth Bella wanted to say that required them to have a coffee. He sighed at his lack of empathy. No doubt Bella wanted to say something about Lauren, perhaps something else that connected her to his father. He really knew so little about her yet she had shaken him from his torpor, made him look properly for Peter. And now, she was gone.

PETER

He pulled into his gravelled driveway just before three o'clock. It would be dark within an hour or so but the December light was clear and precise. Peter hoped for a bustling kitchen, to see his children sat at the table struggling with homework, needing his help with a history project, munching on warm mince pies, but he knew it would be quiet. Empty. His children were having childhoods that bore no relation to his. They had a den and stables and fields. His youngest had his books, his maths puzzles. His eldest had an army of friends. They had grandparents with acres and acres of land and a house with turrets. It was falling into disrepair but that only made it more fun for his sons. They had friends with parents with holiday homes and sound-proofed rooms full of drum kits and electric guitars. They had a hundred places to be and no idea their father wanted them to be in the kitchen.

He walked towards the kettle. He did not want a cup of tea but he wanted some noise. His wife entered silently and leaned against the giant dresser.

'They're so independent now,' she said. 'So busy.'

There was no regret in her voice. She sounded proud.

All Peter could summon was an 'Ah.'

His wife's skin shimmered like porcelain. It always had. It was a constant reminder that she was from aristocratic stock. It would not be right, he thought, to conclude that they had drifted apart. They had always been apart. She was so self-assured, so independent, so confident. Their marriage had followed the path dictated by her and all the while she had been courteous and gentle with him. Why me? he had asked in the early days.

'You're not a knob,' she had said. Or 'I like you.' Or 'You're sexy and you don't know it.'

Now he was almost scared to ask if they could eat together.

'Have you eaten?' he asked.

She did not answer, instead she looked past him, out of the window, where one of her horses was silhouetted against the low hill that was part of their land.

'Peter,' she said and shrugged her shoulders.

'Yes?' he said, fearful now of the distance.

'You know my parents gave us a year,' she said. 'We proved everyone wrong. We were good together, I think.'

She smiled encouragingly. He had an idea he was supposed to say something witty but his mouth was dry.

She stopped smiling. 'No point in dragging things out, though. And no point at all in this being undignified. We will separate smoothly.'

Peter was not sure now he was hearing her properly. He wanted to rummage in his ears for wax.

'Are you?' he whispered. 'Are we...?'

Her eyes widened for a moment before narrowing ominously.

'I'm sorry,' she said. 'I'm not very good at this sort of thing but the lawyers will sort everything. Perhaps you could take a flat in town in the short term. I'll make myself scarce on Saturdays so you can see the children, take George to rugby, that sort of thing.'

She looked again through the window at the horse and Peter thought, *But she always makes herself scarce on Saturdays anyway.* He had questions but no desire to air them, to let his own ears hear them, and she left the room, left the house and walked towards the stables. Her stables.

TIM

A farmer had died and his land was eventually taken on by his neighbour, who had always coveted it, and the inspection had yielded a ditch and in the ditch had been found a skeleton. Tim read about it online and knew immediately they were the bones of Peter Stanning.

George rang the doorbell and Vera answered, her hair in a bun to hide how thin it had become.

'Oh, George, how lovely, do come in. Amber and Tim are here too.'

George knew they would be.

'Awkward this,' he said, 'and please say if it's, you know...'

They all looked at him encouragingly.

'I've always wanted a proper funeral for Dad and we're keeping it small but I wonder if you would attend. It's at the same church as... and that might be difficult for you, so, really, I quite understand if it's asking too much.'

Bob stood and cleared his throat.

'It would be an honour, and I liked your father very much. And we go to the church all the time to place flowers so it's not upsetting for us at all, George.'

'Thank you,' George said, standing a little straighter.

'So, Amber, how's school?'

'Pretty good,' she said. 'Too many exams, though.'

Tim groaned comically and asked his daughter if she would be OK to attend the funeral.

Amber had inherited her mother's sense of fair play and said she would certainly be there.

It was April and the new vicar felt sprightly and pleased to have a funeral that was less emotional than most. He spoke of how proud Peter would have been of his family and Mrs Stanning was astonished to find tears rolling down her cheeks.

She too had needed to say goodbye to him. Her boredom of their marriage had never been so debilitating that she would have wanted him dead. She had wanted him, really, to find happiness with someone else, to do more than work so hard. She had wanted him to be a friend not a ghost. The worst part for her was that she would have taken back her words that final day and stayed with Peter if she had known he was going to vanish. She knew she had sounded cold but that was because she had not wanted to lose her nerve. She no longer loved him but she was fond enough of him, fond enough to save him.

Mrs Stanning knew she would be relieved the day they found him but she was not prepared for the sharp sting of fresh mourning. He was dead, really dead, and it was properly a tragedy because he was too young. She wondered briefly why it all felt so final. She had been to other funerals and wondered about spirituality and afterlives, but not here. This was the end for her Peter. Ah, my Peter, she thought, I'm sorry.

George sighed. He had what he wanted. He was saying goodbye to his father. It had been so hard to sit his mother down in front of Dylan Stenson all those years ago. It had felt he were choosing his father over her, telling her he loved him more than her.

He had asked her if she wanted him to stay with her and the investigator or leave the room. You might as well stay, she had said, as Mr Stenson would tell him everything she said anyway.

Dylan Stenson had been right. There had been a conversation and that conversation had propelled his father out of the door. His father had not seen it coming, his wife's disenchantment, he would have left in a daze, confused, perhaps angry. It was dark, he would have stumbled.

'I'm sorry,' his mother had said, her skin glowing dimly like porcelain, 'and I can't be sure but he might have been unwell. I remember he looked a little grey in the face.'

George had wept later that night, imagining his dad being ill, dying alone in a place so quiet and remote that no one had ever found his body. He hoped that he had dropped dead in his tracks with no time to suffer but George would never know. Not even his mother could shed light on that but she had divulged that when he disappeared Peter Stanning would have been unhappy. Far from hating his mother, it allowed him to forgive her. She had not wanted him to know his father might have died of a broken heart and that was why she had remained silent for so long. Over the ensuing years George had wondered, if his mother had wanted a divorce, why she had not started a new life, and gradually he understood that she had been defined if not by grief then by guilt. If anything, he loved her more, and now as her tears fell as the vicar spoke, George sensed they would all feel able to start again.

Dylan Stenson had pored over the photograph of the Stanning shed and counted ten whole bikes, not eleven, and concluded the body would be within a fifteen-mile radius but that the terrain and passage of time made no sense of a new search. Even so, George, urged on by the ghost of Lauren, commissioned one, so Dylan Stenson drew up an action plan for every ditch to be cleared on common ground. The thinking was that had a man dropped dead on private land, the owner would have noticed. They did not bargain for a reclusive farmer keener to hide a body than have his privacy invaded.

Dylan Stenson had sighed a satisfied sigh when Peter was eventually found. He was within the fifteen-mile radius. The rest of the story, how on earth Peter reached the ditch and why the farmer had been so lacking in common decency, was not something he could have been expected to deduce.

The light streamed in through the church's red, green and yellow glass and Amber smiled as all the dust in the air sparkled. Her mother was here, she thought, right here and smiling at her. Amber wondered at how many particles of dust there must be dancing in front of her eyes. Millions. She felt light-headed all of a sudden and alone. A thought had entered her head. Her mother was in a million different places. Her mother was everywhere but here. The illuminated dust was a greeting from Lauren, a message that somewhere she lived on, was loved and was loving.

I miss her, Amber thought, even though I never knew her. I wonder if she misses me.

And with that thought the sunbeams weakened as if on a dimmer switch and the church became a sad and cold place to be as the new vicar spoke of God's mercy and the sanctity of family life.

Later she hugged George and shook hands with Harry, who she barely knew but could tell was clever in a way that must make him lonely. She looked him in the eye and wondered if his devotion to science meant he never felt spooked or intuitive.

'I'm glad you have said goodbye to your father,' she said boldly, 'and I'm sure my mother would have been glad too.'

Harry nodded but before he could reply, Amber continued.

'But I feel perhaps my mother is somewhere, lots of places, maybe even there is a place where we are together.'

She blushed.

'I have no idea why I said that. I'm so sorry.'

Harry stooped and laid his hand upon her shoulder.

'It is perfectly possible that you are somewhere else with you, mother,' he said gently and Amber was amazed by how level his voice was, that there was not even a hint that he was being patronising.

She walked alongside her father and grandparents towards Lauren's resting place. There was a beautiful posy tied with white ribbon on her grave and a card attached which read, '*The Stanning family thank you, dear Lauren.*'

'I might never have met your mother but for Peter Stanning,' Tim said. Amber linked her arm through his.

'I know,' she said, and she smiled Lauren's gentle smile

which, as always, made Vera blink away the tears and prompted to Bob pull an ironed handkerchief out of his pocket.

'I hope you are happy, my darling,' Bob whispered to the headstone. 'And that, wherever you are, you know somehow that your daughter is loved.'

PETER

The farmer was on patrol. Everything he did was on autopilot. He ate not tasting, he slept not dreaming. He stomped down to the furthest corner of his land aware it served no purpose, it was all rubble and rabble and weeds, but it was his and it needed to be checked. He had found a sheep in the ditch once, many years ago when Hilda was alive. When Frank thought, involuntarily, of his wife he smelled her milkiness, her scones, he felt her sunny practicality like a scarf warming his chest.

He poked among the brambles, keen to avoid the memory of less pleasant smells, of hospital wards and decay, and then he caught a whiff of something real and rotting, looked down and saw a man's face, his eyes wide open, his mouth misshapen, his skin grey. Frank frowned and stomped back to the farmhouse, drank a half-pint of tap water, then collected a shovel and stomped back to the body. He covered it with soil and stones and pieces of shattered brickwork and then teased a wild shrub in the direction of the grave.

Frank had no intention of inviting the police onto his land, of inviting anyone over at all to stare at his dilapidation, his grief, his loneliness, to question him. He had no idea why a man had decided to die in his ditch and he could imagine the cynicism that would greet his ignorance.

Two weeks earlier, Peter's wife had been annoyed he had behaved so dramatically but part of her doubted that he was being deliberately mystifying. He simply would not want to worry his children. They asked her the same question every five minutes.

'Where is Daddy?'

'Where *is* he?'

'*Where* is Dad?'

She sat in the vast drawing room contemplating the irony. Her quest for freedom had inadvertently trapped her. She had to tell the horse breeder who had been thrillingly pushing her against stable doors and then hotel doors to keep away. If something dreadful had happened to Peter she could not be seen to be the cause and neither could she be seen to be so uncaring as to be having fun while he was missing. She baked and then, later, made jam instead. No one could criticise her for making good use of all the fruit in her garden and her jam, she knew, was quite superb. She pictured her children all grown up telling friends and lovers that they coped through their father's disappearance thanks to the homeliness of their mother, hair swept back, spreading her own strawberry jam onto her tall Victoria sponge cakes.

Indeed, the local paper used a photograph of her doing exactly that when they published an interview that was ostensibly supposed to keep Peter's name in the public consciousness but was really a sort of *House and Garden*-style piece on her lifestyle, her kitchen and her horses. Your skin, said the photographer, it is like porcelain. I know, she said.

She later sold the car because it spooked her, the way it had sat there afterwards, taunting her, the way Peter's keys had lain on the table. As Easter approached she began to feel panicked, as if she had murdered him in her sleep. By Christmas, when a year had passed, she asked the local vicar to deliver a special service; not a memorial, but a service of hope. He was delighted to do so, knowing it would draw in the crowds and maybe the local TV cameras.

Not once did she confess she had asked Peter to move out the evening he vanished and she vowed she would never tell a soul until George, tall and successful and attentive George, wrapped his arms around her and said, 'Please.'

The bramble soon covered the stones that covered the body in the ditch and Frank ignored the letter from a neighbour asking to buy the section of land that encompassed the ditch. He would have ignored it anyway.

One year earlier, close to Christmas, Peter had gripped the table edge, a wave of indigestion gripping his chest. He wanted badly to weep. He wanted badly not to weep. He stumbled outside to the driveway and felt in his pocket for his car keys. He must have left them on the table but he could not bring himself to return to the kitchen. He knew he was in no fit state to drive anyway and found himself in one of the outhouses which sheltered all manner of redundant outdoor toys. There were pogo sticks and space hoppers, a trampoline, roller skates and bikes, eleven of them, one or two were even his. He pulled the least rusty away from the wall, rolled up his trousers and left.

Peter pedalled furiously as the light dimmed. He wanted to find exhaustion and isolation so he could scream and not be heard. He turned off the B-road as a church came into view and found a rough track hewn by tractor tyres. He passed a farmhouse and half expected to be chased by a dog but nothing stirred. The track ended and cycling became impossible. The bike's tyres had been almost flat to start with, now he was cycling on metal, not air. He was about to abandon the bike when he noticed in the gloom that there was an incline that would allow him to put yet more space between him and the kitchen and totally destroy his Raleigh. He stuck out his legs and let gravity take over, feeling briefly like a ten-year-old and carefree, his legs stretched out wide, his neck wobbling as the wheels juddered. The lower he went, the darker it became and he knew he would fall, it was just a matter of when. Finally, he hit a rock and let go of the handlebars, laughing as if this were all happening to someone else in an old slapstick film from the twenties.

He lay there, maybe hurt, maybe not. He noticed there was water, a small pond perhaps, and he thought about taking off his clothes and swimming in endless circles but he wanted to cover more ground. In an act of rebelliousness he threw his bike into the water which triggered a fresh bout of indigestion. He vowed to walk until dawn, convinced he could rid himself of the confusion and pain if he pushed himself. It never became pitch-black and the sky retained a blue winter's tinge. The sunrise, he thought, will be spectacular.

He left the land of one farm and entered that of another. He heard the distant bleating of some sheep and he blinked away tears as he remembered his sons cuddling the toy sheep he once brought back from a meeting in Lancaster and the only moment his wife had lost her cool, as her waters broke in the middle of a cocktail party. He felt ill now, nastily unwell. There was a bitter taste in his mouth and his gums were stinging, aching as if all his teeth were ready to leave him, just like his wife was ready.

No, he thought, she has already gone, and he stumbled, his chest sore and tight, into a ditch that was deeper than it looked, steeper than it looked, and the shock of the fall severely winded him. He could hardly breathe at all. I will rest for a bit, he thought, pleased he had found a glimmer of common sense. His body felt numb but he could feel a trickle of blood along his face from his forehead. He was on his side, which was better than being face down, and he wriggled in slow motion to turn onto his back and was rewarded by the sight of the sky lightening as hazy, elongated clouds turned from orange to pink to white.

Peter Stanning did not slip into another world. There was no other universe among the millions of similar universes in which he was still alive. There was nowhere for him to go. There was no alternative path. It was his time.

Acknowledgements

Huge thanks to Clio Cornish at HQ for her intuitive and brilliant editing.

Oli Munson, my agent at AM Heath, with just one short comment, turned a premise into something with a purpose. Genius.

I am grateful to the experts – Philip Diamond, Associate Director at the Institute of Physics, Professor Chris Hull at Imperial College, and Professor David Tong at the University of Cambridge – for their precious time.

Thanks to Sarah Coward for her unwavering faith, intelligence and enthusiasm, and without the (very funny) chiding of my sons, Sam and Conor, I might never have summoned the energy to write at all.

So many dear friends have been supportive but, for not rolling their eyes, I must thank Nigel Taylor, Sarah Squire and my sisters Caroline and Claire. My inspiration is the remarkable Susan Hughes.